Dead Letter Office

Black Lawrence Press
www.blacklawrence.com

Executive Editor: Diane Goettel
Book Design: Steven Seighman and Colleen Ryor

Back cover photo by Crystal Blackburn

Black Lawrence Press
8405 Bay Parkway C8
Brooklyn, N.Y. 11214
U.S.A.

Published 2009 by Black Lawrence Press, an imprint of Dzanc Books

First edition 2009
ISBN-13: 978-0-9815899-4-7
Printed in the United States

*This is a work of fiction. Any resemblance to actual persons, living or dead, or
events is entirely coincidental.*

DEAD LETTER OFFICE

a novel

DANIEL NATAL

Black Lawrence Press
New York

Chapter One

I

Monday, November 2nd, 6:12, pm

Bob Ebersol led a provisional existence. Or so he thought. Because there comes a point when the existence you thought of as "provisional" hardens into your actual life. Sometimes in a bitter frankness he told himself that he was a failure. He was a supermarket manager—a job that was the natural progression of his efforts since first going to work there as a bag boy during high school. Though other kids worked beside him, they had all moved on to other jobs, sought other vocations, graduated to actual "careers". Bob—for who knows what reason—allowed inertia to carry him along. He thought that he was only working at the supermarket to help pay for his car insurance, and then later as a way to earn cash while going to college. It was his intention to do it only until he settled on something else, something more appropriate, more in keeping with his natural aptitude, character and talents. But as he cast about for a career to take the supermarket's place, he was all the while lulled by larger raises and bigger promotions, until finally, at the age of thirty-two, he had attained the dignity of store manager.

It was a world whose noblest vista was composed of colorful cereal boxes and inviting produce departments; a world of cramped aisles, parquet floors and spongy drop ceilings. Though the general trend of opinion from his co-workers was that he was outwardly easygoing and affable, inwardly he struggled under the crushing, desensitizing routine; he ached under the rigid sameness of it all, the unvarying, unimaginative monotony. Somewhere inside him, he felt a pang at the loss of greater opportunities, of greater autonomy inherent in following one's own dreams. If the tenor of his mechanical life could be found in a book, it would not be in a novel, or an epic poem, or a romance. Sadly its flavor would most faithfully be reproduced by a high school math textbook, where X has so many apples, where Y has such-and-such an amount of wood, where the perplexities of his existence are composed of problems such as driving from town A to town B, each at different rates of speed; by which route would he get there fastest?

Yes, the simple humdrum quandaries of a math textbook constituted the deepest mysteries of his existence, and conveyed the boring, mechanical ethos of his life. Although the problems would be less about calculating distances between towns than figuring out how to balance a checkbook under the persistent arrival of new bills.

In the midst of bickering over finances, neither husband nor wife knew that a large manila envelope which arrived in the same mail as their bills would change the current of their lives and upset everything in their hitherto settled existence.

For inside the envelope was a photograph of their son. A black-and-white picture, it captured him at school, suspended in mid-air as he played on a swing.

"Hm. That's funny," said the child's mother, as she gazed at this photo of her boy, a seven year-old who was just growing into an interest in baseball, acquiring extra-familial mannerisms and awaking to a consciousness of the world.

"It's Billy," said Bob, needlessly.

"Do you know what this is for?" asked his wife.

"Is it a school picture or something?"

"No, they took school pictures for the yearbook at the beginning of the year. Besides, those pictures are headshots. This one is him on a swing. They wouldn't do that...would they?"

"Maybe it's for another part in the yearbook?" suggested Bob. "Not the main pictures, but...you know... some section in the middle of the book where it shows students in different activities or something. What does it say inside the envelope?"

"That's just the thing," she returned. "There's *nothing* in the envelope. Just the picture."

"Where's it from?" asked Bob, whereupon both husband and wife observed the fact that the envelope had nothing written on the outside: neither their name and address nor any information identifying a sender, and, furthermore, it came with no postage stamp.

"Maybe Billy brought it home from school with him," he offered.

"No, it was in the mailbox," rejoined Julia with concern.

A current of uneasiness darted between them.

They meant to question their son about the photograph, but he was at a friend's house; and, when he came home, the matter had slipped their minds. It had been eclipsed by a number of other domestic vicissitudes, buried by the swamp of banal crises—such as a broken piece of china coming to light, or a scheduled dental appointment at the end of the week, or the fact that Billy had misplaced his new shoes.

"How do you 'misplace' shoes?" asked Bob, in wonderment. "They're either on your feet or in your closet. How is it possible to lose them?"

Meanwhile, his wife voiced her irritation over their son's forgetfulness and his thoughtlessness when it came to things that cost money.

Bob thought she was a little harsh. She seemed a bit on edge lately. He wasn't sure why.

At any rate, the boy bore up under the stress, promised to find them and went to his room after dinner. No more thought was devoted to the missing shoes until a week later, when Julia was brought up short by a new delivery in the mail. As with the first package, this one arrived with no postage and no addresses. It differed from the manila envelope, though, by being larger and wrapped in brown paper. Bob, who was the first one to notice it on their doorstep, stared silently, speculatively at the strange package. Upon opening it, he was shocked. Inside was a shoebox and, inside the shoebox, his son's missing shoes.

He preserved an air of troubled abstraction as he pulled them from the box and studied them.

Meanwhile his wife's wavering brown eyes searched his face as she stared at him questioningly. "What is it?"

"I don't know," he uttered anxiously. Turning from his wife, he cast his voice toward his son's bedroom, calling: "Billy!"

But Billy, upon appearing in the living room, didn't know any more than his parents did—a fact that they both knew was self-evident, given his age. What child his age, after all, would go to the trouble of elaborately wrapping a shoebox in brown paper and then—for no apparent reason— lay it on the doorstep outside?

The two nervous parents didn't want to overreact. They sought the most rational explanation under the circumstances. Ultimately they settled on a scenario to the effect of a neighborhood friend having admired Billy's shoes. This hypothetical boy stole them. He had a change of heart, however, and decided to return them. Thus the anonymous quality of the plain brown wrapper.

This explanation was unsatisfying because any friend of Billy's would have been as unlikely to have the motor skills to patiently cut a brown paper bag up and wrap it neatly around a shoebox as Billy would, to mention nothing of the elaborate pretense of anonymity.

Despite realizing how unsound their hypothesis was, they allowed it to stand provisionally—until it was refuted by an event that would unsettle the Ebersols and find them contacting the police department. A week after the appearance of the shoes, a new package arrived. Like the very first one, it was a manila envelope. Also, like the first one, it contained a single photograph with no accompanying explanation.

It didn't need one. So horrific was it in its simple menace, so brazen was it in its conception, that they were beside themselves. For there, inside the envelope, was a photograph of their son, lying in his bed at night, asleep.

It had been taken in his bedroom—and recently, judging by the sheets on his mattress.

II

After phoning the police department, they were grateful that the police hadn't dispatched the typical beat cops to pass a cursory glance over their home and make a report. Instead, to their shocked gratitude, they received a visit from an actual detective. As they opened the front door to him, they saw a man who was conceived on a generous scale, just missing by the narrowest margin being an exaggeration of himself. He was at the further end of his fifties. The portliness, soft eyes and white hair all combined to project an image of grandfatherliness. He looked like a conjugation of Santa Claus in the third declension.

He let Bob have his hand. They exchanged a cordial pressure, whereupon he was invited to step over the threshold.

As Bob and Julia looked at him, they observed the fact that he was examining their home critically, making mental notes to himself.

"Would you like a cup of coffee?" asked Julia after the man sat down.

"No, no thank you," he replied, as he took a notebook out of his inner coat pocket. "But if you have a glass of water, I'd be very grateful."

After she returned from the kitchen with the water, he said, "Thank you. Before we begin, I have to apologize. Don't get too close to me; I might get you sick. Seems I'm coming down with a cold and my throat is like sandpaper." After a sip of water, he continued, "So I apologize for my voice. It's not usually this raspy or hard to understand."

"We have a school-aged child; we're used to colds," remarked Bob, wryly.

His wife interjected: "Is that where your partner is?" she asked.

"Partner?" the detective said aloud.

"Don't policemen usually travel in pairs?"

"Well, yes. We're usually teamed-up, if that's what you mean. And yes again to your assumption that my partner's out sick. I thought I avoided his cold, but I guess I finally got it. So try and keep your distance—for your own sakes." Coughing into a handkerchief, he recovered and said, "Where's your son?"

"Upstairs, looking at baseball cards. He collects them," Julia explained.

"A baseball fan, eh?" said the detective. "I might want to peek in on him after we're done here, just to take a look to see if he has any good cards."

"We can go up any time you want," said Bob.

"Yes, yes, in a moment," replied the detective. "But first: tell me what happened."

As they spoke he listened intently, scribbling notes down at intervals. During the course of recounting the events that led up to their contacting the police, the Ebersols started to form an impression of the detective— whose name, as stated on his card, was Gregory Spence. As it developed, he seemed like one of those people whose studied affability had at its source not genuine friendliness but a more impersonal complex of social affectations, the kind of artificial niceness that in doctors is referred to as *bedside manner*.

Underneath this superficial sheen of etiquette, a far more redoubtable personality lurked. He had the inherent formidableness of his type: an ill-concealed cynicism before which even honest people shrank with a feeling as if they had done something wrong and he knew. He had the look of slightly weary tolerance that is sometimes like a frosty coating upon lifelong police officers, people who were too used to being lied to.

So Bob was glad when he could show him the packages as proof that he wasn't making the story up. As the detective fingered them, Bob narrated. He said that the packages appeared to have a pattern. Each one seemed like a stage to represent a greater degree of intimacy with the boy: the first, was simply a snapshot from the distance, the second required the offender to get a hold of the child's personal apparel, the third brought the 'photographer' into the boy's very bedroom at night.

"Is it alright if I take these with me, Mr. Ebersol?" asked Spence.

"By all means," Bob responded, adding, "I wouldn't be lying if I said that I wouldn't mind them being taken out of my house."

"Yes, it was hard to make the decision to keep them—as evidence," interjected Julia.

"Good thinking," replied Spence. "Our job would be much easier if more people were as conscientious. I'll take these back with me and write up a report."

"Do you think that whoever did this will try to hurt our son?"

"I'm tempted to say 'no'. But we can't be too safe, knowing about all the shady people in the world. The fact that he trespassed troubles me. Do you have a security system?"

"No."

"Then you might think of getting one. In the meantime, you should get a dog. Something to warn you if anyone breaks in—or at least to scare off an intruder. Maybe you already have a dog. I just didn't see o—"

"No, we don't have one," said Bob.

"He's allergic to animal dander," offered Julia.

Sighing in scarcely-concealed exasperation, the detective said, "Well, I leave it up to you what you should do. In the meantime, call me if anything else turns up or you have anyone else trying to trespass. As someone in law enforcement, I know I'm not supposed to endorse gun-ownership or encourage everybody to arm themselves. But law-abiding citizens *can* purchase a gun for their own protection. I don't know where you stand on the matter of gun ownership, but—"

"With a child in the house, no..." remarked Bob. "We don't own one."

"Under the circumstances, you might want to reconsider. Just as a precaution. Luckily, other than the trespassing, nothing overt's happened yet. And let's be cautious, too. What if there was no trespassing, either? I mean, what if your son had a sleepover with a friend and the friend—though you didn't know it—had a camera? What if it's a kid and nothing more sending the pictures? It could very well be. Look how the first picture was one of him at school. Maybe that's because the person who took it was a kid?"

"As a theory that sounds as good as any other," said Julia. "But Billy *hasn't* had a sleepover—or any friends with cameras that I know of."

"That you know of," he stressed. "So let's just go forward cautiously from this point on. Just in case it's not as innocent as I just suggested, however, I'll pay you a visit in about a week, okay?"

"We'd appreciate that," the couple said in near-unison.

"Alright. Now—if I may—can I talk to your boy for a few minutes before I leave?"

"Certainly."

Thus the man was led upstairs, where he was brought to the child's bedroom. The grizzled detective struck an incongruous note as he entered that atmosphere of innocent and bounding boyhood. Nevertheless, he appeared to get along easily with the child as the two of them chatted informally—mostly on the subject baseball cards. Afterward, he said: "Well, I have to head out now, Champ. If I find that card, I'll bring it to you next time."

"Thanks, Mr....Mr...."

"Spence," he said to the boy upon parting. Then to his parents: "You have my number. Call me, as I said, if anything happens between now and the next time I pay you a visit. And I hope, in the meantime, you don't come down with this cold. If I've infected you or your son, I apologize."

After emitting another cough, he was escorted back downstairs, where he collected the manila envelopes and the shoebox. Shortly thereafter he said goodbye to the Ebersols and departed.

"Well, what do you think?" asked Julia afterward.

"I don't know. I hope we didn't overreact."

"No, no matter what Detective Spence said: whoever did this *did* trespass. They broke into our house, for God's sake!" Julia exclaimed, hotly.

"Well, do you think we should get a dog?"

"We'll only do it if you think you can handle it with your allergies."

"Who cares if I sneeze a little or itch?" said Bob. Balanced against the possibility of someone breaking into their home again or harming their son, the prospect of hives or rashes counted for very little. "Before we do that, though, let's get the phone book and see about getting one of those home security systems."

"I wonder how expensive that'll be?"

"Whatever it is, we'll budget it in."

But before they could even get a company to send a representative out to their home to give an estimate, an event took place to derail their plans and throw their lives into confusion.

III

"I'm home," announced Bob, the following evening. "Bob?"

"What?" he started upon seeing his wife. "What's wrong?"

"Oh, Bob!" she moaned.

"Where's Billy?" He threw the question at her as he nervously swept the room with his glance.

"He didn't come home after school." Her voice broke. "I called the school, the houses of his friends. No one knows where he is."

The obvious, horrifying answer rose up in Bob's mind. He was just on the verge of mentioning it before caution saw him censor such thoughts as he did not dare to put into words. Because he learned there for the first time that in this life there are words it is impossible to utter.

Though his wife must have been thinking the same thing they, by common consent, refrained from openly mentioning that a phone call should be made to the police. They wanted to wait until all avenues of investigation were exhausted. After all, it would only undercut them if Billy showed up two minutes after the police arrived. It would make the police take any future incident less seriously.

So, talking around matters, Bob said that he was going to drive around the neighborhood to look for Billy—though his wife understood that he was only going to do that *before* placing a phone call to that Detective Spence.

He didn't have to mention it. For she watched him distractedly search through a drawer for the man's business card.

Meanwhile, with an emerging anxiety, she stole glances out of the window in case she should see Billy's young, springing figure coming up to the front door; she jumped with nerves at high tension every time she heard a noise or a sound from outside penetrated the house; she was alive to every creak of their home, every sound of a passing car, alert to all the extraneous noises of distant neighbors that her mind usually filtered out of her consciousness. For in any suburban neighborhood there is always a faint running current of dog-barking, lawn-mowing, the domestic tinnitus of distant telephones ringing. Once or twice she thought it was *her* telephone. But it wasn't.

In the step of the disconsolate mother there was a new heaviness, a new gravity that was brought about by depression. Nevertheless, she tried to control her features in the most ladylike fashion, desperate to mask the anguish she felt and determined to not communicate it to her husband. On the point of tears, however, she decided to calm herself down by splashing cold water on her face.

She went to the bathroom. Bob, meanwhile, found the phone number, placed it in his pocket and started off to go back out to his car. After opening the front door, however, all thought of the hypothetical car ride dissolved as he was confronted by a box on his doormat.

As with all the other strange things they'd received lately, there was no return address on the box, no postage stamp. It took distinct effort for Bob to pick it up and take it inside. It wasn't that it was heavy; in fact, it was suspiciously light. It was just that, coming as the latest issue in a series of strange parcels and packages, as the latest accretion on an ever-building mountain of tension, he found it difficult to treat it lightly.

Carrying it to the dining room, he placed it on the table and set about opening it. His hands lost all adroitness and his fingers fumbled in the penetrating terror of those moments. After a protracted struggle, he finally opened the box. Inside it was another box. He was puzzled. Opening that one, he found yet another box—and another. The series of ever-smaller boxes finally yielded—like a pearl at the center of an oyster—a single slip of paper with what appeared to be a telephone number printed on it.

At least, he assumed it was a telephone number. It had the right amount of digits.

He took it over to the telephone.

Most modern telephones have long since dispensed with the rotary dial in favor of simple buttons. Ebersol's was no different. A pity, since an old rotary dial lends itself so easily to a metaphor related to a safe's dial. With the caution and painful deliberation of a safecracker he dialed the number. With each number in the combination correctly entered, a tumbler was released from the lock. But what would he find behind that door?

He shuddered.

But the door was finally creaking open, the burr of the dial-tone mimicking the squeak of a rusty hinge.

Suddenly a voice came on the line. Something was present in it, a tenor that Bob had never heard in any human voice before. Its echo seemed to set his familiar world rocking.

"You finally phoned. Good. You're being contacted because we have something that belongs to you, or rather *someone.*" The voice paused, and let the syllables drop slowly, one by one, onto Bob's mind. "Your son, Mr. Ebersol."

Bob heard him with a whirling brain. *His son!*

"Who are you? Who is this?"

"It's not important who I am," the voice continued.

"Are you the one who keeps sending all the letters and packages to my home?"

"Who else could I possibly be?" the stranger said with a faint irony, adding, "But that's not important. Your son is."

"Where is he? Is he safe?"

"Would you like to talk to him?"

"Billy?" he uttered, uncertainly.

"Dad?"

An intense, brooding affection held Bob as he tried to command his voice: "Billy?"

"Yeah, Dad."

Just hearing his son, Bob was carried back to that time before Billy was born when he could only be seen via ultrasound technology while in his mother's womb. Having only sound to go by now, albeit the more primitive sound of a telephone, he strained just as much to picture Billy's face, make out the outline of his forehead, imagine the modeling of his features.

His voice pitched dangerously between longing and restraint, Bob said: "Where are you? Are you okay? What happened?"

"I'm fine, Dad. I'm eating ice cream."

"You'll spoil your dinner," he found himself muttering, with tears standing in his eyes. Trying to preserve an appearance of normality (so as not to frighten the boy) he continued in a level tone, "Did you have a good day at school today?"

"I'm not in trouble, am I?" asked the boy.

"No, no, of course not. Why do you ask that?"

"Because I didn't go to school. I...well...I . . ."

"Did someone ask you to get into their car, Billy? You know I told you a hundred times never to get into a car with someone unless your mother or I know them or we say it's okay."

"So I *am* in trouble?"

"No, Billy, no. I love you so much. *I love you so much.* Please don't think I'm angry with you. Can you tell me what happened? What do the people look like? Where are you?"

But Billy was not allowed to answer any of the many questions put to him as the kidnapper resumed the conversation: "That'll be enough. Don't put your son in an uncomfortable situation. Let's not put *him* at risk."

"Why are you doing this?" asked Bob, with a lump in his throat.

"Why does anyone do anything in this world? Money."

"Is this a ransom?" asked Bob. "Because if it is there's been a horrible mistake. We don't have any money."

Bob lapsed into silence and the kidnapper went on speaking with a deadly steadiness: "There's been no mistake. I want $1,634,502.63. You have twenty-four hours to get it."

"What?" Bob's mind spun. *What was he talking about?* Why such a specific sum? It didn't make sense.

But his son's captor didn't wait for him to try and discern reason from the tangle of chaos as he continued to speak.

"If," he pursued with deepening emphasis "you try to involve anyone else in our personal...transaction...you'll continue to receive parcels in the mail, parcels I don't think any father would look forward to opening. But never mind. Let's not dwell on such distasteful things. Hopefully we won't have to even *begin* to deal with such contingencies— just as long as you do as you're told."

"But I—"

"Ut! Ut!" interrupted the man. "No more. There'll be more time to discuss our arrangement at greater length in the near future. Goodbye for now."

Bob's panic and confusion merged into one all-consuming feeling of dread. Meanwhile, his wife emerged from the bathroom. Seeing the phone in his hand, she scanned him with anxious eyes.

"I didn't hear the phone ring. Who was it?" she asked and caught her breath. For she was about to say: "It wasn't the detective, was it? The detective didn't phone us with bad news, did he?" but she checked herself. She gave another nervous gasp, and added in a rush: "Tell me: who were you talking to?"

Something large and uncomfortable seemed to struggle in his throat. With an effort at talking, he tried to clear it; but the sound that emerged from it was as anemic as his face.

"It was a man," said Bob, white to the lips. "A stranger. He says he has Billy."

"What?" she wondered, running a shuddering glance over the telephone.

"A kidnapper," he pronounced, with an edge of panic in his voice.

"That's not possible," she said, as her world began to waver under her.

"I wouldn't have thought so, either."

"It's a prank, a sick, cruel prank," she suggested in rebuttal.

"No, I heard Billy's voice. Someone has him."

She drew back, her air of defiant optimism collapsing. Recovering her self-command, however, she said: "Who? Who has him?"

"I don't know. They didn't tell me."

"Is he alright? What did they say?"

He drew a deep breath. "Billy's fine—so far. They want money . . ."

"Money? We don't have any money!" she interrupted, wringing her hands despairingly.

He sighed his acknowledgement. Then he said, "I don't even know what the hell's going on."

She broke out with a sob.

After less than a minute she collected her senses and said, "Give me the phone."

"Why?" he asked.

"We have to call the police."

He anxiously weighed the proposal, before he said, "No. Not yet."

"What do we do? We *have* to call the police. They have training in this sort of thing."

She was right: they were, as mere parents, definitely out of their depth. Beyond a narrow range of reading in the field of crime fiction, neither of them knew anything about the subject of kidnappings.

"But you don't understand," he said. "If we contact the police, they'll do something to Billy."

"What'll they do?" she asked.

He hesitated about laying a still greater strain upon her nerves by mentioning the threat about cutting their son up in little pieces. So he temporized, saying, "We have to think about this before we call anyone! We need...time. Time to make sense of things."

His wife, trying to keep her head, said, "But that's just the thing. The police will be able to trace the phone call, for instance. They'll be able to track them d—"

She was stopped short by a ringing of the doorbell.

"Who is it?" cried Julia in a stricken whisper.

"I don't know."

They both hastened as soundlessly as possible to the door, but by the time they arrived no one was there. On their doorstep was a nondescript brown paper parcel. They both fastened a look on the package that expressed all their deepest fears and unspoken suspicions.

"What do you think it is?" asked Julia.

He feared that he already knew. That's why he winced when she bent down to pick it up. He almost cried out for her to stop when suddenly a noise started to sound from inside the parcel.

"What is it? What's in there?" he asked.

Upon opening it, they were met by the innocuous sight of a cell phone with an accompanying battery charger. Nothing else was inside the package.

"Are you going to answer it?" he asked.

"I think one of us should," she replied as she handed him the phone.

"Okay," he sighed deeply. Examining the lightweight plastic device, he searched frantically for which button to press. In his great surge of emotion he fumbled longer than he should have, but finally he found the right button and the same voice he had been speaking to before came on the line.

"Your wife is right, by the way," it said abruptly.

"Hello?" uttered Bob feebly.

"Your wife is right about the police being able to trace the phone call you made to a source. It was *this* phone you called, the one you're holding. You'll be saddened to learn that it's a disposable model with no fingerprints on it and no way to trace it. Be that as it may, you're going to keep it so that we can communicate with you."

"You heard what she said?" he faltered.

"Yes, and you made the right choice. Had you given in and contacted the police, there would have been something quite different in the parcel you just opened. Or should I say, 'your wife just opened.'"

"So you can see us, too?"

"You're being monitored. That's all you need to know. And, by the way, your wife was wrong: the police *aren't* very well-trained in matters of kidnappings. They usually call in the FBI. The feds are the ones who are trained. Just thought you should know."

"Can I speak to my son again?"

"Not at this time, I'm afraid. If you'll do as you're told, you'll have him back in only twenty-four hours, and you'll get to speak to him all you want. In the meantime, I'm going to give you a little time to clear your head and recharge the cell phone. I don't want to lose communication with you at any point during our transaction."

"About that," broke in Bob. "I have no idea what you want from me. I have no money. Isn't that the whole point of a k—?"

"All in good time, Mr. Ebersol. You'll get your instructions—as you need them. Until then, goodbye. And remember: recharge the cell phone."

Click!

The voice disappeared, though it continued to ring in Bob's ear long after the cell phone was turned off. His head reeled. What had he meant by "instructions"? Was Bob to be used as some sort of human robot, an automaton to rob a bank at gunpoint? He recalled the gruesome news story from a number of years back where criminals had rigged a pizza delivery man's neck with explosives and forced him to carry out a bank robbery for them. The makeshift human puppet hadn't survived.

What lengths, what sacrifices was he willing to make for his family? Up until now he had never had to think about such a question in concrete terms. All he knew was that he was willing to risk death to save his son, willing to brave torture for his release, willing to commit—murder?

Yes, even murder, he admitted.

In the meantime he was brought back to a consciousness of the cell phone in his hand. It had to be recharged. He laid the cell phone on the counter in the kitchen and plugged the battery charger into it, pushing the other end into the outlet in the wall. As he did so, he winced. Knowing the kidnapper had pressed it to his face before he himself used it, made his flesh crawl.

In a spasm of revulsion, Bob washed his face in the kitchen sink and dried it off with a paper towel. All the while he was aware, almost with a physical sensation, of the cell phone.

When would it ring next? What hellish instructions would issue from it?

His thought was dulled to everything but the throbbing of his temples and the disclosure that he and his family were under surveillance.

To look around at his home now was to look at it with new eyes. Given the fact that they had taken a photo of his son in his own bedroom, it was clear that they had been inside his home. While there, did they plant listening devices, mini-cameras?

Bob, in his agitated state, made a circuit of the house. But he couldn't find anything.

He knew vaguely that security companies occasionally offered the service of "doing an electronic sweep" of a building to detect surveillance equipment. But he didn't have time to hunt around for such a company.

Only twenty-four hours!

It made his head reel. He could scarcely keep his mind focused on a thought for more than a few moments. The one thought that possessed him for any length of time was of getting his son back. He could no longer fix his attention on lesser matters.

Nevertheless, he tried desperately to focus his concentration.

Nothing in his life-experience answered his bewildered wonderment as to what a person was supposed to do in the situation. He dug his knuckles into his forehead in the effort to think of something.

But nothing came.

From vague confusion he drifted into an active resentment at being the victim of such a senseless crime, of being powerless before such an inhumane situation. He burned at the thought of anyone hurting a child—*his* child. He throbbed in a fierce anger at those monsters who would mutilate—or, at least, threaten to mutilate—a little boy. What kind of man would sink so low?

"Monsters!" he repeated to himself silently. He squirmed with murderous rage.

Yet what could he do?

He left matters as they stood, paced the floor anxiously and settled down to a hateful feeling of helplessness and frustration.

Meanwhile his wife suffered, her heart wild with pain. Every throbbing nerve in her seemed to appeal to him.

"It'll be okay," he said sketchily. He agonized with the effort to appear composed.

She looked at him with an expression of gratitude for his façade of bravery. He had a strong, forbearing air that comforted her, as much as that was possible, and gave her a sense of security, as if in walking through a dark room she had found a handrail to steady her. Yet, for all that, the ground was still dangerous, and both remained silent, watching to see what their next move would be.

They lapsed into silence. But it wasn't a blank, featureless silence. For between them was a common history, a shared emotional vocabulary, and now somehow also a greater feeling of unfettered intimacy because of the strain they were both under. For the first time—perhaps in a long time—he didn't take her for granted.

How long was it since he said he loved her—and not in the dry, mechanical sense effected during goodbyes and bedtimes?

It hadn't always been like this. . . .

Chapter Two

I

In retreat from a horrible present and a possibly-catastrophic future, Bob withdrew into the past. It was safe there. And he liked safety. This emotional need was, perhaps, the largest component of the jumble of psychological elements that went together to form his characteristic stodginess. At its most banal extremity, it manifested itself in small ways—such as his always ordering the same meal at a restaurant. Like a little old man, he scarcely ever ventured to order something new, something with which he wasn't already familiar. If he craved a particular dish, instead of driving to the closest restaurant and ordering their version of it, he'd travel out of his way, inconveniencing himself (and others), just to go to another restaurant to which the item was synonymous in his mind. Because of his refusal to experiment with menus, he eventually had a dozen restaurants like this, each—in his own private universe—representing only a single entrée.

At the other extremity of this phenomenon was the effect his stodginess had on work—which explains his tenure at the supermarket. Because of all the ways it limited him, he might have cursed this inner impulse—had it not also inclined him to a long-standing, slow-burning love for his wife. As with the other aspects of his early life that had carried anachronistically over into adulthood, he had met her in high school.

They were both fourteen years old and in ninth grade. As for Bob, he was undergoing a metamorphosis as puberty rushed in upon him. His body was groping toward a new language of pubic hair, of lowered voice, of broadening shoulders; his countenance was losing its childish contours and beginning to set in a hardened, more angular, adult modeling.

Though he could only be vaguely aware of it, a whole world of creation waited within him. Life was building up and pooling in his body, preparing him—though he didn't know it—for that one moment when his whole being would be drained into one soul-shattering point. For under the lavish veil of his shifting flesh, the secret shape of restless life was more truly shown than anywhere else in man's seething, sterile world.

He lived in a continual torment of desire, driven for the first time by his awakening curiosity to steal furtive glances at the flowering bodies of girls: their widening hips, tapering calves, budding breasts, velvety flesh and aromatic hair.

But this new hunger only mounted to something beyond mere concupiscence when he met...her. She had large brown eyes, a pert nose and a honeyed complexion. She had bobbed brown hair that was blondish at its tips, long eyelashes, and eyes shaped like sideways candle flames.

He didn't know what it was about her, but she lifted him completely out of himself and sent a new tremor through the dull mass of his collective experiences.

He didn't understand the pull she had on him, nor could he have given a name to all that was passing at random within him—unless that name was "Julia". For such was her name at the time: Julia Brettloh. But oh, so much more was contained in those two words than just a mere five syllables of identification! Indeed, for him, from the first time he laid eyes on her, it was more than just a name; it was a diagnosis, the description of a sickness that robbed him of his power of speech and threw him into a fever. His blood was in a ferment every time he saw her, or thought of engaging her in conversation. He watched her, in inward agitation, as she talked to this person or that or scribbled notes as she listened in class.

He had the vague feeling that he would like to make her believe in him—somewhat like the God who sends unannounced miracles into the lives of atheists, miracles they willfully refuse to see, calling them mere 'coincidences'.

Yet what else could he do to get someone's attention? Whipping up dubious coincidences, such as when he just *happened* to be in the library at the same time she was. Or the time when he just *happened* to be there when she dropped her book in the hallway, so that he could be the one to pick it up for her.

All of those manufactured coincidences!

His dilemma was the same as a ghost in a haunted house who tries desperately to communicate with the new, living tenants. He felt that insubstantial, that transparent. Accordingly, he tried cover over his obviousness by being oblique. He made friends with all the people around her, and a part of him did this strategically to get her to join in and chat with him; but he never addressed her directly.

He had to solace himself with her pencil. She dropped it one day while gathering her belongings before going home. From his vantage point several desks back, he saw it fall and roll next to the leg of her desk. At first, he was going to call out to her, to let her know what had happened. But that would have entailed talking to her. So he watched, waiting for her to realize her loss and bend down to pick it up. She didn't. After she left, he walked up to her desk. He bent down and took the pencil gingerly, as if expecting a strong sensation from it, a flood of that occult force which primitive man detected in sacred objects. He turned it around delicately in his fingers as if testing to see whether, by having come into contact with her, it had been changed on the molecular level. He knew rationally that it wasn't fundamentally different from any number of pencils already in his own possession. That fact notwithstanding, he experienced a delicious thrill in holding it. He promised himself he'd return it to her the next day. The next day came, however, and he discovered that he couldn't bear to part with it. Besides, giving it back would have necessitated talking to her, and he was too shy. Maybe, then, he should go back and leave it in precisely the spot where she'd lost it. As he debated what course he should take, she produced a new pencil from her desk, and he realized that she hadn't missed it at all. So he greedily kept it, a totem that he used to invoke her memory as he sat in his bedroom after school.

It was the closest he would come to her before a random school fire drill a few days later. With one impulse the mass of students rose and poured out of the building and into the playground outside. The principal was having a hard time controlling the crowd. From out of the whirlpool of faces and frenzied movement, though, lines eventually began to emerge. As teachers shepherded their students into these lines, Bob spotted Julia. Her hair was gorgeously alive against the wind. Her delicate face rose from clothes that spoke an evasive language. Beneath this disguise of decorum, though, she was more than a girl; she was his introduction to all female beauty, the distilled essence of womanhood. It was his first awakening to Beatrice, Salomé, Helen of Troy, all the way back to Eve herself. One woman within another eternally, in a far-reaching procession. The fecund shape of femininity carried across the centuries, so heavy it made his breath labored just to behold it; the sound of her voice so intense it rang in him with haunting resonance.

He stared with an ancient stare. What else could he do? A sweet tumult beat in his veins, the vibration of his heart like a silent music. He ached with the anguish of a desire that had not even acquired a graphic connotation in his young mind. Due to the angle of the sun, her shadow was splayed on the ground in front of him. Unknown to her, he placed his skin in contact with it, as if in touching her shadow he was touching some part of her, some occult piece of her anatomy. As the line he was standing in moved, there came a point where his own shadow almost touched hers. He shifted his position subtly, almost unconsciously, so that they met—a touch of two forms carried out in silhouette if not in reality. Time paused as if suspended by a delicate black thread. But then she moved and the illusion was broken, as when a person notices their own image on the surface of a lake and disturbs the water to see the reflection dissolve in concentric circles.

He had to be nudged to move forward. His mind was still absorbed with the secret that had whirred, sung, hummed around him in the fierce sunlight of his private universe.

It was only some days later that he was brought down to earth. Because he noticed that he wasn't alone in his silent veneration. He heard other boys chatting about her, saw other eyes transfixed on her. And why not? Was he the only one who was supposed to have noticed her grace and beauty?

Carried on the fierce tide of universal admiration, she seemed entirely aloof and inaccessible now. Something about all the boys who liked her dampened his enthusiasm. Why should he be just like all the rest? It cheapened his own emotions, cast doubt on his own taste. No, plainly, he had to renounce all the instinctive urges that she had provoked in him. He pledged to stop stealing glances at her, to put her out of his mind completely.

Of course, since they were in the same class this was impractical, and there were moments when he was forced to look in her direction. But now, chastened, he saw her in a new light. Whereas before he might have noticed the downy blond hair on her body that could only be seen from a certain angle in the sunlight, he no longer felt a pang of longing, but looked upon it as the nearly-invisible fur on a cactus which, if touched, evoked pain in the finger that came away covered in quills. He discovered a small mole on the side of her jaw under her ear, this imperfection like a misprint he had failed to notice before.

Her image after a few weeks started to sting his vision like an eyelash that had fallen into his eye.

His puppy love was now replaced in equal measure by a sort of vague physical nausea as he looked on at the spectacle of unrequited love in others. What monkeys it made of them, what awkward, oafish fools! He didn't mind the quiet, doomed affection that a fat redhead cherished for her in his naïve, solemn way; but he felt the pit of his stomach fall as the more vigorous louts ran eyes of shrewd appraisal over her body and made rude comments to their friends. Or worse: when the raucous elements of school sometimes adopted in her presence a vulgar air shot with flashes of ribald humor, and demonstrated a callous brutality foreign to Bob's nature.

He didn't know what to make of it. His thoughts lingered in a pause. They hovered there, entangled with something confused, remorseless and heartbreaking.

At that moment Bob's anticipations had reached such a decline into disappointment that he wanted to renounce the ugly, bestial thing that love was forever. He had derived such fierce joy in thinking about her before and now it seemed as if he could never pursue her, or anyone else, again.

All this changed when she finally noticed *him* six months later, as he became the object of rather attentive contemplation on the part of the girl. Baffled, he wondered why she was casting a glance at him. Was there something in his hair? Something she was laughing at?

It didn't immediately occur to him that she might like *him*.

But could she really, he worried? She didn't say it in so many words, but her anxious, halting behavior seemed to hint as much. He didn't know how to react. Inwardly, his heart was fluttering.

How strange that she should have taken notice of him just when he had decided to ignore her! Perhaps she mistook his ignoring her for a sort of worldly aloofness.

He was beyond wanting to examine the events too closely. He didn't want to think at all. Thought threatened to get in the way of his emotion; and he felt that he must devour this feeling and possess it all, the rapid pulse, the sweaty forehead, the feeling of panic if "panic" was divested of all its associations with fear.

He decided to put the thought out of his head. What if he was wrong, after all? What if he made a fool of himself?

He wasn't wrong, however, as circumstances confirmed when after school Julia walked up to him. She approached with her glance averted, the hidden eyes communicating their evasive gesture down the length of her body and suggesting an emotion suspended between embarrassed self-assertion and coy invitation.

"Bob?" she said. The touch of her tongue on his name went through him in a tide of delicious agony.

"Yes, Julia?"

Thus they began speaking for the first time. It was only then, in remembering how much unwanted male attention she attracted, that he realized how truly alone she was. It would have never occurred to him that someone like her could be in her own sort of prison.

They both obliquely spoke about their alienation from their peers. And, in doing so, they realized how similar they both were.

"What is it that people want to know about other people?" she asked.

"What do you want to know about me, for instance?" he said only half-jokingly, perceiving the intimate associations her question had when removed from the deceptively abstract form she placed it in.

Sensing that he saw right through her, she was embarrassed. She immediately scrambled to think up some excuses, some artful means by which she could temporize. Her mind lit on several possible replies: "No, that's not what I meant at all" or "God, you're so vain! Why must everything be about *you?*"

Instead, bravely, she decided not to dodge the question, taking him off-balance as she said evenly: "Tell me something that only I will ever know."

Her eyes silently enjoined him to tell her something by which she could remember him should she never see him again.

His flippant mood evaporated before her penetrating gaze like mist dissolving before the hot rays of the sun. Retreating into a gloomy pause, he averted his eyes and considered. Now it was *his* turn to think up clever ways to parry her question. Should he make a joke, he wondered? Maybe ignore the question entirely? Or perhaps answer whimsically, half-heartedly?

His usual conditioned responses to questions like this didn't seem appropriate in the face of such disarming sincerity.

As he sought for words, she watched him dispassionately. *"He's trying to think of something original to say. Or worse: something that'll make him look good."*

"*He's just like everyone else,*" she continued, silently to herself. "*He wants to be seen in the best possible light. Am I any different, though?*"

Of course not.

"We all try so hard t—"

But her thought was interrupted as he finally surprised her by saying something that *wasn't* designed to make him look clever or original or flippant.

After a distinct interval, he broke in upon her silent meditation to say: "I remember my dad. My parents were divorced. My dad came back on one of many failed attempts to reunite the family. I was hoping so much that *this time* things would be different, *this time* he'd stay more than two weeks. He took me to a park at the tail end of one of these doomed visits. Maybe it was his way of saying goodbye to me. Anyway, we did all the usual things fathers and five-year-old sons do. We threw around a ball, bought hotdogs from a vendor, looked up at the clouds as we lay on the grass. But what stays with me was the terrifying possibility that, being so young, this wonderful afternoon would be forgotten one day when I got older. For some weird reason, I had such strange presence of mind that day. I mean, I was only five! Yet even then I knew I'd forget. It's like when you have a particularly nice dream and you will yourself to remember it when you wake up. As a child, your memories are fragile like that. Like dreams. In any case, I promised myself that I wouldn't forget that very moment. It wasn't a special moment or anything. I looked around at bees buzzing around a garbage can in the park. Beyond it was a beautiful green baseball field and a bright blue sky. I forced myself to memorize every detail of that *one* instant: the feel of the breeze, the figure of my father lying on the grass, the strange orbit of a particular bee as it flew around the garbage can. Oddly, all these years later, I still have that memory. Not a dramatic moment, or an exciting moment. Still! I remember it so vividly, so crisply. It's strange how much more present it is in my mind than many other allegedly more important incidents that happened afterward."

As he talked to her at greater length on this subject her curiosity deepened to sympathy. And she drew him out. Over the following weeks and months he told her things he'd never told anyone. He held forth about his turbulent childhood, his parents' broken marriage, his father's stuttering attempts to leave for good.

Stamped across his memory of those times were the images of the maternal hand that would touch his shoulder at one time or another as she would try to soothe him when his father would leave.

"Tut-tut-tut. Don't cry," he remembered his mother intoning as he stared through a window at his departing father. Those panes of glass—at the various homes where they lived—became the natural medium through which to see him, like a pair of eyeglasses given to a nearsighted man. Turning back from the window was like having the eyeglasses torn away from him, so blurry was his vision due to the tears.

Eventually, his father stopped coming at all. By the time he had unburdened himself to Julia, his father had been gone for some years.

He didn't make the revelation of his personal familial melodrama an excuse for trying to stir her to passion. But, on the last occasion where he recounted the events, she had taken and held his hand as he talked, and he permitted it.

That was all.

But it was enough.

II

He looked back with fondness on that time of happiness and new stirrings in youth.

But that time was gone now. He emerged from his reflections to a new world, a darker world. A fact that was brought home to him as he looked outside the window and let the night absorb his soul.

Poor Julia! She had brought him such happiness. And now this!

It was almost like setting eyes on a different human being as he stared at her now. She seemed so inaccessible to him as she sat, trapped in her own thoughts. If he could have penetrated through to them, would he have even been able to understand what he saw? She herself was confused by the impressions and memories that rioted in her brain. Trying to follow the trend of her own thoughts was as difficult as attempting to read a book on a train, consequently reading the same phrase over and over and realizing that you had long since lost the meaning. *What now, what now, what now?* hammered upon her brain.

Bob was also wracked by the agonizing indecision, the prolonged suspense. He looked over at the charging cell phone. After that he tried to ignore it, to go onto other activities. But the thing stared at him from its place atop the counter. He walked around to different parts of the kitchen: sitting in a chair, pacing the floor, fussing with papers on a shelf in the corner. All the while he felt the cell phone like someone might feel eyes on his back, burning into him. Like one of those vulgar paintings where the eyes follow you around the room, no matter where you go.

Soon his wait was brought to an end as the cell phone rang. It produced the same effect on husband and wife, both of their hearts starting in their chests. Bob was the closest to the phone, so he picked it up. Between the "hello" and "goodbye" which parenthesized the conversation, Bob spoke of his son and, in a strain hardly less despairing, of his wife; for he didn't want her to be involved any further in this unpleasantness. As a result, he closed his eyes tightly; then wearily: "I'll do anything you want—on one condition: you leave my wife out of it. You let me take her somewhere where she'll be safe, somewhere away from all this."

"You're in no position to negotiate," commented the man.

"I know," confessed Bob. "But it's not being made as a negotiation point, but as a request, an appeal to your sense of decency as a gentleman, your sense of fair play."

"First of all, I'm not a gentleman—as you well know; and, secondly, I have no sense of fair play." After an excruciating pause, he added, "But since you asked so politely, yes: maybe we can reach an accommodation."

"We can?" exclaimed Bob excitedly, his face irradiated by relief.

"Yes, *but*—"

"But what?" asked Bob, anxiously.

"I know I needn't tell you that if she tries to use this opportunity to go behind our backs and go to the police, there will be a special torment reserved for her—as well as for your son. Anyone she tells, as well, will be killed."

Bob assured him that everything would be kept in the strictest confidence. "I swear!" he begged. "She wouldn't do that, knowing what it means to our son."

"You'd better impress it upon her—or else I might be tempted to change my mind."

"No, no, don't do that!"

"I won't. But...well...my generosity has placed me in a bad position. You see...I phoned to tell you that the next step in your instructions requires that it be carried out by at least two people. If you're not to use your wife then you have to enlist someone else to help you."

"Someone else?" murmured Bob.

It was then that his tormentor issued the command to locate a certain William Frederick Ebersol.

"My father?" declared Bob.

At the mention of his father, consciousness flashed a long light over his past as it related to the man.

His father was a felon, an ex-con.

Criminal! At the word, which brought the seediness of the streets into this respectable suburban home, Bob awoke to a dawning sense of rage.

He didn't know how he figured into the situation, but he knew that *that's* why he and his family were drawn into the turbid current of his father's life.

Bob had broken with his past years ago. It was his assumption that he had left this part of his personal history behind him forever. But now he realized how wrong he was, for however negligible his past seemed up until now, it loomed gigantic before him as he ran up against it like running up against a wall.

"Because even if I *wanted* to, I couldn't get in touch with my Dad," he told the kidnapper. "I haven't spoken to him in years. He's not a part of my life."

"That's not my concern," replied the man, bloodlessly.

"I have no idea where he is!" asserted Bob in frustration. "Aren't you listening to me?"

Unperturbed, the kidnapper remarked in a low, clear voice: "You have twenty-three hours left."

Click! The phone call ended.

Bob raged at the man's unfairness regarding the instruction to find his father. The man ignored his misgivings with a coolness that reduced Bob to a whining servant, diminished him to the level of a plaintive lackey.

Every moment in this situation seemed to be an edged agony. The only possible ground for optimism was the fact that, in what had proven to be a decisive exchange of words, he had successfully won the accommodation from the kidnapper to keep his wife out of it. As he quietly examined the facts, however, he realized that the man acceded to the suggestion because he had no intention of asking him to use his wife as a partner in the operation. He had been meant to find his father all along. After all, his father had criminal experience; his wife did not.

Yes, it was going to be a robbery. He knew that now. *$1,634,502.63.*

So it was a false victory for him to exult over the exemption granted to his wife. The kidnappers probably hadn't meant to use her anyway. Examining the facts under a new light of cynicism, he probably brought them a small measure of relief by removing from the equation a person they considered a "loose end".

Whether he had behaved like a stooge or not, he didn't care—so long as his wife was safe.

It was one less thing to think about as a certain plan was hotly being hammered out in his head.

III

Bob was left in the wake of the conversation to make sense of the situation. At least, he told himself, he had one more piece of the puzzle. In his confusion he had no other choice than to grasp it, to let it carry him another stage in his search for his son. Because to find his father was to find his son.

But as he worked out these facts in his mind a problem of more pressing immediacy was thrust upon him: his wife. For while she had watched him on the phone, the rising flame of indignation rose so high in her that it touched her cheeks and colored her neck. As he talked to the kidnapper he found himself having to silently shush her as she spoke, all the while conscious of her mutinous eyes. After all, she was so thorough a partner to her husband in everything that she just took it for granted that, whatever they'd have to face, they'd face together. Bob had different ideas. And he didn't look forward to facing her when he got off the phone and a torrent of protest would pour through her.

He hadn't been mistaken.

He was proud of her, though. She was trying to be so brave in the face of such monstrous events. But, as he explained to her, he took a careful survey of the facts and came to the conclusion that the situation was too dangerous for her. In fact, it was too dangerous for *him*. But he was (he felt) expendable. She was more important.

"But Bob!" she argued.

"I've thought the matter over, every side of the question, and I can't...I *won't*...let anything happen to you, too."

She thought her husband was too quick to assume nothing but failure. The situation produced a wholly different effect on her, awakening within her the germs of rebellion. The kidnapper's words recounted roused a smothered sense of resistance. A small spark was enough to kindle Julia's spirit and set her in determined opposition to these people. She would fight, do anything she could to beat this situation which imperiled her son.

"I don't doubt that," said Bob. "I know you'd do anything you could to help. And this is how you could help: by letting me know you're safe. It'll be one less thing on my mind, one less thing to have to worry about. Please promise me you'll help me by doing this."

Reluctantly, with tears of frustration in her eyes, she said, "I promise."

"You have to promise me one more thing."

"What?"

"For the safety of our son and anyone I might take you to, you have to promise not to try and be sneaky and call the police. If you do that, he swore that not only would he kill you and Billy—but anyone you told. You have to promise—for the safety of everyone involved."

"Do you really think he'd do that?" asked Julia.

"Yes," said Bob, for more and more he felt the force of this man's sincerity. He was an individual who meant to act on his threats. The last conversation deepened that impression.

"So please promise me," continued Bob.

"Okay. Alright," mumbled Julia.

"Let's go."

"Where?"

"We'll decide that in the car," he said, as he compelled her out of the house that was under surveillance.

It felt good to be in the car (which was almost certainly not bugged), and to be away temporarily from the airless, unnatural, straining environment into which strangers had turned his house.

It gave a luster to his driving which he hadn't felt for years. After all, his car was no longer a symbol of freedom, but merely the cramped anteroom to his office at work. Now it recovered its old ability to impart a sense of liberty (as it had long ago when he first learned to drive).

"Where are we going?" asked Julia.

"I don't know. You tell me."

"I don't think my sister would mind too much if I spent the night," she suggested.

"Okay, we'll go there."

That brief drive gave Bob a deceptive sense of a freedom of will. Emboldened by it, he imagined flouting his tormentors' wishes; escaping their penetrating gaze. In case they had a car following his own, or some way to track him, he decided to vary his tactics as he drove. He took unnecessary and misleading streets, he alternated his speed, he cut in and out of traffic. In this way, he made it to his sister-in-law's house by a very strange circuit indeed. He felt sure, however, that no one had succeeded in following him, his wife that much safer since nobody knew where he was going to drop her off.

When at last he parked the car and they both climbed out, the couple tried to concentrate on superficial aspects of the situation rather than face the all-consuming abyss of their sadness at being parted—most likely forever. So Bob said, "What'll we tell your sister?"

"A cover story, you mean?" replied Julia.

Bob nodded. "Maybe you can say we had a fight and you've decided to spend the night with her?"

"I wonder where she is now," remarked Julia. "Surely, she must have seen us pull up in the car."

"Her car's here; she's home," said Bob. "She's probably just taking a bath or something. You have the key to her house, right?"

"Yeah, it's right here," she said, producing it.

"Well, I guess all that's left, then, is to say goodbye."

Julia, in whose eyes was chiefly a prayer that her husband return safe, drew up to him to imprint a kiss on his lips.

Meanwhile the urge to tell him how much she loved him itched like a cough at the back of her throat. It cost her a great effort not to give into the desire to relieve her impulse. Because she almost said it. She merely treasured up the thought that she would do so when he came back to her—in one piece and with their son.

As for now, she could only fight out the words, "Try to be careful."

She crushed him to her as she stood with him in the same depth of human grief. Pulling away from her, he said, "I will."

They stood rooted to the spot for some silent minutes more, both paralyzed by the unwillingness to leave each other. Had it not been for the consciousness of the passage of time (and what that meant to their son's life) they might have remained there like that for hours longer. But they didn't.

With one more parting kiss, Bob stepped back into the car and, with a lump in his throat, pulled away.

IV

He drove back toward his house and, in a tremor of misgiving, decided not to park in his own driveway. Giving full play to his rudimentary concept of espionage, he parked a block away, around the corner, and resolved to steal homeward as inconspicuously as he could. Maybe (he reasoned) he'd be able to evade any hidden cameras that had been set up—or at least to detect them.

Following a blind instinct, he entered the house through a little-used side entrance.

As he disappeared inside, he felt that he was staggering into a blindness darker than any blackness he had ever known.

As he delicately closed the door behind him, there was an urgent, daring look in his eyes.

Though he didn't know what he was looking for exactly, he gingerly searched the first floor of the house for strange equipment, anything out of the ordinary. What exacerbated his attempts was the fact that he refused to turn any lights on. He conducted the surreptitious investigation in full darkness.

His efforts yielded no results. He cursed himself for his general ignorance when it came to technology. In fact, he could barely operate a cell phone.

Guided by that thought, he produced the cell phone from his pocket and tried to flip it open to use its phosphorescent blue glow as a makeshift nightlight. In doing so, however, he hit the wrong button and noticed something: a mistake that the kidnappers had made!

"How could they have been so idiotic?" he wondered, his excitement verging almost on glee.

In hitting the wrong button, he had accessed a screen that listed saved telephone numbers. There was only one, unfortunately. But maybe it would yield a lead to some law enforcement agency.

He debated with himself to try and furtively contact the police—by some other means than telephone—or to use his own computer to find an online resource that might assign an address or a name to the number.

But he bumbled again; for, hitting the incorrect button in the attempt to scroll down to another function, he accidentally dialed the telephone number.

Before he could figure out how to hang up, it rang— and something happened that made him pull up short and break into a cold sweat. For the cell phone at the other end of the call appeared, terrifyingly, to be *in his own house.*

He started, listening rigidly.

His heart raced. His limbs were full of a frantic urgency. And it was only by a supreme exercise of will that he managed to restrain his instinctive urge to move. He didn't want to give himself away.

Inspired by who knows what latent cunning, he considered the possibility that whoever had the other phone might presently discover that he was in the house if he dialed him back and the phone rang; so, his fingers working frantically against the pressures of time, he figured out how to switch the ringer off and set the phone to "vibrate". A good thing, too, since it abruptly started to do so.

He only hoped that the intruder was far enough away that he wouldn't hear the numb buzz of the phone. He had to "hope," because he didn't *know*. For he had disconnected the call before the first ring was even through. Consequently, he couldn't fix on a location inside the house.

Where was it?

It sounded like it came from upstairs.

Unfortunately, he did not know—nor did he ever learn with any accuracy—the diagram for the veritable minefield of creaks which covered the steps on the staircase, his every footfall lampooned by annoying noise.

He finally—painfully—reached the top.

It didn't take him long from that point to confirm that the intruder was in fact upstairs—judging by a room which diffused a pale light which could be seen under the door.

At the sight of it Bob's roving attention deepened.

He stood, as if rooted to the spot, looking at the door. As he did so, a vague bump corroborated the light and confirmed the presence within.

What luck! He now knew where his pursuer was while he himself remained undetected. But how could he turn it to his advantage?

With as much stomach-churning deliberation as he had exercised in ascending the staircase, he now descended it. His feet pressed weight on the stairs, each step an intrusion on the silence. Fortunately, he made it to the bottom without incident. Creeping as quietly as he could he searched for any household item that could be used as a weapon. He briefly considered getting a butcher knife from the kitchen. But a knife was smaller and required one to get in closer. No, finally, he decided to go to the fireplace where he got a brass poker. He could use it as a club, he told himself.

He tested its weight, its heft. Both would do.

Steeling himself, he rose back up to the second story. The staircase then took on something of the aspect of an ascending musical scale, each step like an ever-higher note that was pitched exactly to the increasing tightness of his drawn nerves. At the top, he hid himself in a distant corner of the landing, taking advantage of an architectural anomaly that provided a full view of the staircase and all of the upstairs doorways.

He waited patiently. Now and then a sound from the room brought before him more vividly the reality of the situation and the horror with which he stood face to face. He didn't know how long he could stand there like that. Finally, after a ten-minute stretch of infinity, the door disclosed the intruder like a dark secret.

Fear charged through Bob.

In a crisis of ambivalence, he vacillated over whether he should spring savagely upon the man or loudly announce himself and give over the fantasy of staging a revolt. With so much hanging in the balance, he would be foolish to do anything to jeopardize his son.

One can imagine his shock when some unchecked visceral reaction overturned the sober ruling of his intellect and he abandoned himself to his rage. Suddenly, all his hatred of these people gathered in one impulse. He swung out blindly. To his horror, however, the man he struck—of forbidding aspect and heroic dimensions—was only stunned by the glancing blow to his shoulder. Startled, confused, the fat, physically-imposing intruder's face tightened with rage as he tried to punch him. Bob pivoted, running out further onto the landing. His attacker, turning around, lunged. But in the dark, and with only a casual knowledge of the house's layout, he miscalculated. Throwing all his weight toward Bob (who parried) the man lost his footing and tumbled down the staircase.

His bulk beat a tattoo on the hard wood as it struggled vainly while in the grip of unforgiving gravity. Bob again felt a stealing indecision. He hovered irresolutely at the top of the stairs. After hearing a gasp from the intruder and, realizing that up until that point he had been holding his own breath, he exhaled deeply. Drawing in a fresh breath of air, he braced himself to go down.

With each step, he shuddered. His shivering seemed to be like its anticipation of possible death, the soul trying to escape through the pores like the screen-mesh in a prospector's sifting pan as he shakes it to allow contents to pass through it harmlessly to the container below.

But Bob had no intention of dying—not on this night. So, getting his shaking under control, he continued down the stairs and found himself on the landing below.

To his astonishment, the man was immobile, his neck twisted at an impossible angle.

As Bob cautiously drew closer, he listened intently for respiration, but heard none. That gasp, he reflected with distaste, must have been his death rattle.

He had to set his addled brain in order, told himself he had to think and observe. Yet if a census of his thoughts had been taken, neither fear nor death, panic nor curiosity about the dead man would have been found, but a half-glad, half-hysterical acknowledgement that he had prevailed.

As he replayed the situation in his mind, he returned with astonishment to the sheer luck of using the cell phone to ferret out the intruder. His self-satisfaction, however, was tempered by the admission that it had been an accident; a serendipitous act. But no, he told himself: even if he hadn't purposely used the cell phone in that fashion, it at least demonstrated presence of mind to have remembered to turn the ringer off on his own cell phone. Under the circumstances, after all, he was surprised by his clarity of thought. Because in his desperation he seemed to rise into a masculine resourcefulness he had never before known.

Inwardly chastising himself he reminded himself how terrified he was, how paralyzed he had momentarily been.

But if his whole body had seized up, it was only temporary. For the atoms within him which had seemed to freeze started picking up speed again—but they did so in the opposite direction. A sort of reverse polarity had taken place, changing the whole character and texture of his soul.

As a result, it was as if he were a different person as he assembled his courage and checked the dead man's pulse.

After confirming that he was dead, he reflected upon the fact that he had killed a man. Having been directly responsible for someone else's death sent a new shudder through him. For, being a fairly moral human being, murder had always been beyond the compass of his hypothetical actions. Having breached that imaginary line now, he felt his whole moral world rocked to its foundations. Every boundary, every prohibition, every restriction was revealed for the illusory thing it was.

Would he have the strength, the inner fortitude to navigate through this new world, this Nietzschean landscape of a reality "beyond good and evil"?

Somehow—though he had successfully drawn on inner resources he didn't know he had—he didn't feel equal to the challenge. Especially when he returned to his senses and realized how extremely stupid his action had been. If that man, after all, had been the kidnapper, how would he ever find his son now? And if he hadn't—if he was only a henchman, a cohort—then, by killing him, Bob could only be further imperiling his little boy. What vengeance would they exact on his son?

He suddenly felt nauseous. It cost him quite an effort to be able to regain a command over himself and search the dead man's pockets for any information, any possible clues. What he found was a gun.

Why hadn't the man used it upstairs?

Perhaps, in the confined space, he didn't feel that he could reach it in time. Being a brutal man by nature, he thought he could rely on the ruthless application of superior force.

Bob could only hazily infer what thoughts must have passed through the dead man's mind. He was only glad that now, at least, he had a weapon.

Even though Bob had no knowledge of firearms and no gun experience, it didn't take him long to establish that it was loaded and that the safety mechanism was engaged.

But he needed more than just a gun. A gun wouldn't get his boy back. Maybe there was some piece of paper, some telltale hint that would lead to where they were keeping him.

As he was groping in the fat man's jacket, he suddenly felt a strange pulsing in his own pocket, an almost insect-like buzz—and then, with a start, he realized that it was the silenced cell phone. Answering it, his stomach nearly rose in his throat.

"I heard a commotion," said the voice, apropos of nothing.

It immediately told him two things: the man lying at the foot of the stairs was *not* the man to whom he had been speaking and, secondly, that there *must* be surveillance equipment in the house since the man was reacting to the noise he heard.

Bob meanwhile hedged.

"Yes, I dropped something," he lied, trying to keep the frenzy out of his voice. "You can understand nerves when someone's in a situation like this, can't you?"

"What did you drop?"

Not a talented liar, he struggled to dissemble and manufacture a satisfying scenario.

"You let my wife leave. Before going, she packed a bag, but—I guess—because of the situation, she forgot to take it with her when I drove her away. I tripped on it when I was at the top of the stairs. She didn't zip it up, so the contents flew down the stairs and all over the place. Sorry. I didn't mean to make such a clatter. Is my son there, by the way?" he asked, another note in his voice. "Can I speak to him?"

"Not now."

"When *can* I speak to him?" asked Bob, fretfully.

"Communication with the boy will be held out as a reward—*after* you reach your father and contact us. You're to call me on this phone," he said, going on to give him a telephone number. "Do you have a pen, by the way?"

"I can find one. Hold on."

After a brief interval, Bob was back saying, "Tell me the number again."

The kidnapper repeated it, adding, "You're to find your father then phone us. Further instructions will follow subsequently. Goodbye."

"But—"

Bob was cut short by an abrupt silence. The phone call was over.

His thoughts now turned to the question of whether they had sight surveillance equipment as well as sound. From the kidnapper's comments, he was left to infer that they only had sound equipment. Just because they couldn't see him in that portion of the house, however, he couldn't assume that they didn't have video equipment in other areas.

To be cautious, he wouldn't assume that it was safe to turn on the lights in the house. After all, he still had the corpse of this dead man next to him. He had to get rid of it before his colleagues found out what had happened and wreaked vengeance on his son.

First, though, he knew he had to resume his search of the dead man's pockets. He didn't want to do it. But he promptly adjusted himself to the necessity of finding any useful or pertinent information that might later aid law enforcement officials in their search for his son.

He winced as he knelt back down and started running his fingers over the clothes on the cadaver. After a frank inspection of the man's pockets, he found a key ring, upon which were car keys. The man's car keys caught Bob's growing criminal imagination. If he could find the man's car, Bob could dump the man in the trunk and get him out of the house.

Bob made his way to the same quiet side entrance from which he'd entered the house. Discreetly slipping out, he stole through his yard into that of a neighbor's, and made his way out into the street.

Re-examining the car keys, he tried to discern what make and model of automobile the man drove. In his study of the keys, however, he saw something that might save him time: a car alarm switch. By pressing down on the button, he could hear the sound of a surprisingly close car. He didn't want to draw attention to himself, though, so he only tapped the button with the result that the alarm made a quick chirp before dying back into silence.

Fixing his attention on the noise he hunted around for the man's car breathlessly. Upon locating it, he was shocked to discover that it was parked around the corner, a mere two car-lengths away from his own car.

Sparing an instant of amusement regarding the quaint similarity of their sham attempts toward espionage, he unlocked the door and entered the car. He cursorily searched through it for any possible address books, papers, or incriminating evidence that might help the police. Finding nothing, however, but two old magazines and a crushed paper coffee cup on the floor, he abandoned his search and climbed into the driver's seat. It gave him a repulsively close sense of the dead man's presence to sit in his car, to touch the steering wheel *he* had touched, to feel the cushion under him that *he* had felt. Suppressing a twinge of nausea, though, Bob stabbed the key into the ignition, started the engine and drove the vehicle closer to his house.

He got it far enough away that any hypothetical surveillance equipment might not notice it, but close enough to help him when he had to drag the body out and get it to the trunk.

"God, now I have to go back inside!" he muttered to himself.

Forced by circumstances, he had to choke down his repugnance, forget his little private store of superstitions and haul the still-warm corpse out of the house.

He gasped as he bent over his task like a novice longshoreman struggling with a sack of potatoes. He fell and promptly struggled up to his feet.

"Jesus, he's heavy!" he exhaled, as he started again.

Eventually, he got a firmer grip and managed to drag him to the side-entrance of the house. Now came the hard part: getting him outside and to the car with no one noticing. He knew that nothing short of a miracle could ensure his inconspicuousness while carrying out his grisly enterprise. But he had to try.

Once outside, under the illumination of a full moon, he could see better. For the first time he got a good look at the dead man's underbred, overstuffed face. Bald, with a big shiny pink head, his face presented to Bob's startled gaze a weird resemblance—by some a strange perversity of association—to a man's thumb. Looking at his own thumb, he was shocked by the familial resemblance.

"God!" he whispered breathily, pausing.

After a minute his wits returned to him, and he could think again. An idea seized him. Leaving the dead man where he was, he ran out to a shed in his back yard. He returned with a tarp and a wheelbarrow.

The prospect of lifting the heavy corpse from the ground and into the wheelbarrow was daunting. But, after some minutes of effort, he finally—with a smothered exclamation—managed it. Once his gruesome load was in place, he threw the tarp over top of it. Staggering behind the lurching wheelbarrow, he managed to push it out to the car. He had to rest for a minute to regain his breath. Due to his terror of being caught out, however, this brief respite scarcely helped him. For in the quiet suburban evening, he knew that, at any moment, someone might peek out a window, or some car might drive by and inadvertently witness what was going on. So, getting back to his work, he struggled to tip the lip of the wheelbarrow into the back of the car and let it disgorge its contents into the trunk. He had to help it along, of course; and, after a series of painful stages, he succeeded in pushing the body into the opened trunk.

Chapter Three

I

Thursday, November 19th, 9:05 pm

After driving the car ten blocks away to a public park and abandoning it there, Bob returned to his home on foot.

How long would it be before someone discovered the body, he wondered?

It didn't matter. Regardless of when it was found, it would be long after the time period set for his son's release: *twenty-three hours.*

Or was it twenty-two now?

Yes.

He found himself jogging faster as he made his way home. What would happen there, though? He'd have to come up with some plan to track his father down. But how?

The simplest way of getting more light on the question would be to visit certain family members who might know.

With that thought in mind, he settled on his father's Uncle Leo. He always seemed to know how to get in touch with people. Bob climbed into his own car and drove to Leo's house.

He never liked his great-uncle. He had the look of a man who perpetually has to go to the bathroom, the kind of person whose life appeared to have been passed in a protracted bout of painful gassiness. The expression of his face in repose was that of physical discomfort; and it looked as if one was exacerbating it whenever one addressed him. His natural crabbiness colored his whole manner. There was more impatience and discomfort than vigor in the character of his features; and the same bad-natured disposition may be traced to the aforementioned spiritual dyspepsia that described the nature of his turbulent soul.

He had white hair (what was left of it, that is), with a face channeled with deep wrinkles and a neck that was as saggy and loose as a turkey's.

When he spoke, his voice was raspy with all the odd crackles and strange pops that one would expect from an ancient vinyl album: "Bobby? I haven't seen you for a while!"

Bob winced, made vaguely uncomfortable as he was by the usage of an anachronistic diminutive that he hadn't used for himself since the age of nine.

Passing over the fact in silence, he greeted his great-uncle and apologized for just barging in.

"Well, it's not *that* late," said Leo. "What? About nine?"

"Yes."

"So what brings you here?"

"Well, it's complicated," began Bob, nervously.

"What is?"

"Well, you see it's like this," plunged Bob, lying anxiously to someone he had never lied to before. No matter what else he might have thought about his skill at prevarication, his great-uncle seemed to accept without reservation that he wanted to make amends with his estranged father.

Leo said grimly that he thought it was commendable—despite their differences. Leo himself had differences with his nephew, William. And on the old man began to talk, his narrative veering off, away from the subject at hand, and ending up (somehow) about a problem he was having with his spleen. Bob smiled appreciatively and tried to get in a question or two about his father. He did discover vague intimations that his father had recently contacted his cousin, but beyond that Bob could find no evidence that the old man supposed him to have come to see him for anything but his long-winded stories.

The fact that Leo was gossipy filled Bob with hope, reassuring him about the communicational possibilities of the William's existence.

Somehow, though, his mention of various family-members always coincided with some new bodily ailment he experienced while in their company. Bob shifted uncomfortably as the old man pulled a long face and talked discursively about his myriad physical ailments.

Eventually Bob found himself panting at his uncle in a controlled voice, "Please...about my father . . ."

The agitating old man relented, talking about William again. But then, before Bob knew it, he'd digress again into some fruitless conversational tangent.

Ever fearful of exploding in hysterics, Bob marshaled all his patience, put all his anger under a tight rein, and kept firmly before him the vision of finding his son.

With the thought of the boy, his eyes flashed up to a wall bound clock.

Tick-tock, tick-*talk*.

Overwhelmed by the stalking specter of failure, he suddenly became more assertive and said, "Please, Uncle Leo. Can you tell me where he is?"

The old man finally began to concentrate. "No, I'm sorry that I can't quite remember his address. But I know my sister will. She writes things down. And she sent him a package recently."

"Which sister? You have two," said Bob.

"May."

"Does May still live at the same address? On Oak Road?"

"That's right. The blue house."

On the strength of that vague remark, he wished his great-uncle goodnight and set off for his aunt's house.

II

Bob's heart nearly gave out when he drove to his great-aunt May's house only to find that no one was home. The passage of time affected him physically, it would seem, each second that slipped away feeling like a grain of his own soul peeling off and becoming lost forever. He paced outside her home. He ran his fingers through his hair. Just on the point of harassing her neighbors for information, a car pulled up in front of her house.

For a fleeting moment, he feared that it might be someone who had followed him. But it wasn't. It was merely a car filled with his aunt's friends from church.

After the passenger door opened, a woman who was far older than he remembered climbed out. She was soon assisted by her great-nephew—who was, in turn, assisted by the driver of the car.

His great-aunt May looked positively fresh, with her healthy indifference to the aging process. She was a traditional, no-nonsense "old lady". Eyeglasses perched as high as attic windows under a thatch of severely-parted hair, and a sallow complexion made her look like an old yellowed photograph.

In seeing her now, objectively, she looked exactly like her brother Leo—but with a wig on.

After helping her to the door, he asked his aunt if he could trouble her for some information.

"Anything," she replied. "But come in, Bobby. I don't want insects to get into the house."

"Sorry," he said apologetically, as he crossed the threshold and closed the door behind him.

Meanwhile the old woman went about the house, turning on lights. "Would you like some tea?" she asked.

"No, I'm afraid I don't have time. Would you like me to help you off with your coat?"

"Thank you," she said.

After returning from the closet, he remarked, "I'm really in a bit of a hurry. I apologize. I don't want to get in the way of your nightly routine. I just came because Uncle Leo said that you might have my father's current address."

"I do, as a matter of fact," said the old woman, who absented herself to look up the information.

As she rummaged around in a desk, Bob stole a look around. The windows were hung with curtains, vague as shadows, next to which on the walls a whole series of family photos were arranged, which spoke of past happiness and hinted at bygone get-togethers.

For the old woman it was home, though for her adult children the living room was more like an actor's green room—a place to find snacks, kick up one's feet and idly thumb through magazines before being called out onto the stage of Life.

Because of these photos of his widowed Aunt May's adult children, his mind sprang back to his son. Where was he now? Was someone hurting him? Anguish made him look at his aunt with impatience. She struck him as positively doddering, and he wondered how much time she'd waste as Billy, by imperceptible degrees, drew closer to death.

Bob hated himself for becoming frustrated with the old woman. She finally found the address and he reflected upon his selfish pushiness in the face of her own contrasting saintliness.

He was effusive in his gratitude.

"I'm sorry I don't have a phone number. Just an address," his great-aunt said.

"That's okay," smiled Bob, excitedly. "I can contact him with this. You're the best. Once again, I'm sorry for barging in on you and breaking up your routine."

"Oh, it was no trouble at all," she insisted.

Bob, having made his hasty goodbyes, decided to carry the results of his investigation to a public telephone. Knowing that the cell phone he had been given was likely to be tapped, and skeptical of his own telephone at home, he drove to a nearby convenience store and sought out a telephone there. Dialing information, he got the area code for the city and state where his father lived. Using that information, he called a local operator and asked if she could give him the telephone number for the address he read off to her.

"I'm sorry, sir. But I can't do that," she said.

"Why? Is it an unlisted number or something?"

"No, it's just not our policy. FCC regulations state that f—"

"Well, don't reverse directories exist?" he interrupted.

"Yes, you can find them on the Internet, for instance. But we, on our end, can't—"

"Thank you. Sorry to disturb you," he said, hanging up.

It was getting late. Would a library be open where he could access the Internet? Probably not, he concluded. Not wanting to drive home and enter the house where so much unpleasantness had recently occurred, he decided to drive to his office at the supermarket. Once reaching it, he hastened to his work computer, gained access to the Internet and tried to look up the information. Within ten minutes, he had a telephone number. He dialed it. No one answered. It rang and rang, but no one picked up.

Sweat stood out on his forehead as he considered the very real possibility that his father no longer lived there. So he dialed his great-aunt, and got her confirmation that she had only very recently sent him some photographs.

"So he's still there?" pressed Bob.

"Yes. As of two weeks ago," she replied.

Saying goodbye, he ended the call and again tried the telephone number associated with his father's address. Still, it rang and rang—to no effect.

Anxious, but somewhat reassured by his great-aunt, he decided that he would just have to risk it, to go there himself and see if his father really lived there.

It was the only option he had left.

Should he call the airport and try to get a flight? He started looking for the telephone number for the airport, but stopped. To book a flight this late in the evening was manifestly impossible. Though he was disconcerted he was not demoralized by this new obstacle. A train, then, perhaps? Yet after another interval of uncertain meditation, he realized that that also would be too slow.

"God, why did he have to move so far away?" raged Bob.

But his father wasn't so far—maybe a seven-hour drive, if he hurried.

Would he be up for such a long drive—after having had no sleep? Thinking of his son—and his wife—he knew he'd be able to rise up above his own personal weariness and make the insomniac journey.

After driving to a gas station and buying a map, he decided to set off there and then. Why not? What did he have to pack? Anything he would need, he could buy on the road. He didn't care about anything else. Shouldn't he at least phone work and tell them he'd be absent the next day?

Such a commonplace thought never occurred to him. For far off and dim were the banal responsibilities he was supposed to attend to the next day, all thoughts of the supermarket fading. Everything connected with his existence as he had known it seemed curiously remote and unimportant as he set off on a journey that, in one way or another, would change his life forever.

Chapter Four

I

Thursday, November 19th, 10:44 pm

Suddenly it was as if two enormous gates had opened in his life, gates giving upon an immense unknowable darkness—through which anything might come. Even death. As he drove, he reflected upon how surreal it was: the kidnapping, the cell phone, the shadowy people giving him orders. It was all so ridiculous that his mind, even expanding to its full dimensions, failed to grasp it. What he knew, he knew intuitively, not intellectually. And what his blood whispered to him was *Hurry!*

He obeyed that impulse, and he drove. Fast.

He was cut off from his old life now—and it brought about a revolution in his thoughts. Driving past the city-limits and seeing the familiar landmarks of his existence it all looked so familiar, but so different—as if it were part of a dream. The city where he had spent so much of his life seemed to become instantly divided from him by a great distance, a greater distance than could actually be accounted for by physical space.

Though he didn't yet realize it, with the sole decision of embarking on this journey to save his son, he had already stepped outside his own life. Consequently, the artifacts of his old existence took on a foreign cast, a strange appearance. These fluctuating lapses from one life to another carried with them a sense of dissonance. And he was not immune to distress arising from these divergent strands in his own mental composition.

He felt himself developing a headache.

62

Yet this paltry physical discomfort was as nothing when weighed against the larger psychological upheaval he was experiencing. Bob began to look out over the tremendous vistas of possibility that his fugitive status now opened, and he lapsed into a phase of imaginative release. Things that had seemed set in stone were now visibly in flux, things that had previously appeared as dry as dead bones put on flesh and were now startlingly alive.

It was so foreign to him—this sensation of blind motion; manic propulsion. Nevertheless—in some inappropriate way—it was almost exhilarating. It was as if the familiar scenery of banal routine had been drawn aside and Life stood unveiled. *Real* Life. To have stated it before as standing before two gates was limiting it. In fact, there weren't two doors in front of him but two hundred, two thousand, two million. Any direction he turned in this new existence of adrenaline and chaos was a new door past which he'd never traveled.

It was bracing, but scary, confusing.

Would his father even be at the address he had been given? And, if not, what would he do then?

Where would he go?

The crossroads is the cross upon which the indecisive are crucified. Knowing that, he kept driving without questioning himself. So long as he was in motion, all would be fine. Movement, speed, action.

It was better to look forward, rather than allow himself to be drawn back into painful doubt. Because it was there that the memory of his son waited for him. In those crowded moments, he thought it was best to avert his mind from the thornier, more emotional elements of the situation. If possible, he had to compartmentalize his emotions, so that he wouldn't allow them to gain the upper hand and trip him up, weaken him.

The speed of his driving helped him, producing a peculiar exaltation. The old Bob Ebersol was gone—the Bob Ebersol of strict behavior, repressed tendencies, faultless punctuality, priggish adherence to all the rules. This Bob Ebersol, who had seemed so satisfactory and complete and final, had been thrust aside like a mask.

Now there was something more living and vibrant and urgent underneath.

At last he came into contact with it.

And then all the heat and energy of this tumultuous, subterranean layer of his identity resolved itself, coming into focus like a diffuse light tamed and concentrated by a lens. Then the light that was in him—the light of defiance—flashed in his eyes as he resolved to find his son.

A strange numbness began to spread through him.

He was bracing himself. For never before had he truly been tested by those events that show in the light of day the inner worth of a man, the marrow of his essence, the fiber of his being; that reveal the quality of his resistance and the secret texture of his most-hidden character.

But now he was challenged, spurred forth and upheld by one desire: To save his son.

II

Though Bob was concentrating on resolving one crisis, another series of circumstances had uncoiled to complicate the situation. Though he didn't know it, his wife was in danger almost from the second he had dropped her off at her sister's house.

Bob's headlights had only been gone a few moments when Julia thought she saw another pair. Since her sister's home was in a remote area, it was unusual to see much traffic. At first, she assumed it was her husband, having turned around for some reason. That assumption was refuted when the outlines of a van became visible. What made the van's appearance suspicious was the slowness at which it moved. Its headlights swung into view like lightning strikes that threw Julia off balance. Her mind seized, her eyes riveted as she tried to adjust to the Improbable. But the Improbable had just happened. What now?

She swallowed, the panic in her rising.

The vehicle came to a jolting stop.

With mounting hysteria she struck out, running from her sister's yard to a stretch of woods behind the neighborhood. Her eyes followed the line of trees in the distance. Trying to keep low, she dashed toward them. Guided by instinct she abruptly decided not to make for the safety of the foliage itself, but to hide before she reached it. With what seemed like her last breath, she dove in an attempt to hide in the tall starched grass.

In the meantime, her worst fear was borne out: her pursuers had seen her. The doors of the van swung open with the menace of a cobra's hood, disgorging two men who broke into a rapid stride toward the woods.

Julia cowered in the grass, trying to moderate her breathing, silence her body. Her heart thundered in her ears so loudly that she was certain they would hear it.

As she clenched her eyes shut the two men split up, going in different directions, trying to flush her out. One man had a flashlight while the other had to make due with what appeared to be a penlight from a key ring.

The lights probed every moving branch and twig.

The glowing lights weaved around trees like mythological sprites moving through the woods.

Though she cautiously opened her eyes, the next minutes were a blur for Julia.

She knew that time was now measured in moments, apportioned out in heartbeats. If she was going to get up and make a break for it, she would have to do it any second.

Calling as little attention to herself as she could, she tried to draw herself up into a crawling position. But her fear was such that her body would not cooperate. Any attempt to rise instantly provoked a sensation of paralysis. She could only tremble in place. Julia caught sight of one of the men as he swept past her on his way to another series of trees. Eventually, however, he came back. Stopping and looking around with his bestial, penetrating gaze, he then turned and shouted for his cohort.

Her mind was racing, her eyes darting everywhere.

Overhead, a bruised sky swept by cold wind produced a radiant moon. Like the stars, it gave off a platinum light. Looking up, she wondered at the revolving heavens—in awe of such distances which were capable of leaping across eternities of time and space to drizzle down around her, each distant star's light like a rain-drop kissing the earth.

But the moon—oh, the moon— filled her with dread, as it stared down like a third, all-seeing eye, one that threatened to give her away. She could think of nothing else as pockets of darkness were pierced by intersecting shafts of light behind her.

The insects around her fell silent. For some seconds everything seemed to listen.

The place, the frenzy, the darkness all conspired to create the impression that this situation was part of a fevered dream. She felt that at any moment the sound of the men would cease, and she would find herself stirring in bed.

"Hey!" shouted an out-of-breath voice just paces away from her. "We know you're here somewhere."

Julia closed her eyes and tried harder to become invisible and blend into her background. It was futile because they hit on the one thing that would override her self-protective instinct: threats against her sister and her family, if she didn't come out.

"You have ten seconds."

Julia winced at the peremptory commands the man issued. But, faced with that ultimatum, she capitulated.

"Okay, okay," she heard a female voice say, as if from a distance. Had she herself spoken? It sounded remarkably like her own voice. Yet she was too overwhelmed to have remembered giving away her own position as the men converged on her.

She was lifted to her feet by one of them. Feeling dizzy at first she staggered, but slowly found her balance.

Julia, meeting his eyes, looked into them down a long vista of brutality and moral anomie, and perceived that unmistakable stamp of bad breeding and cretinism on his face. A different reaction met her as she looked over at his partner.

The second man, somewhat taller and younger, stopped in his tracks when he saw her, looking at her round-eyed, almost frightened.

She didn't understand his reaction. But it made little difference as she looked around herself in panic.

"You did the right thing," said the shorter man, trying to keep her under control.

Held firmly in check by her two captors, a shaken Julia was led into the back of the van. She got inside the vehicle and another nightmare began its dreadful course, played out in the dirty interior of the van. It was there that one of the two men issued a command that she take off her jacket and lift the sleeve of her blouse to expose the flesh of her upper arm.

"Hold your arm still," said the shorter man, his voice frigid in its flat delivery.

The next impressions she had were of the smells of gasoline and motor oil as her face pressed against the van's blue acrylic carpet, the coarse scratchiness of the fibers making their vague challenge to human pubic hair.

As she lay there, she felt the effects of the drug wash over her. Before she knew it, her thoughts were as tangled and nonsensical as they usually were when she was about to fall asleep. In her wandering and enfeebled thoughts, she held onto the image of her son and husband for as long as she could and sank ever deeper into the black quicksand of unconsciousness.

Chapter Five

I

Friday, November 20th, 4:12 am

The hours passed before him with a sluggish tread.

In Bob's ears there was a continual sizzling of the question that haunted him, *What if my father's not there?*

The very real possibility that he wouldn't be able to find him, despite having an address, laid its cold touch upon him. But not being able to find him was exactly the factor he wanted as much as possible to keep out of his talk and his thoughts. The address was right because it *had* to be right.

As he continued to drive he began to grow afraid of his solitude, fearful of the maddening round of his thoughts. Concentrating on the road made him feel better, distracted, perhaps. Speed felt like some sort of protection.

Life, so recently a congested monotony darkened by boredom, became exciting, mysterious and alien.
In some perverse way, he blossomed under it. It sharpened his senses, called upon the full resources of his mind. The world surrounding him now seemed more vivid; new sights sprang into his eyes.

In the past, when driving, the scenery went by but it made little or no impression on him. Now, however, he took it all in. For the current of the urgent activity on which he was gliding called for all his attention; and never had its tides been so swift, its gulf streams so dangerous. Therefore it was a relief to relax in the numb grip of velocity—if only for a little while.

II

His speed only abated when twenty miles from his destination a storm started to rise. Nature added increased drama choking the sky with clouds, as rain softened the outlines of the landscape. He gave a start at thunder which was like a detonation, a bomb set to shatter the sky. The resulting lightning like a "spider crack" running up the side of the Night, its light merely the Day peeking in briefly from the other side.

The storm affected his mood profoundly, demoralizing him, making him superstitious. He took it as a good sign, then, when within two miles of the address, the storm abated and moved on to the east.

It was no longer raining as he got out of his car in front of an attractive villa on a quiet suburban street. Standing there before the door he experienced a throb of apprehension. He had no clear idea of what he was going to do or say, beyond the definite conviction that, whatever obstacle stood in his way, he would secure his father's compliance no matter what was requested of them. He would threaten him himself, if need be.

He was determined that his son wasn't going to die.

In fact, he had a clearer image of that son than he did of the child's grandfather. Bob's memory of his father had less the sharp, clean lines of a photo than the dull, hazy blurriness of a rude lithograph.

He expected to find a man who was woefully coarsened, grown cynical, if not entirely broken. What he discovered was something quite different when the bright face of his father signaled joyful recognition after he threw open the door. Bob was surprised to find a florid, big-chinned man who looked less like a criminal than a tan and well-fed businessman. He was handsome and full-blooded, with the physical distinction that comes after a lifetime of refinement and healthy dieting.

As for his nice villa and expensive furnishings, he enjoyed his son's amazement. Smiling and watching the effect of it all on him, he waved Bob in. "Well, just don't stand there," he said.

As Bob crossed the threshold, he wondered, "Were you expecting me?"

"Well, you called on the phone earlier," began the older man.

Cutting him short, Bob said, "How did you know it was me? You didn't answer the phone."

"Caller ID," said the man. "I didn't know it was you, *per se*. But I saw the area code and I took a chance and called Uncle Leo. He told me that you were trying to locate me. So I just assumed that...well...who else could be phoning me? No one other than one or two members of my family there knows my phone number."

"Why didn't you pick up?" asked Bob.

"I rarely answer the phone when I don't know who it is. I tried to call you back at the number on the caller ID when I realized that it must be you, but no one answered at your end. It just kept ringing."

"So you *did* try to call me back?"

"Of course."

"I made better time driving here than I thought. Since there was no traffic at this time of night—or, I mean, morning—I shaved nearly an hour off. It's what? About five in the morning now? Sorry I came so early."

"That's okay, that's okay," assured William. And then, after a pause of brimming enthusiasm, he said, "So what brings you here—after all these years?"

"I don't know," began Bob, nervously. He brought forth a few commonplace phrases, but his father scarcely

71

listened. He was so happy to see his son again. He felt like he had stepped back in time. Every line of his son's face, every plane of his features, the very set of his jaw, while contributing to this effect, sent forth each a separate appeal to some sensitive memory. So fully was he an anthology of his progenitors that it overwhelmed Ebersol, senior.

His nose was his mother's, his hairline his father's; his gray eye-color belonged to the Ebersol line, while his voice was purely from his mother's family. Every word and every tone of his son fed some starved sensibility in the man.

Had he examined the feelings that overtook him at the sight of his son, he might have reflected upon the fact that, though he had outwardly broken with his past years ago, many memories still lingered in his mind. Certainly, he was a criminal, a bad person (and he kept himself away from his son mainly for these reasons), but he had never totally surrendered his feelings for him or came to terms with his loss. He thought he had. That is to say, the old identity that he used to have—that tiny "father" that was still a part of his composition, even if in an attenuated form—only stirred in its sleep at the reports he'd every so often receive after he discreetly sent away to learn about his son. But he could never have anticipated the emotions he had now, as the young man stood before him.

His son could not be made to fit into any of the patterns of his current life; yet there he was, ensconced in his heart and mind as deeply as the day on which he was born and William held him in his arms at the hospital. Sometimes, half irritably, he said to himself that with an effort he could forget about him once and for all; yet he lived on in him, unseen yet ineffaceable, like a ghost that haunted his very body—a second soul to clatter about inside him next to his own soul.

As for Bob, the sight of his father awoke in him a confusion of feelings, of which only the uppermost dealt with the immediate situation at hand. His heart was icy toward the man. Yes, he had once shed hot tears over him. But to these recollections Bob could shut his heart. They seemed so irrelevant—as if they were the memories of someone else, someone who—thank God!—he no longer was.

He had solved the problems of his upbringing years ago by closing tight his emotions, shutting himself off from the past and learning to be more forward-looking, more future-oriented.

It was the only way he could get beyond the scars of his childhood. But now these scars were re-opened as his old emotions at his abandonment combined with the new element of resentment for what the man had caused in the present. After all, his father was the one possible point where his life made contact with the underworld. Because of that fact, his own son was now in danger.

He wanted to yell at the man, but somehow that expenditure of emotion would strike too intimate a note. All he could do was keep his distance and address him in the stilted, overly-polite tones that he might have reserved for a stranger.

Because of that constraint, they engaged in a fluent exchange of commonplaces by way of conversation. William asked his son about his hometown, their mutual relatives, his job.

"Job?"

"Yeah, what do you do?" asked William.

Embarrassed, but desperate not to show it, he said with a steadied voice, "I'm the manager of a supermarket."

"I'm glad," grinned his father. "That's a stable choice. You're obviously a very stable person."

"Stable?"

"I've always respected stable people," continued William. "I never was. All the problems of my life can be traced to that fact. Because of that I've always admired people who were like you. You know...good, hard-working, reliable."

Bob, in his agitation, felt as if his father laid an unkind emphasis on the word "reliable". To Bob, his own worst sin in life had been "reliability", because it connoted laziness, stodginess, conformity. And he no longer wanted to be the sort of person who goes through life paralyzed, the sort who tries to make a virtue out of their paralysis by calling it "stability".

Though he didn't adduce his philosophy on this matter, his father saw that he wanted to say something more.

What Bob really wanted to say, however, had nothing to do with careers or jobs or life-philosophies; it had to do with his son. Yet what he had to say choked in his throat, for it was so disturbing, so terrifying that he didn't know how to open the subject.

The one or two times he tried, the thing died on his lips.

His father, however, realized that his son had something to tell him, for the younger man's look suddenly arrested him.

"You didn't really come here just to chat with me after all these years, did you?" he asked.

"No," confessed Bob, sheepishly.

His father's face fell. "Well, then why did you come?"

Bob seemed to brace himself for a great effort, and then began speaking. "It's about my son...it's about Billy," he began.

William arched his eyebrows. "You named him 'Billy'? You named him after *me*? You did, didn't you?"

Bob, who thought of himself as beyond the reach of his past, felt tricked when his father's "You did, didn't you?" pierced him, made him a son again.

Reluctantly, he said, "I suppose so. Maybe. I don't know. But that's not what I'm here to talk about. Billy, as I said, is the reason I'm here."

Thus he began to give his father a full account of the situation—a set of circumstances that troubled the older man greatly. He didn't know what to make of it as Bob finished his narrative and stood there, fluttering with nerves yet desperately determined. But Bob could tell something about his father: with his veiled expression and his troubled silence, the man clearly knew something.

"What is it?" he demanded.

"It's a long story," his father hedged.

"I'm listening."

William Ebersol ran his fingers through his hair and paced the length of the room. He seemed to be weighing his words before speaking. Moving back toward his son, he said, "I know exactly what's going on. I'm sorry. I'm sorry I had a part in this."

"What are you talking about?" uttered Bob, anxiously.

Not directly answering him, his father said, "Well, why do you think they asked you to find me?"

"I don't know. I just assumed that they wanted you to help me rob a bank or something."

At this, William's wounded vanity cried out. For, he stressed to his son, he wasn't a thug. He had advanced his fortunes by more sophisticated methods such as money laundering, stock manipulation, Ponzi schemes, not by the vulgarity of armed robbery.

"I wouldn't know what was involved in robbing a bank any more than you would!"

"Then why you? I don't understand."

His father then sketched quickly, in broad outline, the situation in which he and a number of other men had carried out a "job" together.

"But one of the men got greedy," he continued. "He did something that he should never have done, something that breaks every code—"

"Honor among thieves?" interjected Bob.

Passing over the remark in silence, William told his son about how the mission's ringleader had contrived to place one of his colleagues in a precarious position, and how it led to his death. Considering the untrustworthiness of the man, the circumstances surrounding the death seemed open to suspicion.

"Why would he kill one of his own?" asked Bob.

"An amount of money that's split six ways is bigger than one that's split seven," he answered, with suppressed anger. "But not all of us took it. I, for one, refused to accept it. When it came time to apportion the money, I took my share—a share that was made on the assumption that it would be split six ways. So I netted an extra $1,634,502.63."

"That's exactly the amount they want for Billy!" exclaimed Bob. His father, with a darkened countenance, made a gesture which implied that the significance of the sum was not lost on him, whereupon Bob returned, "So then you know who's behind this?"

"Yes. Again, I have to say that I'm so sorry. I never would have done what I did if I knew that he would go after you or your family. I kept my personal history and connections scrupulously hidden. Many of my closest friends have no idea that I ever even had a son or a grandchild. I did it as a protection, but—"

"But what?" asked Bob, irritably.

His father's face went white and a look of suddenly remembering something crucial swept over his face. Interrupting the flow of his previous comments and diverting the conversation into a different conduit, William asked, "I'm sorry to go off into a tangent, but something just occurred to me. When you were telling me about the kidnapping, you mentioned them instructing you to contact them once you reached me . . ."

"Yeah. So?"

"How are you supposed to do that?"

"They gave me a disposable cell phone to c—"

Interrupting his son, William said, "God!"

Confused, Bob defensively said, "What?"

"They didn't give you a cell phone to communicate with you; they gave you a cell phone because they can use it to track you!"

"What are you saying?" asked Bob.

"I'm saying that I hid my whereabouts, and I hid them well. They couldn't find me. So they used you to find me. Your whole function in this wasn't to rob a bank, but to lead them to me!" The deplorable precedent of his murdered colleague being present in his mind, he added, "It's not safe here now."

"Jesus!" wondered Bob, his head spinning.

"But we probably still have time," his father returned calmly. "You just got here yourself. We just need to get rid of the phone."

Against his express advice, though, Bob was determined to keep the hateful thing because it was his only link to the kidnappers, hence to his son. As William listened his thoughts slipped back into the old groove; and, after some brooding contemplation, his face was transfigured by inspiration. After emerging from his sibyllic trance, he asked, "Is it possible to still make it *seem* as if you have the cell phone while not actually having it at all?" By way of explanation, he said that—though he couldn't speak with absolute assurance—he vaguely knew that business calls could be forwarded to another telephone number. What if Bob got a second phone and got the phone company to forward the calls from the first phone to the second. Meanwhile, he could ditch the first phone. Stick it on a train going east, dump it in a landfill, post it in a box to Mongolia. He then asked his son to imagine the kidnappers trying to follow it while, meanwhile, he'd be elsewhere—and still in communication with the ignorant kidnappers.

Though Bob told him that it was a brilliant idea, he said that he wasn't the owner of the phone. So even if the phone company had representatives up at this ungodly hour, and even if this call-forwarding feature could be activated immediately, he'd still be at an impasse since he didn't have the information to be able to pass as the owner of the phone on the account. No customer service representative would let a stranger change existing service.

"But it's a disposable model," said William. "There is no 'account' attached to it. You just buy it in a store. They're usually in big bins. Let me see the cell phone they gave you."

Bob dutifully handed it over.

His father flipped it open and studied it. Going over to his own landline telephone, he picked up the receiver and dialed a number.

"Who are you calling at this hour?" asked Bob.

"Shhh," intoned William. "Yes, hello. I'd like the customer service number for Seria Communications. Yes, thank you. Uh-huh..."

Scrambling for a pad, he wrote down a number. After finishing his call with who Bob could only assume was an operator, William dialed the number for the makers of the disposable cell phone in his hand. Though it was just before dawn, there was surprisingly—agonizingly—a long wait before the man could speak to a customer service representative.

Bob peeked out a window which gave a prospect of the quiet street beyond. He didn't see anything suspicious.

Coming back to his father, he watched as the antsy man waited. After ten more minutes, he was connected with a human being.

"Yes, thank you," Bob heard him utter. "I have a disposable cell phone that I bought from your company. I made the mistake of throwing the package that it came in away, and now I need to know about what features I can get on it. What I mean to say is: can I get the call-forwarding feature on it?...*I can?*" he smiled. "Thank you. That's very helpful. Can I do it right now, with you? Great!"

Bob's heart raced with vicarious elation as he watched his father conduct the call.

"The phone number I'd like the calls forwarded to is (502) 864-9221. And the number for the disposable cell phone is (612) 968-9555. Uh-huh...uh-huh...Yeah...I understand...Here. Here's the credit card number . . ."

After reading off a series of numbers (from memory, no less) William perked up. "Then that'll do it?" he asked the person on the phone. "Thank you."

Bob's face brightened. "Well, I'll be damned!" he exclaimed. "You actually pulled it off?"

He abruptly took a cheerier view of his father as the older man said, "It wasn't so hard."

His father's manifest competence gave him the first real comfort he had had since this whole situation began. Nevertheless, Bob's spine stiffened when his father made motions to leave the room. "Where are you going?" he asked.

"To get you the second cell phone. *My* cell phone. Whatever calls come through will come through to that.

You can carry it with you. All we have to do now is drive somewhere and ditch this one."

Bob waited as his father disappeared for a minute and then returned with the aforementioned cell phone.

"Where should we take it?"

"Anyplace that will move it, make it look like it's *you* traveling. I like the idea of the train myself. We can stick it on a train car or something. There's a station not far from here."

"You confuse me," declared Bob.

"How so?" asked his father.

"Think of the life you could have had if you had used your brains for something other than crime," replied Bob, censoriously. "Imagine."

"I know, I know," sighed William. "I wish things had been different myself, that I'd had different opportunities, a different background. But sometimes you just have to take what you can get."

"Did you have to 'take' that money, though?" returned Bob, tartly.

"Why not?" argued William. "Who do you think we scammed? Orphans? The state treasury? No, the job I told you about revolved around a drug dealer. It was drug money. Why not take it? If I played Good Samaritan and turned the money over to the authorities, they'd only end up stealing it themselves. After all, they only need one or two major busts a year. These, they push in the news in order to get funding. As for the rest of the time, let's just say: drugs and cash have a way of disappearing before arriving at the police station property room."

"You're so cynical," said Bob. "You've been having shady dealings for so long you think everyone else is, too. I remember that about you when I was a kid. You seemed so intelligent, so worldly; but now—"

"But now *what?*"

After hesitating and being prompted to continue, Bob said, "You come off as a bit paranoid. You probably believe in a whole bunch of conspiracy theories."

Insulted, William—whose social axioms had been gathered in the soil of bitter experience—challenged his son by saying, "Would you be surprised if I told you that the man who has your son is a police detective?"

The words had the impact of an explosion. He stared at his father, dismayed. All his confused, contradictory impressions assumed a new aspect at this announcement; and to hide his shock he added defiantly: "How can you know that?"

Seeing the blood drain away from his son's face, William felt as if his point was gained.

"I know who's doing this," he replied, "because that's who's angry that I took a sixth-part of the take, and not a seventh. A man named Spence."

Bob's eyes were fixed on his father in a gaze that contained neither distrust nor doubt, but only a chilling wonder.

The revelation suddenly opened a new view of Detective Spence to Bob's wonder. It threw the whole picture of what had happened out of perspective. Shifted everything he thought he knew about the situation. How could Spence have been so cold-blooded and seemingly at his ease while talking to the very people he was planning on victimizing?

Suddenly as these memories chased across his brain, he thought about all the things Spence asked about and realized why he plied them with all those questions about home security or whether he owned a gun or not. He was trying to ascertain his victim's vulnerabilities. Likewise with the remarks he made to Billy about baseball cards.

Was that how he lured him into his car? The boy's defenses would have been lowered both by the offer of a baseball card, as well as by the approval his parents showed toward this figure of authority. Of course, Billy would have gone quietly and with no suspicion of danger.

"Oh, God," he moaned.

"What?" asked his father, impatiently. "Let me get dressed and then we'll drive and go ditch the phone. I'll be right back."

He dressed faster than Bob would have imagined, but the younger man was still consumed with dread.

"What's wrong?" asked his father.

"What you told me...It still doesn't change anything. If they don't get the money, Billy's dead."

William met this quickly. "No, they'll have the money. Don't be afraid on that account."

The acquiescence was so unexpected that it routed all of Bob's resolves. He, as he stood looking at his father, reflected that his character, for all its seeming hardness, its flashing edges of cunning, revealed a personality no less human than his own. He had not expected the older man to yield so quickly to his demands or to confess his sense of guilt that way.

As William went off to gather what funds he had on hand, Bob didn't know what to say. What words of gratitude he had came with an effort.

William's gesture brushed away the thanks he was given.

"It's my fault, after all," he said, manfully. "Here's the suitcase."

"The money's in here?" asked Bob.

"All of it."

"What are you doing with millions of dollars in cash, just sitting around?" wondered Bob.

"Try taking it into a bank," replied William, dryly. "If you bring in any cash over $5,000 to deposit, they have to write up a report and people will audit your bank account. It's set up that way to hinder drug dealers. So..."

"So what?"

"So I have to have a suitcase full of cash until I can deposit it little by little. So far I only deposited a few thousand. When I went to my bedroom I didn't put money in, I took it out. I took the rest of the money that was seen as my legitimate 'cut,' leaving in the $1,634,502. As for the sixty-three cents, he'll just have to make due without that," said William, his remark larded with sarcasm. "Here. Take it."

"Thank you," said Bob.

"Now let's go."

But before they could get out the door, something happened to arrest their progress: a sound. William heard it and paused. Bob looked around the room, as if seeking the clue to his father's agitation. Then came another sound—a slight creak. The older man looked up, and their eyes exchanged meanings for a rapid minute. His gaze was as troubled as his son's.

"Maybe it's nothing," he murmured. "The wind."

"Okay. Let's go," said Bob.

"No. Wait."

The two men just stood there, listening. Perhaps thirty seconds afterward they heard another sound and recognized it as someone standing close to the front door. The faint movements had ceased for a moment and then there was silence. Then came a subtle shifting. Neither man made a move, and after an interval they saw that the doorknob was being tentatively turned.

"We gotta get out of here," broke from William, who turned on his heel and scurried out of the room.

Bob felt a deep inward trembling. The immediate effect of the feeling had been to send him forth in quest of his father. But which way should he go?

He had never been in the house before and didn't know its floor plan. Nevertheless, he stole away as softly as he could in the direction down which his father disappeared. Passing through a succession of rooms, he made it to a kitchen that appeared to have a back door. But just as he got close to it, he saw that someone was trying to jimmy the lock.

With the claustrophobic feeling of being trapped, he scrambled out of the room. He didn't know the layout of the house and the exits he did know about were blocked. His hope had to be in his ability to hide and his capacity for maintaining silence.

He passed through another series of rooms when the sound of the opening back door reached him. His eyes roving over the room he was in fixed on what appeared to be a linen closet. As he squeezed inside and closed the door, his body sank into a breathless hush.

Intense attention created a furrow in his brow as he listened to them. His nerves were twisted with anxiety as he tried to infer their movements in the house.

It was clear to him that there were at least two intruders, on opposite sides of the house. They were closing in like pincers. He knew that once they closed their grip on him, he'd be shown no mercy.

He jumped nervously as steps rung on the tile floor of an adjacent bathroom.

Then the steps drew closer. The door opened and the steps were in the room, coming cautiously toward him. He remained motionless, holding his breath as if he were trying to listen to the heartbeat of a sick person. In this case, however, the heartbeat he noticed was his own. Fear welled in him. There was a pause, then the sound of a wavering soft advance, the rustle of movement just a pace away from him.

Bob stood motionless, without opening his eyes. He saw only the face of his son. It rose before him and pressed upon his vision with the same distinctness as the objects surrounding him. More so. Because they were in the dark, and Billy's countenance was lit up as if by the flame of Bob's imagination.

But suddenly another sight jostled the first one from its position and asserted itself with greater authority: that of the muzzle of a gun as it was being pressed into his face.

Chapter Six

I

Friday, November 20th, 6:53 am

Denied sleep, his eyeballs were bloodshot, his eyes looking like they had sustained rope-burns. Almost as if he had clenched his eyelids so tight in order to fasten onto the image of his son, to hold onto it—just as the picture was being torn away from him.

And what a face there was that replaced it! Behind the barrel of a gun, the visage of a middle-aged man came into focus. It was alcoholic-red with giant pores, making his skin look like a needlepoint canvas—which accounted for his thick eyebrows which looked like they were done by the same technique of pulling yarn through an embroidery frame. Thick nose hairs sprouting from various other inappropriate pores added to the impression of a work left sloppy and incomplete.

He commanded sharply. "Step out!"

Bob complied.

Leveling his weapon at his Bob, he said in a raspy, static-prone voice, "Where's your father?"

qBob was surprised to discover that fear had tightened his throat, and that he could barely find his voice. Recovering it a few moments later, he spoke slowly, with great deliberation, picking over his words like a man picks over food in an unsavory meal. "I don't know where he is," he said, "If I did, I'd be there with him. Not here."

He addressed his captor nervously, but the man turned on him a face as blank and inexpressive as a statue. If he had had a fleeting and cowardly impulse to throw himself on his mercy and offer to do whatever he said, it died there in the contemplation of that brutal and remorseless countenance.

Luckily, however, the man seemed to believe him, because Bob was indeed alone; abandoned. In reflecting over this fact himself, Bob seethed. That his father had left him corresponded with the set pattern. He was humiliated that these strangers knew his shame.

Motioning with his gun, the intruder said, "Move."

Fear seemed to have loosened Bob's joints and dulled his brain. He felt mesmerized by the horror of the situation, paralyzed. It cost him quite an effort to be able to control his limbs. But he did, falling in with the man's peremptory commands in a kind of dream.

As they walked out of the room and down a hall, Bob was in front with his captor behind, pressing the gun into his spine like the metal key of some wind-up doll. Bob's legs moved accordingly. Then, they crossed the path of a second man. He was stocky, barrel-chested, with short-cropped gray hair and a knuckle of cartilage at the tip of his nose. With weapon drawn, he was still apparently busy canvassing the house.

Bob was led to the living room.

After what seemed like a long time, the second man returned to his partner.

"Did you find anything?" asked the first man.

"Only this," he said, indicating the suitcase with the cash.

The two men seemed pleased—but it was a pleasure vitiated by the loss of their intended target: Bob's father.

"Where is he?" the second man asked, addressing Bob.

Both men read his face for a reaction. To them, Bob seemed wholly sincere in his avowals that he had no idea how his father had escaped.

"So then he's not hiding somewhere in the house? You know he left?"

Both men looked at Bob narrowly.

"I don't know if this house has some secret escape hatch or a hidden room. This is my first time here," replied Bob logically, adding, "Whether he has a hidden room here or not, your guess is as good as mine."

The captors fixed upon him a look of mingled curiosity and distrust, which unnerved Bob. He felt with trouble and mortification that he was beginning to go pale under their scrutiny.

Marking this, one of the men passed a significant glance to his partner. Afterward, the second captor broke eye contact and turned back to Bob, uttering, "Well, whatever the case, he's gone now. Let's go."

Transferring their attention from the hostage to the suitcase, one of the captors picked it up and gestured for Bob to walk toward the front door.

"Move," they said.

Flanked by the two men, Bob was led outside. They ushered him out toward a car. Instinctively heading toward the passenger-side door, he was prodded in the direction of the trunk.

Before being forced in, however, he was fitted with handcuffs.

The bitter irony was not lost on him that, so soon after callously stuffing a dead man into a car's trunk, he found himself now forced into one.

But as for the handcuffs—

He wondered momentarily if he should fight. After all, he knew that he would be either taken to be tortured (in the hopes of extracting information about his father's whereabouts) or else summarily killed and dumped somewhere.

In whatever case, they already had the money. He was useless to them now—as was his son.

In the brief time he took to reflect upon these facts, his opportunity had passed and the handcuffs were wrapped securely around his wrists. They were biting into his flesh. His captors were indifferent to his discomfort as they shoved him down into the trunk and slammed the lid down over his huddled figure.

II

Bob had no idea that, even as he was a hostage, so was his wife. Julia was in a hell of her own. She awoke to it slowly, though.

It was late autumn outside, but it might as well have been winter, for the weather was cold and raw. This circumstance added its chill to that already imparted by the tone of the rough concrete walls, the cobweb-strewn ceiling and the dusty floors. It was a dead space, all the more dead since it was also dark.

A grim scene, especially to the woman who discovered herself a prisoner there. She awoke confused, and in a kind of remoteness from the crisis of the preceding hours, through which it loomed mistily. Then she looked around herself, at first in a sense of mystification and then with dawning incredulity, as she discovered that she was no longer in the back of a van but tied to a chair in an unknown room somewhere.

In those first moments of halting consciousness it was as if a deep hypnotic stupor possessed her, depriving her of all personality. Struggling against this interior indolence which lulled her, she tried to regain possession of her faculties.

Initially, it was difficult to reflect on the circumstances that led her there, to trace the meshes in which she had been caught. A thousand thoughts crashed against each other. Trying to overcome mental congestion, she attempted to focus in on a few key images, a few concrete words. Yet the words circled in her brain till repetition robbed them of the last vestige of meaning.

At last, she thought about crying out for someone to hear her but she suppressed the impulse, with an instinctive perception that nothing could be more dangerous for her. Whoever had done this might be alerted to her resumption of consciousness; and it was to her advantage to quietly try and escape.

Her spine was pressed against the back of the chair due to a length of rope tied around her chest; her hands, likewise, were tied tightly to each arm of the chair. Her legs, in a lapse from the same system, weren't tied to the legs of the chair, but rather bound to each other. So she could lift her feet, but not enough to make any difference with regard to her bondage. She only managed to disarrange her legs so that she was resting on the chair awkwardly, like someone riding a horse side-saddle.

It was uncomfortable, so she swung her legs back into place below her.

Turning every way she could, she could not escape from the fierce clutch of the rope that bound her to the chair. Consciousness of her powerlessness stirred up an inner violence in every fiber of her rude strength. She writhed, she struggled, she twisted—all to no purpose. Tears rose to her eyes, fed in equal portion by frustration and outright fear.

What was going to be done to her?

Whatever the truth of the matter, her headache only seemed to grow worse. At least, she was waking up more.

She grew restively conscious and tried to govern her body, but it trembled.

She tried to hide this fact from herself, or else use it to her advantage by attempting to shake so much that she would capsize the chair. In hypothetically falling to the ground, the chair might break, allowing her to free herself from the rope. So she undertook the project of moving the chair—until she realized that it wasn't moving. Apparently, its legs had somehow been fixed to the floor below. She tried to see if they were nailed, but she couldn't crane her neck far enough to make the inspection.

In a fit of exasperation, she tried to shrug herself out of the ropes again. All she succeeded in doing was giving herself rope burn. She gave up.

Finally, her head hung forward over her breast. She caught her breath once or twice, like a person who meditates a struggle with superior force and then remains passive in its grip. The acceptance of her utter helplessness crept upon her.

The gathering terror was too much for her nerves. Whatever repressed superstition that lurked beneath the exterior of her life, this situation brought back to the surface. She had had a religious upbringing. The Bible's stories of demons had made quite an impression on her mind.

Could it be right? Could such things really exist? She remembered times as a girl when the paralysis of her mind yielded at times to a sort of nightmare. She would lay in bed at night, trying to fall asleep, all the while seeing demons crouching in every shadow, the sound of devils in every twig brushing against a window. She expected to see these otherworldly beings at any moment, freed from the abstraction of books, and stalking through the real world.

At those moments, she fell under the spell of a sort of horror.

She would tuck her head under her blanket. Occasional peeks outside brought her the realization that nothing was changed in the order of nature. Through the turmoil of her thoughts, she could still see the furniture around her, the artifacts of mundane reality ranged comfortingly about. She solaced herself, then, admitting that she was just being silly. In any event, she scarcely slept a wink some nights, taking refuge in slumber only after the sun rose up in the morning sky.

If only she knew that life would furnish real things that she should be afraid of. But she didn't.

And so now she sat there, many years later, as an adult. She was aware of a presence of evil so powerful as she had sensed it as a girl, as it had seemed to her at certain other times in her life. Irrational moments, when it was almost as if she could divine an otherworldly presence. Abruptly, she shot a glance around at the shadows in the room. What did they conceal? Was there a person hidden there in the darkness, watching her, waiting?

She closed her eyes tightly and listened carefully. All she heard was the sound of her own throbbing heartbeat, racing in the stale air of the dusty room.

"How long before they come back?" she wondered, laying hold of one definite thought which she could grasp in the turmoil of horror that whirled before her eyes.

She had to do something. But what?

Gradually mounting from the mental numbness in which her drug-induced torpor had left her, there still clung to everything the feeling of unreality. The situation gathered substance and weight again as she craned her neck to look behind herself after she heard something shift.

To her shock, it was the younger of the two kidnappers. He stood on the other side of the room regarding her with candid curiosity.

For a full minute they gazed at each other.

Finally, he broke off the glance and looked around the room with evident interest. Suddenly he shifted and appeared to have reached some decision. His whole body seemed to indicate this fact. With pious eyes and nervous hands, he at last addressed her.

"Mrs. Ebersol?" he began.

She acknowledged her identity with something like a clearing of her throat.

"You're awake now?" he continued.

Once again she gargled a syllable—not like someone surly who refuses to answer, but like someone who has eaten too fast and experiences a painful hitch in the back of the throat that momentarily keeps them from swallowing. Despite that, she managed to get out the word: "Yes."

"Are you in any discomfort?" he asked.

"I'd like to get out of this chair," she said.

"I think we can do that," he uttered, to her relief, adding, "You were only tied up like that because you were unconscious and we didn't know when you'd wake up, and we had to step away for a little bit to attend to...some other things."

"Oh."

Although he asked a number of questions after that and listened attentively to her replies, Julia felt that his real interest in her was centered elsewhere. In fact, she had the strange sensation that he was getting to know her in some silent region to which he had access, and whether he gave or withheld his confidence did not depend on what was said between them.

The passage of time and the fact that they were enemies seemed equally irrelevant. Though she desperately wanted to know where her son was, she decided to ask no questions and let the conversation go its own way.

"Larry says that the stuff he injected you with would probably leave you feeling cotton-mouthed when you woke up," he continued. "So I brought you some water. Would you like a drink?"

Julia sheepishly said yes.

The man ducked back out of her field of vision for a moment to return with a jug of water.

"Drink," he said.

A tremor of anxiety passed over Julia's face, on which her captor kept his eyes steadily fixed as he put the lip of the jug up to her mouth.

Over the objection of her suspicion, she drank the water which was passed over her sandpapery tongue. That cloudiness of mind that she had previously experienced disappeared before it, but her anxiety remained.

After examining the taste in her mouth and concluding that nothing had been slyly added to the water, she offered her thanks. "What's your name?" she ventured.

"Rah—" he began, breaking off abruptly in an effort to recover himself as he said, "I mean, it's not important. We're not supposed to use names."

"Did Larry tell you that?" she asked.

"How did you know *his* name?"

"You used it a minute ago."

"I did?" he remarked, in sincere perplexity.

"I guess it doesn't matter," rejoined Julia, adding, "I just wanted to thank you, Ron."

"It's Ronnie," he corrected her, shyly.

"Well, thank you, Ronnie."

"You're welcome," he replied, and then turned to leave.

Chapter Seven

I

Friday, November 20th, 6:22 am

Back in the trunk, the handcuffs were not the only metal implements attributing to Bob's discomfort. Some kind of hard, awkward object was also digging painfully into his leg. Upon inspection, he determined that it was a shovel. Did they intend on killing him and then burying him as he calculated moments before? The matter was beyond all question.

Bob felt the trunk bounce as the two men climbed into the front of the car. He heard the slam of their doors and the sudden beat of the engine as he sensed the car gathering speed. The vibration of the engine reverberated in his skull. He lay there, the rolling, disruptive noise beneath him as the car was pushed along. Meanwhile his mind drifted along its own dark currents as he oriented himself to his new, claustrophobic environment.

He took in the close, stale air of the trunk, which smelled of motor oil and dust. He adjusted his body into the space allotted for it. Panic affected his coordination. He breathed deeply, trying to control the involuntary trembling that had seized his whole body.

Keeping calm was paramount, but a feeling of despair swept over him.

Suddenly, the car hit a pothole or something in the road. Bob, momentarily weightless, came down with a hard thud, and became abruptly conscious of the hidden weight in his belt.

A thought intruded upon his panic, a memory: so blind with terror was he that he had forgotten that he was armed.

They didn't know he had the gun. And as the reflection darted across his mind he saw a slender chance. It was a huge risk, but against it was an absolute grim certainty.

He could use the gun, but first he'd have to get his arms from their position behind his back.

Being in the fetal position made it easier to free his hands. Given enough time, he worked his arms into a better position and threaded his legs through the loop made by his bound hands. It was difficult. His wrists got caught on the tread of his shoe and he felt some of the soft flesh scrape off; but, finally, he did it. His hands, though still bound, were now in front of him. From this position, he could retrieve the gun from its place underneath his belt.

Blind in the trunk's darkness, he tried to feel around for the gun's safety catch. He had to disengage it. After locating it he flipped it back and forth, not sure if he was taking the safety off or putting it on.

He suddenly paused in his efforts and raked his memory. If he could only picture the gun as he originally saw it, he might be able to know which way the safety catch went.

"Damn-it," he screamed internally, "Which way, which way?!"

After several minutes of indecision, he finally made his choice and prayed that he was right. If not, he'd lose precious seconds during the confrontation.

But he couldn't think of that. It was too horrible. If he died, his son died.

It was just that simple.

He had to stay alive for Billy. His own life, by this point, was irrelevant. He was only important insofar as he could save his son.

It cost the sleep-deprived man an effort to remain lucid as the car continued on. The trunk acted like a sensory deprivation chamber; the hum of motion, of darkness, was lulling.

In his fetal position, it was like being in a womb—with the difference that, on the other side of that door, death might be awaiting him.

He had to concentrate to stay sharp. He was of two minds about reaching whatever destination his drivers had selected: he wanted it to come as soon as possible before he lost his courage, but at the same time his stomach was wrung by apprehension, terrified of the possible consequences that awaited him there.

Finally, though, the time came. He could feel the gears shift on the car, the pulse of the engine slowing, the tick-tick of the tires losing their beat. At last, they were stopping. The smooth sound of the blacktop gave way to the crunchier sound of gravel. Sharp pebbles pinged against the wheel wells. Bob heard no other vehicles. In fact, he heard nothing. They must be on some desolate back road.

After an agonizing pause, he could feel someone climb out of the vehicle. His would-be executioner would soon be standing directly outside the trunk. That had been the first point in his sudden consciousness. The second was the heavy feel of the gun in his sweaty hand. The third was the pounding sound of blood in his ears as his heart thundered in his chest.

Suddenly, he heard the scrape of a key, followed by the opening trunk door, which revealed his captor's face. The man's dark gaze seemed to rest on him without seeing him. "Of course!" realized Bob. The man's eyes, used to the well-lit road and the glare of illuminated billboards and businesses that lined the highway, needed time to adjust his eyes to the darkness of the trunk's interior. To Bob quite the opposite was the case. To him, the opened trunk threw in a torrent of light and fresh air—and the man above him fairly glowed.

He didn't know if he had successfully released the safety mechanism. Nevertheless, he staked all his chances on it as he seized the initiative and raised the gun toward the man.

Fear and ambivalence went down in a tempest of adrenaline. He pulled the trigger and suddenly the figure recoiled. In those terrifying moments, which seemed slowed in time, he kept his eyes fixed on the man's face. Bob watched as horror, disbelief and confusion converged in his captor's eyes.

Then a blankness.

Afterward, a collapse.

Bob climbed out of the trunk with a sense of liberation. He was fairly choking to be out of that confined space. He stretched his limbs and tested his legs. His body was vibrating. He couldn't fix whether it was a holdover from his ride, or the beginnings of a tremor from what he'd just done. He'd killed a man. His breath came back to him in shallow gasps.

Stealing a look around, his eyes saw wide expanses of forest on either side of the car.

But that sense-impression was interrupted by the sound of a voice: "Goddamn it, Ted! Couldn't you wait? Now the trunk's gonna have to be cleaned! I'm not cleaning it. You're cleaning it. Un-fucking-professional!"

It took Bob a second to realize that the man wasn't addressing him, but his slain colleague. With the trunk lid up, and obscuring the view from the back windshield, the driver couldn't see what was passing behind him, and it was his assumption that "Ted" had murdered their captive prematurely.

Bob saw the car rise and fall slightly as the second man got out of the car with an oath and started around to the back of the vehicle.

There was not a moment to spare. The man had a gun. Before Bob even realized this consciously, the thug pulled the trigger of his weapon. Oddly, nothing happened. His gun, making an impotent click, appeared to be jammed.

For a split second their glances crossed; and, in that brief time, that fleeting flicker, Bob watched as something sprang into his captor's eyes. That something was terror. It was a look pitched between the shock that he had miscalculated his prisoner's grit and the horror of actually having to face death himself. Bob raised his weapon, took rapid aim and fired. The man arched backward and with a low-throated grunt, he fell to the ground.

With both his captors dispatched, Bob was left in a state of panting wonder.

He was relieved to be alive, yes. But that circumstance didn't provide the occasion for his total relief, because the situation itself opened up the possibility for a whole new set of worries when he thought about how he would get his son back now, or where he would go to deliver the money?

He drew up short before these seemingly insurmountable obstacles.

His thoughts hovered over various courses of action. His mind began to labor busily over the problem of his cuffed hands, though. How would he get them off?

Recovering his self-command, he knew he'd have to find the key by going through the pockets of the dead men. He didn't want to touch their still warm, bulky shapes, and shrank from the thought that one of them might have an after death spasm. It took all his resolution to pick past the bloody garments and gingerly fish around in their pockets.

Ted had nothing but a few loose coins, some thread and a battered leather wallet. Bob felt like he was going to throw up.

He had to stop for a moment and swallow down the mass in his throat. As he paused, he stole a look around. Morning was finally approaching. Had it been spring or summer, daylight would already have been there— consequently denying him his one opportunity to mount an ambush. Luckily, it was late autumn and the days were shorter. That bought him some extra time — he would have to hurry.

Bob collected himself, as he stood under the wash of dawn colors, the glow of the new day coming in as unobtrusively as the spilt light of a fallen table lamp.

He knew that he couldn't waste any more time. He was in a desolate wilderness, true. But that was no proof against someone driving by soon and stumbling upon the scene. He saw the horror in front of him objectively.

A singularly chilly feeling crept up his spinal column.

He had to press on.

After going through the pockets of the second man and finding nothing, panic started to gather up inside him again. He went to the driver's side of the car.

"Yes—!" the man had left the keys in the ignition. Relief surged up in him as he observed the fact that on the key ring was a small handcuff key. Using it, he was finally free.

He rubbed the reddened chafe-marks around his wrists. He knew that he'd have to move the bodies and hide them at once. But what would he do with them?

He recalled the shovel in the trunk, and savored the irony that it would be used on *them*. Reflection upon this fact, though, brought him little glee. He didn't look forward to the task. Nevertheless, he squared his jaw, set his eyes and met the details one by one.

The first thing he saw to was the collection of any pertinent information from the dead men themselves. By taking their wallets, after all, he'd be aiding future law enforcement officials while also—in the immediate future—making it harder for local police to identify them. Missing wallets would also imply that there was a theft-motive in their deaths. That might buy him sufficient time to carry out whatever actions he needed to before finding his son.

In coolly weighing these considerations, he was shocked by his presence of mind. He had never been in a situation like this before, yet he was already starting to learn to see certain contingencies he would've never thought about in the past. He was beginning to be able to see many things—as when your eyes become accustomed to the darkness.

Racing daylight, he continued combing over the corpses and taking anything he thought he might be able to utilize: weapons, handcuffs, wallets. Into his pocket their money went against future emergencies, where he might need to draw on any petty cash. After he had brought this act of pillaging to a successful conclusion, he set about burying them.

First he pulled the bodies by their feet until he could drag them down the steep embankment on the side of the road and out of direct sight of any hypothetical passerby. Then he went back for the shovel.

Anticipating the sweat that would arise as a consequence of his strenuous physical exertion, he took off his jacket, pulled off his shirt and continued to dig. All the while, he reflected upon the slipping away of precious time. As the sun rose and the blueness of the sky deepened, he experienced the slipping away of minutes as an almost-physical sensation. That sense of haste might explain the shallowness of the grave as he dumped both men into the same pit, their bodies tumbling on top of each other in a vaguely lewd embrace. Filling the hole back in, he covered it with leaves and twigs.

He had no illusions about the competence of his impromptu burial. Animals, he knew, would probably disturb the grave before the day was up. Decomposition would be rapid and pungent.

He wondered how many days it would be before some camper came across the remains or some cocker spaniel on its owner's leash would nose around the area.

Bob put his shirt on, sat on the rear bumper of the car and took stock of his position

He was in the middle of nowhere, without his own car, with two dead bodies that might at any time be discovered. Then he went back to wider considerations. Abandoning the immediate thoughts about himself and his own well-being, he thought about how his actions would affect his son. If the death of the first man hadn't yet been noticed, certainly the sudden disappearance of these two individuals would attract attention. And then what would happen to his boy?

He shuddered, thinking about it.

And then he remembered: the mission of his pursuers was most likely twofold: get the money and—their chief mission—administer a punishment that was supposed to serve as a warning to others. Bob wondered if the henchmen had phoned their boss before that personal account was settled or if they were waiting until after their task was complete. They had never caught Bob's father, so, he reasoned, they probably didn't contact their leader. They might have. But somehow he didn't think they had, and to that he clung.

He had to believe it, or else he wouldn't have been able to work up the courage to phone the kidnapper himself. He knew that he must. After all, he had to confirm that his son was alright.

So, hanging onto the outside hope that the ringleader had no idea that three of his underlings were already dead, he took out the cell phone and dialed the telephone number fear had stamped onto his memory.

It rang. Then rang again. And again.

His heartbeat started to race, almost matching the trilling of the dial tone that rang in his ear. What if they're gone? What if no one ever answers the phone again? What if B—

"Ebersol?" a voice suddenly uttered.

"Yes," Bob said, at a handicap.

"Did you reach your destination?"

His throat tightened. His voice edged with anxiety, he said, "Um…yes…uh…Hold on…"

Bob was beside himself. Listening to the voice now, he compared it to the voice of the police detective that still vibrated in the far regions of his skull; and he could confirm that both voices belonged to the same man. He recalled, too, that Spence had feigned a cold and kept complaining about a sore throat. In retrospect, it was obviously a primitive ruse to justify modifying his voice. He intended to disguise it as much as he could before then going on to talk to his victim on the telephone, this time with his own natural voice. But he was lazy. There weren't obvious and irrefutable similarities. He couldn't keep up the masquerade for that long, and now, listening to the voice again and recalling that of the detective, Bob realized that his father was right.

It disturbed him, a qualm that was offset by the comforting fact that the kidnapper, *Spence*—the man who set in motion the nightmarish events that upended his life— carried on as if he had no idea that anything was amiss.

"Yes, I'm right here in front of my father's house," lied Bob, still trying to appraise his tormentor's reaction.

"Good, good," said Spence.

"You said that after I got here you'd give me further instructions."

"Did you talk to your father yet?"

"No. Not yet. Why? Should I?"

"How can you confirm that it's his house if you don't t—"

"I've already spotted him, through a window," Bob prevaricated again. "I'll knock on the door, if you want me to. So far, though, I've just been waiting outside."

"How long have you been there?" asked Spence.

"Not long. Maybe fifteen minutes."

"Good. Wait there."

"For what?" asked Bob, knowing full well that Spence wanted him to wait for henchmen who would never arrive.

"Um...you have to wait for further instructions. But I can't give them to you now."

"Then let me talk to my son. You said, after I got here, I'd be able to speak to him."

"Alright, alright. Hold on. He's sleeping. It's early. Wait a minute."

Bob hung in suspense. He released the breath he didn't know he was holding as he heard the sound of his son's voice.

"Billy?" he exclaimed, his heart in his throat.

"Hi, Dad."

"Are you alright? Are they treating you well?" he asked, trying to infuse naturalness into his voice.

"I'm okay," Billy replied, sleepily. "I had the strangest dream last night."

"Really? What was it about?" asked Bob, trying to steady his voice.

"I dreamed that I was in this big field, and it had a house. It wasn't our house, but it was supposed to be. You know . . ." he prompted.

"Yeah, I know what you mean."

"And there were these weird animals. Like panda bears. But almost like half-panda, half-koala. Strange . . ."

Bob gave a start as his son's voice trailed off and Spence resumed the line.

"As you can see, your son's fine," he said icily. "You can talk to him again, if you want, after you receive your next instructions."

"But how will I get them?" challenged Bob.

"Just wait where you are. That's all. Don't move."

"And that's it?"

"Don't move. Do you understand me? Just wait right there," he said, closing the subject.

"Okay."

The connection was broken.

II

Bob placed the cell phone back in his pocket. And, before he could move, he heard a cell phone ring. It took him a moment before he realized that it was not his own cell phone, but that of one of the dead men. It was inside the car. Apparently, no sooner had Spence terminated his conversation with Bob than he tried to contact his subordinates.

Bob located the phone inside the car and held it in his hand as it rang. He worried that Spence would grow suspicious over his men not answering the phone. It continued its insistently shrill call. All Bob could do was hope that Spence would chalk up their inability to answer as interference from the mountains.

Perhaps it would buy him some time.

He had desperately little. He knew that.

The phone stopped. His attention was drawn to the interior of the car. The suitcase with the money was sitting right there on the passenger seat. Hopefully, he might find other clues, some telltale hint that would lead him to his son.

In his previous conversation with Spence, Bob hoped that he'd get something useful out of him to locate Billy's whereabouts. But the conversation was controlled by the kidnapper, not by him. All the hope he had left relied on something, anything he could turn up among the artifacts the men left behind in the vehicle. Some impulse made him slip his hand under the seats, and there he found something that set his pulse racing: a map.

It was crumpled and stained, but legible. To his shock, it charted a course directly to his house. They had printed it up from an online mapping service, so it contained a destination address, but also an address for the starting-point.

Pieces were finally falling into place.

He would drive back to where the map led.

His luck had held, but for how much longer? He didn't know. All he knew was that he had to continue on with his mission.

There was no plan of campaign in his head, only the map, a starting point that could mean nothing.

Chapter Eight

I

Before setting off on his journey back home, he decided to make a quick detour. His father was right: they had been using the cell phone to track him. It only made sense to follow through with the plan and get rid of it. If he discarded it on the side of the highway, it would make his position look stationary. It would be more confusing and convincing if the signal moved about.

Yes, his father had had the right idea about placing it on a train traveling in the opposite direction. He even mentioned that there was a station relatively near his home. After stopping at a gas station and getting directions, Bob got back into the car he was driving and located the station.

He approached its entrance with his cash-filled suitcase in the hopes of impersonating a real traveler. Pushing past the revolving glass doors that looked like a camera's flashcube, he emerged into the interior of the large building.

It was his intention to slip onto a train, tape the cell phone beneath a seat and slip back off again. But first he needed adhesive tape. Looking around, he saw what looked like rows of church pews, peopled intermittently with waiting travelers. Beyond those his eyes settled on an array of employees inside various booths. An arcade with concessions trailed off to the left.

Surely, someone's got to sell tape, he thought to himself.

Bob went up to a woman at the ticket counter. She didn't know of any stores that sold tape at the station, but was kind enough to give him the last of the roll from her desktop. He gratefully accepted it.

"Thank you," beamed Bob. "That's very helpful. Thanks a lot."

After she handed it to him, he started to walk off, but the woman cleared her throat.

"Huh?" uttered Bob, distracted.

Her mouth set in grim disapproval, she said, "You can't go beyond this line without a ticket. You forgot to show me your ticket."

He paused, his eyes wavering. "Ticket?"

She nodded.

Bob went through a theatrical ruse of searching for his nonexistent ticket before claiming that he must have dropped it.

"Hold on. I'll be right back," he said.

He felt the press of time at his back.

Running to the other side of the station, he went to a ticket booth and secured passage for a destination he would never see. He comforted himself with the thought of the use he had been able to make of the money he had cadged from the killers' wallets. Bob was back at the ticket counter in five minutes; he showed the clerk his ticket, melded with a throng of people down a hallway and erupted onto the train platform.

Once there, he saw the train for which he bought a ticket. As he ran along its length, he passed a succession of windows, each presenting a different scene, like panels in a comic book. His hands were sweating and he almost dropped the phone. Finally, he arrived at the door and gave his ticket to the conductor. He immediately darted glances around the interior looking for a seat under which he could tape the cell phone.

He had to be careful. In the age of terrorism, taping a cell phone to a seat might be misconstrued as an attempt to hide a trigger mechanism on a prospective target. He didn't have time to be hauled off the train for to await interrogation by the transit authority.

With all these thoughts in mind, he sat down as inconspicuously as possible in a relatively deserted section of the train car and set about his task. He fidgeted, pretending to settle into his seat. Looking around to make sure no one was approaching, he lunged down, with his head between his knees as he busied himself with the tape and the phone. The packing tape held remarkably well, he reflected. He only hoped that the cell phone wouldn't lose its charge before too long.

Sitting back up he commanded a view of the people in front of him with the domes of heads visible from overtop the seats, like a cinema but without a movie screen.

Confident that no one noticed him, he stood up, grabbed his suitcase and started for the door. Just then a conductor said, "The train's about to pull out."

"I know, I know," muttered Bob. "I'm getting off. I forgot something."

"You'll miss the train if you get off. We're about to leave."

"I know," huffed Bob, anxiously.

Pushing past the man, he emerged back onto the platform and ran back up the stairs to the depot.

He stopped in front of the ticket office and thought about buying another ticket, which he would *really* use. He quickly scanned the time-tables and routes, and realized that train travel would not be faster. It had too many stops and didn't go directly to his hometown. He'd make better time in a car. It was only then that he relapsed into thoughts about taking an airplane. Certainly, he'd confront the problem of having to get a ticket on such short notice. But maybe, he considered, that obstacle could be overcome. He might take

$5,000 out of the briefcase and bribe someone to give him their seat. For the slight inconvenience of having to take the next flight, they'd make a tidy commission.

Just as he was getting excited about this possibility, the very thing that made it possible (the money) also made it improbable. After all, on second thought he reflected upon the difficulty of getting through airport security with a suitcase full of cash. He'd have to submit to people placing his luggage through an X-ray machine. How would he explain what they'd see inside?

Furthermore, there was the little matter of getting through the metal detector with the firearms he'd acquired.

He'd probably be mistaken for a criminal and detained by security until the proper authorities could arrive and question him. The disastrous loss of time inherent in any detention could spell the death of his son.

No, he'd have to drive back, after all—even at the steep cost of losing another seven hours on the road.

He hurried back to the car, put it in gear and headed out.

II

With the long hours on his hands, he reflected on the insanity of the last thirteen hours that had propelled him into a madness beyond his understanding. He had no idea what was going to happen to him, and it caused him an acute pain that, by the end of his drive back home, he would have lost twenty of the twenty-four hours allotted to him.

But he couldn't think about that. He had to drive out all doubt, suppress all conscious reflection.

He let the sound of the highway run on as the musical undercurrent of his thoughts.

Hill folded into hill as the car turned west, the landscape compressing like the accordion doors of a bus, like the folded pages of a map.

By that hour of the morning, traffic was already starting to thicken. The cars that plied the road were comprised chiefly of morning commuters for work. Among their number were also insomniac truckers, wayward vacationers and weary salesmen.

The highway tapered away to the blue horizon. His glance strayed down the winding roads in front of him. He had a fixed purpose ahead, and could only push on.

Chapter Nine

I

Friday, November 20th, 1:12 am

Outside events that take place on the plane of logic, Julia sensed that—in some strange way—she exercised a pull on her captor. The quality of that attraction, and the region from which it emanated, evaded her.

She couldn't help but feel that Ronnie had spoken to her not to exchange information or ideas but merely to hear her voice, to test it against some pre-existing model. It was as if he were acknowledging a confused feeling of recognition—like he was familiar with her with the elusive familiarity of a person encountered in a dream.

For Julia, of course, the present circumstances were less dream than nightmare. She was left alone for some time and lapsed back into a sort of torpor, a protracted period of mental blankness. In its own way, this period of wavering consciousness was like sleep. She recovered her presence of mind abruptly when she became aware of someone in the room again. As she lifted her head she saw the second captor hovering over her sleep like an accusing spirit.

Her heart nearly burst in her chest as the grim reality of everything rushed back in upon her. She tried not to jump, but an anxiety had hold of her before she could resist it, and she gave a start. Her firmly set jaw told of an underlying determination not to let her captor see that she had been frightened as much as she had, so she lowered her head again and remained still, in silence and languor.

The second man—Larry—took up a position ten paces away and settled down with a weary sigh that implied that he meant to keep a vigil for a while.

Julia wondered if Billy were here too, somewhere. The realization that he must be made her stomach clench with pain. Her baby—did they feed him, was he scared, was he alright? She felt her cheeks flush and the warmth spread behind her eyes as they threatened to overspill with the anguish of it all. She resolved to observe the men and try to learn something of Billy's whereabouts.

It was clear to her that the two men were taking shifts. While Ronnie was with her, Larry had probably been with her son; and now that Larry was with her, Ronnie was with the boy. Why was the decision taken to separate them? She couldn't make sense of it.

Over the next hours—and the next "shift change"—the two men who had captured her interacted. There were repeated mutterings interchanged between them. At first they spoke only in isolated sentences. But, as time dragged on, Julia gleaned more about them. They turned, by stages, into different people, their identities succumbing to the slow process of individuation.

As for Ronnie, the younger, taller one, his face expressed only moderate intelligence, but the lines that were the worn pathways of habitual expressions were those of kindness, friendliness. Talking to Ronnie (as she discovered little by little) was invariably tedious, because one seldom got a word in edgewise. Conversation with him was more like tuning into a radio station. You could, if you so chose, listen; but your presence didn't really have an effect on the programming.

He was a talker. Put another way: to speak to him was to indulge in bibliomancy—that superstitious game where you let a book fall open at random in the hopes that a sentence arrived at haphazardly might cast a light on a particular situation or provide a clue from Fate with regard to some course of action. Similarly, peering into Ronnie's mind was to peer into a book that had been randomly thrown open; a finger stabbed onto a random line.

"... the what's-his-face on the who's-it's gone ..." heard Julia at length, wondering, "Now, what on earth could *that* mean?"

Her eyes glazed over and Ronnie continued his flow of talk until, at wide intervals, the figurative finger came down on a random sentence again: "... dodge the issue with camel-like carpet thingees ..." or "... the gap between the empty everything ..."

Julia grew fixed in the resolve to pay attention in the hope that, if she did, Ronnie would start making sense. That hope, as she discovered, was ill-founded.

The other man (Larry) was smaller—of average height and stout, with leathery skin and a gnarled, weather-beaten face. She put him down at forty-five, but had no idea how old he really was. His eyes were spaced too far apart, in a face whose features were branded by permanent distrust. There was cruelty in his pronounced frontal lobe, brutality in his squat, neckless physique. With the raw aspect of a thug, he held himself as if always primed for violence.

The dominating impression caused by his appearance was the feeling that here was a man to be feared, an unstable man, a man capable of any outrage.

It was therefore comforting to see his malevolence moderated somewhat by Ronnie's influence, for, whether he knew it or not, he acted as a foil to his surly partner. In that sense, he undercut him. This was illustrated when Ronnie would add little footnotes to everything Larry said. The effect on Julia was that of reading text in a book where a previous reader has scribbled notes to themselves in the margins.

If Larry said, "You'll get food in a little while," Ronnie would add: "Crackers. I had some earlier; they're pretty good. Peanut butter." Or if Larry would scowl and say, "If you want anything else, don't bother asking," Ronnie would interject: "Unless, that is, you have to use the bathroom. You can. Just give us a call."

He was a great balm to Julia in those nerve-wracking hours when fear and horror lay like a weight on her heart.

But she didn't have the benefit of Ronnie's calming influence when he went off to his shift with her son and left her alone with Larry. She, understandably, felt uneasy in his presence. Even though this was her second time with him, it didn't enhance her opinion of him.

He produced a stack of letters from his jacket. He picked up one envelope mechanically and gazed at its sheaf of pages—although it wasn't clear if he was really reading because he hadn't gone on past the first page, even after fifteen minutes.

He coughed, his raspy utterance jarring the room. Silence soon reestablished itself. Yet the ruffled silence resettled itself along new lines. It wasn't the silence of absence, but that of someone listening.

It made Julia nervous. This man had the same effect on her now as he did when she first laid eyes on him. With trepidation, then, she resumed her survey of his features. She took an almost perverse interest in his broad, worn-out face, in his Troglodyte build, and the uneven, yellow teeth that looked like broken crockery in his mouth.

She observed something new that she had missed before: when especially agitated, his left eyelid produced a series of involuntary twitches. At certain angles, when his eyelid hung lower than the other, it imparted to his face the look of a doll with counterweighted eyes, the kind that, when shifted into a recumbent position, assumes the appearance of sleep. Since his left eyelid hung a little lower he had the look of a doll with a broken eye.

Her scrutiny reinforced her initial impression of him. Having exhausted her interest in him, she transferred her attention to the wall.

She despised her powerlessness, her inaction. She tried to imagine escaping in a general sense, but whenever she attempted to wed it to her particular circumstances, her imagination staggered and failed the task. Fear rose like a stone wall at the end of every proposed path.

Staring at the wall in front of her, she was conscious that it was a living metaphor—since her thoughts had run up against a wall of their own.

Her interest was quickened by the fact that the wall vaguely suggested the interior of a bank. Is that where they were, then? An abandoned bank, perhaps?

If that was the case, she might be able to figure out where they were. *Are there any closed bank buildings around where we live?* she wondered.

Nothing came. She tried to think, but thinking became harder and harder. Soon she just let her mind wander. How else could she hold onto her sanity in the midst of the lean, nondescript hours which concealed among them the seeds of the answer to whether the situation would end in life or death, in triumph or tragedy?

Minute succeeded minute, hour followed upon hour.

She experienced a strange mental isolation which alienated her from her own thoughts. It seemed easier to shrink away from her memories and emotions as she turned her attention outward. Toward that end, she made the observation that night must be thinning, morning was approaching. Like the bluish cast on mountains seen from a distance, dawn set its electric-blue haze on all the objects of the morning, its color even in some imperceptible way suffusing Julia's own windowless cell with its faint tremulous light.

Why blue? When you get closer to a mountain the blueness vanishes by slow degrees; likewise with morning. The further you travel into it the less it has of an azure glow.

Julia watched this process as hours slipped past and dawn deepened into the new day.

Gradually, the room ceased to be a blur as light slowly restored contours and shapes in the room. Objects began to emerge. First into view were the walls, floors, and the scant furnishing of the room—which was composed of a few cheap, wooden folding chairs. Second, she noticed that the walls weren't uniformly gray as she had thought earlier, but that three of the four walls had been painted a sickening shade of light green. There were also some cardboard boxes in a far corner.

A funereal calm lingered over everything.

Meanwhile, her captor—having long since abandoned his stack of envelopes—shifted somewhere outside the range of her vision. Something unusual in the sound of his movement arrested her attention.

She tried to ignore him. She tuned the strings of her nerves to fit the key of the circumstances in which she found herself. Consequently, she became a shell of herself—withdrawn, quiet, circumspect. But, occasionally, she would look up with a start as she felt his eyes on her.

On this particular occasion, he reacted to her suspicion by trying to allay it with a question related to whether she wanted the peanut butter crackers that had before been mentioned. She shook her head, refusing even to utter the word no. She wanted to let him understand that even under these circumstances, he couldn't extort friendliness from her.

One effect of this rebuff was to make him even surlier in his bearing.

She almost immediately regretted her action. She had to make up her mind whether she was going to keep up a protective barrier of defiant taciturnity, or whether she should make an attempt at reaching an understanding with her captors.

Certainly, it *felt* better to keep a protective distance between them, but tactically, she realized, it was probably smarter to establish a common ground with them.

With Ronnie, it would have been easier. With Larry, however, she didn't see how she could mask her natural fear and aversion of him.

These thoughts affected her head much as her bladder was now affecting her body. For, even as she tried to remove herself to a safe intellectual sphere of contemplation, the need to go to the bathroom was becoming increasingly imperative. She moved restlessly on her chair.

"Do you have to pee?" a voice startled her.

Julia tensed, and regarded her captor with dignified amazement.

Unflappable, Larry pressed, "You keep tapping your foot. Do you have to use the bathroom?"

She didn't want to show weakness by admitting that her bladder was beginning to cause her discomfort. So she remained unresponsive as he put the question to her a second time. He seemed not to understand her reluctance. "Well, do you have to or not?" he said a third time, somewhat pointedly.

Julia fantasized about flouting them as much as she could. But, when it came to bodily functions and her own surrender of dignity, she decided that the kidnapping was *their* doing, and they must accept the responsibility for their captive during the time they had her. She finally acquiesced and said, "Yes, I have to use the bathroom."

At first, she expected them to hand her a bucket. To her great relief, however, her captor started to untie her. She paused and looked forward to her release in a state of anticipation, qualified by apprehension.

He too must have felt a sense of apprehension because he added with telling emphasis: "But I tell you this: if you try anything funny, you're dead. Your son'll be dead, too."

The threats were expected given the situation, but something in his manner carried conviction.

"I understand," she breathed.

"Good," he muttered, and piloted her outside of the room and up the hall to a bathroom.

When they got to a row of stalls and she walked over to one, her tormentor alarmed her again by saying: "I'm coming with you." His tone indicated clearly that there was only one side to this question.

Even if proprieties clearly counted for little with him, she still had her standards.

"You can at least let me shut the stall door."

His tone was flat. "No".

"No?" she asked, making a despairing gesture.

"No," he said, in a tone that was an even blend of annoyance and sadism.

Her eyes flashed uneasiness, greatly to his satisfaction. Meanwhile his eyes bore into hers as she backed toward the toilet. She shifted her glance away from him as she lowered her pants and installed herself on the seat. She sat there abjectly, trembling with agitation. To all outward appearances, she stared into vacancy. By a feat of imagination, she imagined herself in her own home, using the bathroom in monastic seclusion. It was her way of psychologically absenting herself as she struggled to empty her bladder. For several minutes she couldn't. Finally, with the fear of her hesitancy soliciting comment, she overcame her timidity.

She listened shamefacedly to the sound of her own bodily waste splashing against the water.

Her warder stood there with the easiness of conscience of a man indulging in his own form of recreation. He managed to convey the impression that he was quite at home in this voyeuristic activity.

Finally she rose, a trifle unsteadily. With a sudden swift movement, however, she assembled herself and moved to leave the stall.

She took a step forward and their eyes met. Anger and shame were pretty evenly balanced in her expression. Cheerless mirth stood in his eyes.

She bristled as his teeth showed like bone breaking through the skin, his smile like a compound fracture.

Speaking in a low voice that vibrated with anger, she said brusquely: "Excuse me. I have to wash my hands."

"Oh, pardon me," he replied with weighty sarcasm.

Flushed with rage and humiliation, she walked over to the row of sinks that stood against the wall. She turned on a spigot and a thin gray braid of water descended into the basin below. A mirror hovered on the wall above it. She looked into it with unseeing eyes as she scrubbed her hands. It was as if she wasn't staring at it, but beyond it— as if it were a mirrored one-way observation window with police on the other side whose glances she could meet if she just pressed her face to the glass and cupped her hands around her eyes. But she knew she wasn't standing in an interrogation room; she was standing in a bathroom. And there were no helpful law enforcement agents watching out for her.

Chapter Ten

I

Friday, November 20th, 3:22 pm

After nearly seven hours of driving, Bob was finally within the city limits. He hadn't made as good time as he had hoped. Though he had sped as much as he had on his original journey, congestion had slowed him down.

He was seized with a sense of physical sickness as the succession of remembered landmarks pressed upon his eyes. His stomach roiled. It was dizzying to be back—surreal. In his hometown this aspect of "otherness" became the strangest of unrealities. Not because he was in a familiar place, nor because the sensation of incongruity had flung a mist of dreaminess over everything; but because hidden away somewhere in that vast unheeding labyrinth was his son....

Ever since Billy had been taken, Bob's mind had been saturated with him: he had never seemed more insistently near than as their separation lengthened. But though the time between them lengthened, the space between them was contracting. His heart began to beat a little faster at the thought that he was closer to his son. He became conscious that he was driving too fast, as if no speed, short of flight, would be swift enough. He was keeping pace with some inward rhythm, seeking to give physical expression to the mad rush of his thoughts.

He knew, once off the highway, though, he'd have to observe traffic laws. It would be counterproductive to be stopped by the police, his foreseeable run-in with the law costing him precious time.

So he slowed down, falling back into what felt like a crawl as he searched out the address left to him on the map. Within twenty minutes, he found it. The address on the map was a gray ranch-style house in a working-class neighborhood on the east side of town. Tall trees surrounded it, almost obscuring it. The evergreens—pine, spruce, fir—seemed to hide the structure, while sucking up all the sunshine around it.

Having no overriding urge to make himself conspicuous, no desire to give away his position, he parked two streets away. At that hour of the afternoon, most of the people who lived in that neighborhood would still be at work. Hardly anyone would be around to notice him.

He got out of the car, a lack of sleep apparent in his bearing. The long thrum of the road made his legs unsure of the pavement. Yet controlled fear and channeled anger kept him steady as he walked to the house. His anger was the rallying-point of many scattered impulses. It kept him lucid, focused.

He was fatigued, though. To his strained senses there appeared to be no one in the house—or at least no car in the driveway.

He crept closer, using the trees as cover. His palms were damp. He blotted them on his pants. Turning a corner and reaching the side of the house, he stood on tiptoe and glanced into a window for a glimpse of people inside, but obtained none.

He walked back around to the rear of the residence and saw a glass peephole in the back door. Looking through it was like looking through the telescopic sight of a rifle. He expected to be shot any instant.

Curiosity compelled him to try the doorknob. It was locked. So he tried a nearby window. It, too, was locked.

It was getting cold. Winter would be coming early

this year. As he stood outside, in too light a jacket, his teeth chattered, an occasional shiver wrenching through his body as a brisk wind blew past him.

He was grateful when he eventually found a basement door with a rusty lock on it. He couldn't break it, but he could push against the door until, in relatively short order, there was a splintering sound and the wood around the hinge gave way.

After a struggle, he had the door open. He drew a deep breath, wavered a moment and then went inside.

As his eyes acclimated to the unlit interior, he became conscious of rough concrete walls, a low ceiling and dusty floors. Looking up, he saw various pipes which ran along the ceiling like thick roots to some unseen tree. His eyes followed them until they reached the end of the room, after which his glance descended to see cracks in the concrete walls which looked like fissures on a human skull. There was an acrid smell of water-damage and mildew as dust hung in the air like TV static.

The only sign of life in this dead place was a spider web, the intricate whorls hanging in midair like a transparent fingerprint—a smudge of a thumbprint, say, on a pair of eyeglasses. The spider itself moved about its web with the disturbing adroitness of a hand on a Ouija-board, the construction and design of its home as if communicated to the industrious creature by some unseen intelligence.

Seeing nothing of particular interest there, he decided to follow the staircase up into the main body of the house. He walked slowly, his heart in his throat, as he tried to avoid any creaks that fate had placed in his path. Every time he mis-stepped and elicited the tiniest crack, his whole body tensed up as if the report of a gun had rent the air.

Anxiously, he slowly but surely made his way to the

top of the staircase—armed only with the hope that there were not additional locks on the door from the outside. His mind raced with alternate scenarios. If the door were locked, he could try to pick it with the metal pin from his belt-buckle. Or else he might try to—

His thoughts trailed off as the door in front of him opened.

No, it had not been locked from the outside.

Short of being relieved by this stroke of good luck, he was visited by doubt—wondering if a sinister fate was sportingly extending him a handicap, just to make the inevitable ambush all the more brutal and heartbreaking.

But he tried to fight down these misgivings as he realized that the basement door opened up into the kitchen. Turning the doorknob quietly, he eased into the room.

It was deserted, the house eerily quiet.

His heart, which had been fluttering faintly, gave a great leap, as he realized that no one was there. He'd stepped into a galley kitchen, a long narrow room devoid of much space or convenience.

He darted glances here and there, trying to get a broader sense of his surroundings. He looked uncertainly at the corner which led out of the kitchen and into a hallway.

The rooms and closets could conceal someone quite easily.

His head ached with the effort of listening. The pressure building up in his skull pressed against his eyeballs. He pinched the bridge of his nose as he cautiously began to advance.

He started working his way from the back of the house toward the front, affecting a sense of casualness he didn't feel. Every muscle was primed for a sound, every nerve alert in anticipation of a movement, a shifting, a telltale creak in the brittle silence.

Fear eased its grip somewhat as he realized that the house was empty. There wasn't even a pet. But the absence of a dog wasn't the only thing that struck him. The house seemed to lack a number of other things that would imply active habitation. For, having started in the basement and methodically canvassing every square inch of the house, he noticed some conspicuous absences. There was a stark simplicity to the home, granted. Yet even the sparest house would have food in the refrigerator. This one didn't. The kitchen floor had the roots of pipes where a stove should have been. Likewise, there were no paintings on the walls, no decorative touches. No mementos of past trips, no bookshelves with old novels, no photographs of family.

Opened drawers held no secrets, either.

His suspicions were further aroused by the fact that there were no clothes in any of the closets.

A moment's reflection made it clear that it wasn't a home, but some sort of safe house. Perhaps when crimes were being planned or meetings held, they used this property as an informal meeting-place or staging area. Bob felt as if he were at a dead end.

Beyond looking up the deed and trying to ascertain the owner from the public documents, he had no other avenue to pursue. He hoped that he would find something more. Accordingly, he stood on the threshold of the house with a sinking heart. Just about to close the door, his eyes were drawn to something they had previously overlooked—a small rectangle of cardboard that had fallen to the floor and was pressed up against the baseboard.

His attention constricted until his whole being focused on it.

It was a baseball card. It required no muscular effort of memory to arrive at the conclusion that it belonged to his son. Seeing something that belonged to Billy caught Bob off guard. It was as if he'd been punched in the diaphragm and his mouth worked but he couldn't find any air.

It took him a moment to recover his equanimity. His feeling was a strange compound of sadness and excitement. He was excited that he had found a clue that implied he was a step closer to his son's rescue, yet it was an excitement balanced by the sadness of just having missed him.

All he felt about the boy, all the love and kindness, the affection and worry, trembled through him at the touch of the card.

The discovery of the item was a fresh incentive to action. Because this occurrence determined his next move, a trip to someplace with Internet access. It seemed to him that the first thing he had to do was to get as much light as he could on the whole situation, and the obvious way of doing that was through the deed to that safe house. Who owned it? Property deeds were open to the public and could be accessed via the Internet. Before he had bought his own house, he had done research and looked up the records online to see what the previous owners had paid for the property. Surely, he could do the same thing now—with this new address.

II

Bob's first impulse was to drive home and use his own computer. But between the safe-house and his own home was the supermarket where he worked. Because it was geographically closer Bob decided to use his computer there. At first he considered the possibility that they might be staking out his place of employment. But even to his alarmed imagination this seemed improbable. An instant's thought told him that they assumed he was hundreds of miles away. It would be a waste of manpower to place someone in front of the supermarket to keep an eye on things. With the number of people who come and go in any such business, it made such a stakeout even more daunting and unlikely.

So he decided to drive there. While driving, though, he thought about the possibility of stopping by at his house afterward to grab a heavier coat as the day grew chillier. In an aside, he thought about the storm he had driven through the night before. It must have been part of a larger "front" that was moving through the region, bringing with it colder temperatures.

"How can I even think about the weather at a time like this," thought Bob, amazed at his inability to filter out everyday minutiae.

As he walked inside the supermarket, he had the sense of passing out of a nightmare into the reassurance of kindly and familiar things.

"Hi, Mr. Ebersol," one of the stock clerks called out to Bob as he moved past the main body of the store, toward his small office in the back.

On the way there, however, he encountered two more staff-members; Donna—a young and struggling mother of two, and Chrissie, a bubbly and sweet-natured teenager.

He found a blessed refuge from his perplexities in his co-workers' unawareness. They simply greeted him and made vague remarks about his absence earlier in the day.

By himself he had been too agitated, too preoccupied to give his thoughts over to anything other than horrible contingencies, but the banality of the supermarket steadied him. The commonplace sights, the mercantile noises, the inane browsing of customers, the music filtering from the ceiling, all wove around him a spell of security through which he felt he could almost re-energize himself, be restored to his natural place in the scheme of things. It felt good; it felt normal.

He looked back at his life as it had been up until twenty-one hours ago, and its colorless uniformity took on an air of dignity and self-respect. Was it because of his current crisis that it now wore that look to him?

He reached his office, where he closed himself off from the rest of the supermarket. He stood there, strained, harried, fatigue pressing down on him. Bob's sense of relief at sitting down showed him for the first time how tired he really was. He stifled a yawn. He was also lightheaded from lack of food.

Massaging his forehead with his fingers, a knock came cautiously at the door. Before he could even think to be nervous, a head poked its way through the crack in the door as his assistant manager, Judy Finch, said hello.

"Oh, hi, Judy," uttered Bob, his tension abating.

"Is it alright if I come in for a second?" she asked.

He was too tired to do more than nod his head.

Closing the door behind herself, she said, "You weren't here this morning, and you didn't call in sick or anything. So no one knew what was going on. Eddie had to open because you weren't here. Are you okay?"

"I'll have to thank Eddie for covering for me," replied Bob. "You, too. You're supposed to be off today."

"I can use the extra money, I guess," Judy returned earnestly.

"I'm sorry, Judy. I didn't mean to inconvenience anyone. Least of all you."

Bob spoke with a visible effort at composure. She picked up on his strained attempt to be "normal," but somehow he didn't seem his usual self. Beyond his pale complexion and drawn face, he appeared to Judy to be changed in a way she couldn't quite articulate. He seemed like a different man somehow: as if he were not her boss, but a man who looked remarkably like him.

Bob could feel her uncharacteristic constraint in his presence.

"Are you not feeling well?" she asked.

"No. I'm fine...I guess."

Whereupon she asked him why he hadn't come in, but he clouded at that and replied that he had experienced a family emergency.

"I hope it wasn't too serious," she probed. "Is Julia alright? Billy?"

He weighed his words as uncomfortably as a tourist who tries to compose a response in a foreign language he barely knows. Then he stammered out assurances that, after the accident that had overtaken Billy the night before, he had had every reason to believe that he'd be okay in a couple of days, perhaps.

"Is it the flu?" persisted Judy, concerned.

"No, no. It's nothing like that. But don't worry; he'll be okay. I just feel bad that, because of all the confusion, I caused a bunch of people an inconvenience."

"It was no inconvenience," she protested. "Don't worry on my account. I have two small children myself. I know how it is."

The hard tension of Bob's face thawed to a thin smile.

"Was it an allergic reaction to something, then?" she continued.

Skirting the subject, he said, "At the risk of inconveniencing you even more, can I ask you to do something for me?"

"Of course."

"I haven't really eaten anything since yesterday

morning. I'm starved. I don't want to let everyone see me in this condition. If you'll notice I have the same clothes on I wore yesterday. Could you run over to the bakery department and get me some bread, maybe. Something to eat."

"Of course. I'll be back in a minute."

As he waited, he remembered the small coffee maker in his office. He wanted to set a pot brewing. Standing up from the chair Bob nearly fainted from the blood rushing to his head so fast. He steadied himself, however, and made his way over to the coffee machine. With trembling hands, he measured out the coffee, filled the machine with water, and then turned the button on.

Judy came back, warmth and concern in her eyes. While she handed him the loaf of fresh-baked bread, the coffee machine was in operation behind them, giving forth a reassuring and jovial note as the fragrance of coffee slowly rose in the air.

"Want to wait for a cup?" he asked her.

"No. I can't drink too much coffee and I already had a cup with lunch. Not good for the digestion."

"Judy, I'm not officially here. I know I'm causing problems by doing this, but I have to run back out after this. I only stopped by for a few minutes to check a few things before getting back to...the hospital," he lied.

"I understand," she said, stoically.

"I appreciate all you're doing," he returned. "I won't forget it."

"Just tell Billy I hope he feels better soon."

"I'll do that. Bye, Judy."

After she went back out onto the floor, he lowered his head on his desk. He just wanted to rest for a minute while the coffee brewed. He knew how dangerous it was, however, to get too comfortable and didn't want to risk falling asleep. Just as a hidden watermark is revealed when a stamp or bank note are held up to the light, so his closed eyelids seemed to produce the same effect, summoning up the hidden image of his son whenever he dared to shut his eyes for too long.

He forced himself up and tried to focus his thoughts.

"The coffee's done," he breathed to himself in a mumble. Drawing himself up from his chair, he prepared a cup for himself and sat back down.

As he did so he looked at a nearby clock, the loss of time goading him back into action.

Turning on the computer on his desk, he sipped at his coffee. The caffeine entered his bloodstream rapidly. Because of it he felt that he was able for the first time in hours to clear a way through the darkness and confusion of his thoughts.

He accessed the Internet, and went immediately to the county's website, where public documents and deeds were posted online. Unfortunately, the website offered no enlightenment.

"That's odd," thought Bob. The property wasn't owned by an individual but by a company: the Murex Corporation. He had a moment's bewilderment, followed by the immediate thought that maybe someone had made a mistake and left the real estate developer's name on the ownership line after the property had been sold. But, no, listed in the records of ownership on another section of the deed was the original real estate developer, Triton Industries. Perplexed, he checked all the neighboring properties. What he discovered was that they were all homes built by Triton Industries and owned by individual citizens: one Boris Erickson, one Brian Walls, one Kevin Clinton and his wife Laura, and so forth.

Toggling back to the deed to the house he was

researching, he saw only the enigmatic "Murex Corporation" as the listed owner.

"Is it common practice for corporations to own real estate in residential areas?" he wondered.

He wanted to look into the Murex Corporation and how it related to the kidnapping.

His heart was racing. He wondered if he could address himself so composedly to his task. He did; he had to. He brought up a search engine and typed in "Murex Corporation". The search engine came back with a long list of references and articles. Bob's eyes plummeted down the page until he reached a particular line. His concentration narrowed to a sentence in an article which mentioned the company and his own city.

It seemed to be part of a larger investigative report on private companies gaining government contracts. Murex was just mentioned in passing. Beyond this, the article had no information to impart.

"Damn!" Bob's breath came out in a rush, as he looked at the clock.

He needed something to go on, anything. One thing struck him as curious. The article was listed as the first installment of a sixteen-part report, but so far as Bob could determine there were no further installments—even though the initial article had come out more than a year before.

Bob's mind brimmed with speculation. Yet he didn't want to jump to conclusions.

Presuming that the author of the article would know more, or at least, be able to point him to somebody who did, he decided to contact the newspaper. He found their phone number on the Internet.

He grabbed up his office handset and dialed the number.

"Daily Journal. How may I direct your call?"

"Um...Is Ned Bissel there?" he said breathlessly.

"He's no longer employed here, sir. Would you like me to direct your call elsewhere?"

"Ned Bissel no longer writes for *The Daily Journal?*"

"No, sir."

"Why?"

"I couldn't say," responded the feminine voice. "Would you like me to direct your call to the managing editor?"

"Uh...sure," he acceded.

"His name's Louis Webb. Hold on. I'll send your call through."

Bob waited on the line as the girl's voice snapped abruptly off to be replaced presently by a ringing sound. He expected to get the man's voicemail, but was pleasantly surprised when a human being answered.

"Louis Webb," the older, craggy voice said by way of greeting.

"Hi, Mr. Webb. You don't know me, but I'd like your help if you could give it," began Bob.

"I'll see what I can do," responded the editor with astonishing tractability. "What's it about?"

"It's about an article—or, rather, a *series* of articles— written by one of your writers, a certain Ned Bissel . . ."

There was a sudden change in the tenor of Webb's voice as he broke in, "He's no longer employed here."

"I know," rallied Bob. "I was just wondering if you could tell me how to get in touch with him. I had a question regarding one of his articles and . . ."

"Well, I can give you his phone number, if you'd like it—"

"Thank you."

"—But I can tell you that he probably won't be there."

"Is this a number where he works now?"

"Well, if by 'works' you mean drinking himself into a stupor—then yes."

"Oh, I see," uttered Bob, embarrassed in the face of such unprofessional behavior on the part of the managing editor.

"But if you're calling about giving the guy a job, I don't see how I can stand in your way. This *is* about a job, isn't it?"

"Yes," lied Bob, wondering how the man had gotten that bizarre impression. "I write for a magazine called *Weekly Springfield* and I was wondering if he'd be interested in doing a few articles for us. I've always been a fan of his."

"What did you say your name was?" asked the editor.

"Chester Biggs," blurted Bob, the name surging up from his subconscious (stolen, though he didn't know it at the time, from a boy he had in class during second grade).

"Well, Mr. Biggs, I hope you can do something for ol' Ned. He's been in a dark place for a while. He could use a hand up. Here's his number. Hold on. Wait a minute. Okay, okay. Here's his number. Are you ready?"

"Yes," said Bob, grabbing a pen.

"It's 281-0303."

"Thank you."

"If you don't get him there, you might try him at his other haunt, the Blue Horse Tavern."

Bob waited awkwardly for the man to explain that he was merely joking, but that assurance never came. So he thanked the man for the lead and said goodbye.

He was frustrated. The phone call brought no aid to solving the problem; but it gave him, at any rate, the clear conviction that no time was to be lost.

Minutes were slipping by, opportunities were fading fast.

Anxiously, he dialed the number given to him by the editor. But no one answered. It rang and rang and rang.

Finally, a recorded message gave him the opportunity to leave his name and number, but he felt too nervous about leaving any information.

Out of desperation, he thought he might risk a drive out to the Blue Horse Tavern, and went online again to find their address.

He moved so quickly that he was surprised when he suddenly hesitated upon reaching the exit of the supermarket. He had an ominous sense that to leave his job that day was to step out of more than a building: it was to step out of a whole life. Who knew what lay beyond that threshold? It all took on a different aspect because of what he knew might happen before the day was through. He memorized it all in with one sweeping glance. His eyes lighted on his coworkers, the aisles of products, the design of the ceiling and floor. There was something eerie and mystifying in the airy naiveté of the place, which floated aloof from the evils and passions of the world outside.

All of this was crowded out of his mind as he prepared to drive to the bar.

Chapter Eleven

I

Friday, November 20th, 4:21 pm

Before even making it out to the parking lot, something jarring suddenly intruded on Bob's thoughts. Abruptly, as if commanded by an inner voice, he looked up and saw a tan late-model sedan in front of the supermarket. It crawled through the congested parking lot in a way that sent a shudder through Bob. When he stopped and looked up at it the car sped off, leaving him to his racing thoughts.

Was it someone conducting surveillance on him?

"No, it was nothing," he told himself decisively as he found the car he had driven up in. He started the engine, slipped the car into gear and started off for the bar.

"I'm just being paranoid now," he concluded, feeling the weight of his strained nerves.

It was natural, after all he had been through, to start at the slightest sound, to feel a knot in his stomach at the most insignificant sight. He had to get a tighter grip on himself, he determined. It was no good to allow the situation to propel him into panic, whereby he'd lose what little control he had over events.

"Maybe I shouldn't have drunk that coffee," he mused, although he was glad for the effect of the caffeine.

As he drove he thought about his gamble, for he hadn't obtained Bissel's home address. If Bissel wasn't at the bar—as his former boss snidely joked—Bob wouldn't know how to get a hold of him. He could phone back and leave a message, but how long would it take the man to return the call?

Twelve minutes from that thought, he drove into the graveled lot in front of the bar. He pulled up next to a beat-up old pickup truck and cut the engine. He gave the front of the building a speculative stare and then opened the door and stepped out.

Pushing past the door, he entered a bar as he had never entered a bar before—in the afternoon. His experience of bars was always at night. Because of his younger days, he associated such establishments with revelry: people unwinding after a long workweek, others on informal dates with the opposite sex; still others, young people out for a night of unapologetic intoxication. The Blue Horse Tavern at four o'clock in the afternoon was at variance with that image. He encountered a decidedly different element: regulars. Bob wondered if Bissel was one of them.

Looking around, Bob saw one man who bore a resemblance to the photo next to the newspaper column he had read. He could only see a three-quarter view of the man's face as he sat on a barstool. He had brown hair, a chin shadowed with stubble, and a dark blue sports coat. The man he needed to talk to was sitting no less than six paces away from him. Bob seated himself at the bar close enough to speak to him but far enough so as not to incur initial suspicion.

Now all that was left to do was to somehow open a conversation with him.

Do it! Go talk to him now, an internal voice urged him. Just then the reporter was approached by the bartender. Bob waited. From what he could gather, Bissel must have entered the bar shortly before he did, or else the bartender was just starting his shift, because the two men started catching up on events since they last saw each other.

"You look terrible," said the bartender to the reporter.

"Is it that obvious?" he replied.

"Yeah. Have you slept at all? Here. Let me get you something to calm your nerves. . . ."

"I had a bad week," said the reporter.

"Why?" asked bartender as he briefly stepped away to get his patron a shot of whiskey.

"Oh, a lot of reasons," he continued, vaguely. "Victoria's back at her mother's. We had a big fight, too, before she left."

"Why?"

"Said I was a drunk."

"That's odd. Better have a drink and tell me about it."

Bob smiled at this exchange, which neither man seemed to find ironic. The bartender stepped back to place the bottle of whiskey on the shelf, leaving the reporter to brood alone over his drink for a moment. Bob saw this as his second chance to introduce himself. *Now!* the voice rang out from the muddle of his thoughts, more imperatively than before.

"Excuse me," he ventured.

"Huh?" asked the reporter.

Bob controlled his breathing and tried to adopt a sociable smile calculated to put the man at his ease. Toward this end, he was largely successful, showing no sign of anxiety. He was not only smilingly calm but absolutely chipper; and yet, beneath his affable mood, the reporter caught now and then a hint of serious purpose. Because of that, he studied Bob's face, his voice growing cautious. "What's this about?"

Bob swallowed, meeting the troubled gaze of the reporter. "This is about an article you wrote, mentioning something called the Murex Corporation."

"What?" The reporter tried to gather together his startled thoughts.

"Do you remember the article?" pressed Bob.

Bissel's eyes blinked through his fixed stare. "Are you serious?"

"Yes."

"That's the article that got me fired. Who are you?"

"My name's...Bob," he said, at a risk. Something about the reporter made Bob feel as if he could trust him. "Bob Ebersol."

"Why do you want to know about the Murex Corporation?"

"There have been...things. 'Things' in my life recently, bad things, and I think they might have something to do with this company," answered Bob.

"What kind of bad things?" asked the reporter.

"It looks like you've experienced your fair share of bad things connected to the Murex Corporation, too—I gather from what you've already said."

"Yeah," smiled Bissel wryly as he devoted himself to his drink and lapsed back into silence.

Bob's curiosity was sharpened.

"So...tell me," he continued.

"What's there to tell?" asked the reporter. He subjected Bob to a searching scrutiny before he spoke again: "Are you with law enforcement? The District Attorney's office, maybe?"

"Me?" smiled Bob. "Nothing like that. I'm a supermarket manager."

"Are you kidding me?" chortled Bissel. "Why on earth would *you* be asking questions about the Murex Corporation, Mr....Mr. . . ."

"Ebersol," supplied Bob.

"Mr. Ebersol," finished Bissel on a breath that smelled of whiskey.

Bob gave him to understand that it was far too sensitive a matter to go into at that moment, but added,

"Will you tell me all you know if I promise you a story after it's all over?"

"With a pitch like that, how can I refuse?" joked Bissel. "Okay. I'll play along. First I request something from you."

"Alright," said Bob. "What?"

"A drink. Spot me another whiskey and I'll tell you what little I know—for whatever it's worth."

Bob agreed. Calling the bartender over, he ordered two more drinks for the reporter while ordering a beer for himself.

After the bartender furnished them with their respective drinks, Bob placed a rather large bill on the bar, peeled from one of the two appropriated wallets he had on his person.

After Bissel took a sip, Bob urged him to continue.

"Where do I begin...?" he asked rhetorically. "Let's see..."

"You can begin," said Bob, "with why the initial article promised to be the first of a series, yet there were no more installments—at least, no more installments that I could find."

"No, you're right," confirmed Bissel. "There were no more installments. It was killed after that first article—and so was my career."

"Why?" demanded Bob.

"Pressure was brought to bear," remarked Bissel. "Phone calls were made. I was fired."

"But why?"

Suddenly, Bissel looked distinctly more sober. Perhaps to counteract that sensation, he took another swig from his shot glass of whiskey, finishing it off.

Before picking up the fuller shot glass next to the now-empty one, he tried to set forth the object of his series of articles. "Do you know anything about government contractors?" he asked by way of beginning.

"No. Not much, I guess," answered Bob, honestly.

"Well, it's no secret. Our government's being hollowed out, gutted. It's happening everywhere, on the federal, state and local level. Private companies are getting contracts to do things that used to only be done by the government. Budgets are being slashed for state and federal agencies, people laid off, downsizing happening left and right. Private companies are picking up the slack, sometimes getting very large contracts. Sometimes it's legal and there's nothing outwardly untoward about it, but sometimes...well, sometimes there are questions of corruption. A government bureaucrat will decide which cuts to make, which agencies to de-fund—and then suddenly retire to get hired by the very private companies that get the contracts which resulted from the government downsizing. It can get pretty sleazy."

"Yeah, I've read a little about what you're talking about," commented Bob.

"It doesn't depend upon any particular branch of the government; it's happening in all sectors," added Bissel. "People who've put in decades of service are being fired, downsized as the men who made the cuts are being hired with fat salaries at the private companies who are awarded the contracts to do the work previously done by the civil servants. Murex is really a very small part of what's going on. I only mentioned them in passing, and only because they're local. They're small-time. But they're part of a bigger trend."

"What do they do?"

"They're supposed to be good at coordinating efforts with law enforcement agencies."

Bob's mind was racing ahead. "Rent-a-cops, you mean?"

"No, nothing like that. More secretive stuff," said Bissel, who wanted, as he explained, to study the secret, to ferret it out.

"What do you mean by 'secretive' stuff?" asked Bob after a period of silence, of concentration, fighting the clouds of fatigue.

"Most of these contractors generally operate below the radar," continued Bissel. "Do you know anything about the Pinkertons?"

"What's that?" asked Bob, interrupting himself almost immediately to say, "Hold on. Bartender, can we have another round of drinks?"

When the bartender responded, Bob asked him to leave the bottle of whiskey. Bissel thanked him as Bob closed the distance between them, moving from his own barstool to the one directly next to Bissel's. Meanwhile the latter resumed his monologue: "The Pinkertons were a famous detective agency in the nineteenth century. They had an eye as their symbol. It was supposed to stand for constant vigilance. That's where the phrase 'private eye' comes from for detectives in general."

"Oh, yeah," declared Bob, his features brightening with recognition. "I think I know what you're talking about. They were big around the time of the Lincoln assassination."

"Yeah, and the famous strikes of the late nineteenth and early twentieth centuries. They had field offices in every major city in North America. Have you ever read anything by Dashiell Hammett?"

"No."

"He's the author of *The Maltese Falcon* and a bunch of other famous novels," said Bissel. "He wrote his detective stories from his actual experiences. He used to be a detective with the Pinkertons. That's how I got interested in the subject."

"What do you mean?" asked Bob.

"I was reading a collection of short stories by Dashiell Hammett," answered Bissel. "And I was struck by the number of cities his fictitious detectives would go to and the fact that they all had field offices. It was amazing, especially considering the fact that there was no CIA back then. Nothing even remotely comparable. I did some research and Hammett wasn't exaggerating: the Pinkertons were everywhere. It was like a proto-CIA before there was a CIA. In fact, the CIA was based, in large part, on the Pinkertons. It was just like an intelligence service before nations had official intelligence services. In one story, for instance, a detective is tracking some criminal and he calls ahead to a bureau in a distant city and has them assign half a dozen men to shadow him. He could do this in just about any city in North America. They had a massive infrastructure, thousands of agents and operatives. I wanted to research it some more, to see if the Pinkertons still exist."

"Do they?"

"Yes!" declared Bissel. "It shocked me. They're still quiet and unobtrusive, but, yes, they still exist. It's a testament to their power that neither you nor I gave them a thought. I mean, in this day and age when every kid knows about the FBI or CIA, no one talks about the Pinkertons anymore. They're *that* powerful."

"Are you serious?" broke in Bob. "Do they still have field offices in every major city?"

"Yes. But they don't go by the 'Pinkertons' title anymore. That's part of what helps them stay underground—and quietly ubiquitous. They were bought out by another private security agency and go by a new name—Securitas. They're international and very, very good at what they do."

"So what does this have to do with Murex?"

"Absolutely nothing. Murex isn't affiliated with Securitas or the Pinkertons or anything else. But they're riding on the coattails of these companies in the age of the private contractor. Murex is small-time, as I said before. Mostly staffed with retired law enforcement types, people who get lured away from the military or SWAT units. Stuff like that. They get paid much better working for private firms."

"What's wrong with that?" asked Bob.

"Rome fell because of mercenaries. They stopped using their own citizens and outsourced everything until finally the mercenaries turned on them and the 'barbarians' seized control. We're so busy outsourcing our military, bringing in private contractors, soldiers of fortune, gutting our own infrastructure, undermining our own federal and state agencies that— Well, there's always a risk of these private companies acting as if *they're* the government, the law—when they're not."

"They're rent-a-cops," piped in Bob.

"Yeah, but they act like stormtroopers. There have already been a bunch of cases like that, where mercenaries given government contracts overstep their actual authority. Overseas, one group of mercenaries actually pulled their weapons on *our* soldiers! They're totally out of control."

"Well, what does this have to do with Murex?"

"Sorry. I'm ranting again on my soapbox," apologized Bissel. He moderated his tone, embarrassed that his voice had grown too strident, adding, "Murex isn't involved with mercenary soldiers, just mercenary law enforcement."

"What do you mean?"

According to Bissel, rumor attributed a diversity of motives to their operations, the least damaging of which was their private consultation services to law enforcement agencies. "But," Bissel added, "there was something more going on."

Bob took a pull at his beer, then said: "Like what?"

"Imagine a sort of temp agency for criminals."

"Murex did that?"

"Imagine people in law enforcement, or, rather, people who *used* to be in law enforcement using their expertise and connections to recruit criminals to pull jobs for distant crime bosses. In this age of outsourcing, even crime syndicates rely on temping every once in a while. It helps distance them and their people from a particular crime pulled off in their city. They can place a phone call, get people tailored to a particular heist, a particular job."

"Is that what Murex was doing?" asked Bob, mystified. Because, if true, this operation was larger than anything he had conceived of before. His eyes were lit with anxiety as he reflected upon it now.

Meanwhile Bissel methodically unfolded the vast narrative. Slowly and with much resistance Bob assimilated the details. At last, his skeptical mind was turned away from its mundane preoccupations as the new conceptions opened out before it.

"God, what a world we live in!" he said.

The truth about how the world really worked depressed him; and the perception gave him a startled sense of hidden darkness, of a chaos of wills and purposes far beneath the ordered surfaces of life. He looked back with melancholy derision on the impression he had had earlier—as recently as when he arrived at the supermarket. In going back to his old life, he thought at first that he had reentered reality, while in fact the opposite was the case. The supermarket, his neighborhood, his whole domesticated existence fell away like a stage set, a mask covering over the seething tumult of bestial drives and desires which constituted reality's truer nature. All else was artifice.

Coming back to his senses, he thought to question Bissel on one more point. "So this is why your series never appeared in print? Why you were fired?"

The reporter commented that the timing seemed charged with significance. "At least, I thought so. Unless it was all just a coincidence," he remarked, laughing mirthlessly.

"Sorry," muttered Bob.

"Although, leaving the subject of coincidence aside for the time being, I can't pretend there weren't other reasons, if you wanted to look for them," affirmed Bissel, his eyes dropping below Bob's gaze. He sat there, looking alternately at his alcohol and his benefactor.

"I see," responded Bob, letting the remark ride on the silence for a moment.

He paused and when he spoke again his voice was pensive. "Do you remember anything about a man named Spence, Gregory Spence?"

"Doesn't ring a bell," mumbled Bissel. "But Murex is a huge corporation. They have a bunch of different branches. The 'criminal temp agency' aspect of the company is a smaller part of what they do. It's a clandestine operation under the 'criminal profiling' division, if you can appreciate the irony of that. Aside from that, they have a branch that deals with consulting, one that deals with home and business security systems, one that d—"

"Home and business security systems?" echoed Bob.

"Yeah. Why?"

Bob's eyes strayed, his thoughts obviously racing. Answering Bissel after an interval, he said, "Spence—the Spence I mentioned—is a police detective. He encouraged me to get a home security system. But never mind. It doesn't matter."

"You think he might be mixed up with Murex?"

"I don't know."

"He's a cop; it's possible. They're always recruiting."

Bob sat silently, trying to mentally filter the information. It would take him time to make sense of it all; he knew that. Meanwhile, he would have to say goodbye to Bissel and thank him for his help.

"Is there a way I can get in touch with you later, if I need to?" asked Bob, by way of valediction.

"Do you have a pen?"

"Um...no," uttered Bob, after patting down his pockets.

Bissel borrowed one from the bartender and proceeded to scribble his address and telephone number on a paper napkin and handed it to Bob.

"Let me know what happens," he muttered as Bob folded the napkin and stuffed it in his wallet.

Bob himself, waving goodbye, had no idea what was going to happen. Not even in the immediate future. Walking back out to the parking lot, he was hard put to think of where to go to next, what direction to take.

Even though he longed to check some of the facts Bissel had given him on the Internet, he shrank away from the thought of going back to the supermarket. At loose ends, he felt like he couldn't go back. He was afraid he would lose what momentum he had already built. No, in inner turmoil, he decided to go forward, whatever forward meant.

Since Spence was the last subject he had broached with Bissel, Bob fastened onto that. Maybe Bob could track him down.

He knew the risk of calamity he ran, but it didn't turn him from his purpose. His estimations of his own courage and competence were too mixed and indeterminate for him not to feel the risk of such an action. The one element he had to his advantage was that his enemies had no idea how close he was, and he intended to exploit it.

Chapter Twelve

I

Friday, November 20th, 6:52 am

Larry stood like a sentinel at the door leading back out into the hall. Quivering with indignation, Julia had to submit to his authority as she left the bathroom. He grabbed her roughly by the shoulder as he ushered her back into the room that was being used as her holding cell.

When she got there, she was glad to see Ronnie waiting. She looked at him despairingly.

"Hi," he said. "It's time for my shift."

His tone was softer than it usually was, more sympathetic. Though he didn't know what happened, he gave her a commiserating look. Larry shrugged to signal that his captive must be a high-strung woman given to hysteria. Why else would she make such a big deal about being taken to the bathroom? Larry implied that his intention in doing so was to spare Ronnie the irritation of having to do it later himself.

He let his glance wander toward Julia, hang there a few seconds, and then go back toward the wall. A flickering, anxious scowl played across his features, alternating with an expression of blank preoccupation whenever he thought he was being observed.

Ronnie broke in, saying, "Well, at least you're out of those ropes now."

"Uh-huh," mumbled Julia, making a gesture expressive of her hatred for the chair. She welcomed freedom. Gratitude and irritability contended within her for supremacy.

In the meantime, Larry emitted a series of banal comments, remarks designed to initiate a conversation with his captive. But Julia refused to give him an opening. She tried to retrieve her dignity by pointedly ignoring him.

"Oh, well," he concluded, addressing Ronnie by saying, "She's yours now."

With that, he left.

Coming somewhat out of Larry's dark shadow, Ronnie recovered some of his oddly childlike and loquacious personality. She was glad that, in listening to him, she didn't have to think about her trip to the bathroom, or the fact that Larry seemed to derive deep inner satisfaction from watching her. Even thinking about it afterwards saw a sudden blush invade her face.

She was glad that Ronnie didn't seem to notice. She allowed herself to relax as he poured into her ears an endless flow of rambling comments.

It was touching, in a way, that he expected people to have a bottomless interest in the small trivia concerning his own affairs, like what food he liked, what shoes he preferred, the latest gossip about people she didn't know and would never meet.

"I just got a hold of some reading material," he began, "I was bored out of my mind and Larry is never any help, he's always so quiet so moody and besides we're on shifts here so I don't really get to pass the time talking and there are no books here so I just get crazy staring at the wall and b—"

"AnywayasIwasabouttosayInoticedLarryreadingallthe seoldlettersandIaskedhimwherehegotthemandhesaidthatthey wereinaroomoffttotheleftonthesecondfloorhesaidtherewerestack sandstacksofthemboxloadsinfact."

Julia's attention trailed off. Only as if from a great distance did her mind still catch what he was saying.

When she emerged from her introspection, she realized he had a strange habit of pursuing his thoughts aloud. Often, when he had been silent for some time, he would say something which seemed to assume that his listener had shared the succession of thoughts that led up to his sudden outburst.

Of course, Julia hadn't been following. So she said, "Huh?"

"I asked if you wanted something to eat," he repeated, producing a few plastic containers of crackers.

Just the sight of them made her stomach turn over. Perhaps, she told herself, she should try to eat something. She would need to be strong for whatever the upcoming hours would bring.

So against her better judgment, she accepted a packet and ate the crackers. They left her mouth dry.

Ronnie, anticipating her need, ran and brought her a glass of water. Whenever he came into the room—whenever he did anything for her—he assumed a confidential air, as if there was a secret understanding between them. Moreover, he adopted the habit of glancing over at her during quiet periods, as if he were willing her to talk to him. And when she did, he always had the air of trying to prolong the conversation.

He seemed so lonely.

His whole attitude denoted solitude, emotional isolation. As strange as it felt, some maternal strain in her composition reacted as pity stirred in her.

She remembered how, when he first saw her, he stared at her as if she were an apparition. Even now, he would talk and talk—but as soon as she met his eyes and returned his stare, he immediately looked down at his shoes.

"Why do you stare at me?" she asked abruptly.

Ronnie started, unaware that he had been staring. He fidgeted, averted his glance and indicated by his whole manner that—on this one subject, and perhaps this one subject alone—he preferred to remain reticent.

"Um," he said meditatively. Then changing the subject, he added: "I have to go and get something. I'll be right back."

With that, he hastened away. She had wanted him to talk. But her attempt at a conversation with him had served only to increase her perplexity.

Did she remind him of someone? An old girlfriend, perhaps? Someone he had met many years before? Each possibility in turn captured her mind to the exclusion of everything else. Instead of one mystery she found herself confronted by two.

She had no time to explore either one of them now, for his absence reminded her of more pressing things. Because for those precious few minutes, she was alone.

Her primary need, at the moment, was to obtain some degree of mental perspective. She withdrew into herself and reviewed her situation.

She thought about her options for a considerable time and ended on rather a pessimistic note. *How realistic is it to believe that Bob can lay his hands on over a million dollars?*

The question had the force of a blow.

She knew that, statistically, it was very improbable that—of modest income and limited prospects—he'd be able to raise the funds. It was a better gamble from her point of view to try and get her son out of there herself and escape.

But how?

Her only plan was to concentrate all her energies on formulating a strategy. With an effort of will, she became interested in the room around her, in its architecture, in the possibilities inherent in it for escape. She thought that the bathroom up the hall was significant, but its significance eluded her.

Fear gave concentration to all her energies, if not any particular definition to her plans.

Nevertheless, she studied her rather stark and severe surroundings. The walls, the ceiling, the few cardboard boxes in the corner; all were objects of intense interest.

As Julia came away empty-handed, she returned in thought to the bathroom, its size and design, the fact that it had a number of stalls and not just a single toilet, all fostered the belief that this was a large building of some sort, a commercial building.

Gradually other certainties presented themselves, such as the fact that it was abandoned. She heard no one— other than the kidnappers. The sounds of traffic never penetrated to her cell, nor did noise reach her in the hallway.

It *must* be an abandoned building. But was it a bank, as she had first wondered?

Maybe not.

As she turned over these possibilities, she remarked the stale air. The room's air was to oxygen what apples were to apple cider. It was as if someone had fermented oxygen, aged it, stored it in a cask, and then released it. Old, dusty, moldering air.

She had reached this point in her deliberations when Ronnie came back.

"Hi," he said, almost shyly as he closed and locked the door behind him.

Deeply absorbed in the study of her environment, she returned his greeting but then tried to concentrate. Meanwhile, Ronnie sat down on one of the chairs in the room.

He held in his hands envelopes much like Larry had had earlier. Noticing her observation of the envelopes, Ronnie said, "I grabbed a stack. You want some? I know it must be boring, just sitting here, doing nothing."

"I don't understand," she returned, puzzled.

"Letters. See?" he said, holding them up. "You can read some if you want."

"Are they for...me?" asked Julia, diffidently.

"They're not for anybody."

"I'm still not sure I understand."

"Well, if you get bored, you can have some," he said, and proceeded to open one of the envelopes. As he folded open the letter and set about reading, Julia tried to bring her thoughts back around to plotting plans of escape.

She kept trying to think, to organize her thoughts, but her mind was hobbled by the flood of emotions washing over it as she thought about her plight, her position, her son.

There was nothing she could do about it now. It was time to concentrate on the task at hand: formulating a plan of escape.

She began to work it out in her head. She could try some ruse. Perhaps ask to go to the bathroom again. Then, as she walked up the hall she could make more mental notes about escape possibilities—or at least get a better idea about the building. Even if she obtained no useful information, she could think of some way to trick him eventually and make for an open window, an unlocked door, a staircase—anything. But, not now. She had to bide her time, find the right moment. First, though, she would trump up a reason to get back outside the room and reconnoiter.

As she hatched out these plots, her attention kept reverting to the envelopes that sat on Ronnie's lap.

After fifteen minutes, he seemed to be losing interest in his reading material. For the first time, she realized that—as captors—they were allowed as little sleep as she was. Less, in fact. Ronnie seemed to be getting drowsy. Apparently the letters failed to hold his interest. He let them fall to the floor by his feet.

After fifteen more minutes, when sleep overtook him, Julia, with sudden resolution, decided to pick up the envelopes. She thought that they might offer her a clue.

Retreating to a far corner of the room, she read letter after letter without deriving any clear conception of their significance. None of them were part of a cohesive whole. They seemed to be from a number of different people, and covered a huge range of different topics. Examining them more closely, she determined that they were from not only vastly different people and social types, but from remarkably different time periods. From the oldest to the most recent there was a disparity of over fifty years.

"Anything interesting?" a voice rang through the room as her heart jumped in her chest.

She saw that Ronnie was looking at her intently. Apparently, he had woken up.

"Uh . . ." she muttered.

"I read some but I don't see why Larry likes 'em so much," he said. "Did you get any good ones?"

"I'm still not sure what they are," admitted Julia, her features softening when she realized that she wasn't in trouble. Sighing in relief, she added, "What are they?"

"Letters."

"I know that. But from who?"

"I don't know. Do you want some more? We can get some more."

"Where from?" she asked, warily.

"Right up the hall."

"Can you show me?"

Ronnie paused for a minute, turning over the prospect in his head. "Well, I don't know," he began. "Larry might not want me letting you out. I should probably get them myself and b—"

"But Larry let me out to go to the bathroom," she hastened to interject.

"That's right; he did," mumbled Ronnie.

Julia existed in a limbo of torment as her captor weighed the pros and cons of the act. Trying to shift the balance in her favor, she decided to psychologically manipulate him by rising and moving toward the door.

"Hold on there. Hold on," he called after her.

Because Ronnie couldn't see her face, he was unaware of the expression of pain that masked his captive's features, the anguish in the tightly closed eyes as she stood frozen in place. When he caught up to her, he occasioned her relief when he said, "Don't walk so fast. I have the key."

Drawing a deep sigh of relief, she stood back as he unlocked the door.

Once outside the cell, he said, "Shhh. Now be quiet. I don't want Larry finding out I let you see the letter room."

Letter room?

They moved through the halls like restless spirits haunting a mansion. Meanwhile she glanced around, noting architectural features and possible escape routes.

God, I wish I'd studied more, she thought to herself, returning in thought to her life as a student, before she'd dropped out of architecture school.

She had the nagging feeling that, had she completed her course of education, she would have been able to use that knowledge to ferret out likely escape routes now by having a better understanding of the building around her.

All the while—despite enjoining her to be quiet—Ronnie prattled on in a muted undertone. She was only dimly aware of the few commonplace remarks he made, for her essential attention was occupied wholly by the layout of the building. Its appearance surprised her, for it contradicted her expectations based on the dilapidated storage room in which they kept her, and those collected in the long hallway leading up to it.

The rest of the building was clearly abandoned, but not nearly as decrepit, at any rate, as she thought it would be.

As for the "letter room," it was a large, oblong room with a counter in the middle of it and a whole wall devoted to cubbyholes which called to mind a rabbit warren. On the floor were dozens of large canvas sacks stuffed to capacity with what appeared to be envelopes.

She looked round the room, nervously at first, then with startled interest. "What is this place?"

"I don't know," replied Ronnie. "I guess it used to be a post office or something."

"A hub, maybe," she mused aloud.

"For some reason, they never sent on these letters and packages."

"So this is a dead-letter office?"

"What's that?" asked Ronnie.

"It's where they send letters that don't have addresses or aren't capable of being delivered. I'm surprised they didn't destroy them when they abandoned the property."

She thought more about the possibilities that this discovery opened up regarding her own location; then, after a moment's indecision, she picked up an envelope.

Ronnie had wandered away from her and started digging through the bags for himself—perhaps looking for the odd package that was buried among the envelopes. As he did so, she scrutinized the envelope in her own hand.

Reverie captured her. A thousand voices seemed to rise to her from the moldering letters.

Which would she open?

She grabbed a small stack and glanced through them. The names interested her: L. Wallace, Claude Oldfield, Mary Griffith-Johnson, Mr. And Mrs. Edward Bright.

The very sound of them seemed to create differently colored lights in her mind.

One by one, she delved into a different life. A lawyer named Horace Marsh had written to a dry-cleaning establishment in order to find out about a missing jacket. Elena Sadowska wrote to inquire about the health of her sister, Mashenka. Samuel Stubbs who sent a greeting card to a cousin for Christmas—a greeting card that, though he didn't know it, would never arrive.

A fever of curiosity possessed Julia. She marveled at these lives which flashed into her consciousness with the fantastic reality of a dream. It seemed as if she was looking down on life from a great height.

Of course, most of the letters she opened were banal—Christmas wishes from children to Santa Claus, letters to distant relatives who had died or left no forwarding address, catalogs mailed to people who had moved away.

But one or two of the communications she came across were heart-wrenching. One was a father's letter to his children after he had left the family, explaining why he had to leave "Mommy" and how he still loved them and always would.

These children would never receive this note, which might have helped them to understand the torrid world of emotion and loss all around them. In fact, as Julia examined the envelope, she realized that these "children" would be, if they were still alive, in their eighties.

She staggered under the weight of that realization.

Another communication—charged with emotion— was a love letter, written from what appeared to be a mining engineer of some sort to the girl from whom he was separated. He was apparently in South America. The letter was dominated by a respect and knowledge of love which extended to every detail. The writer transformed the most banal acts into studies of adventure and mystery.

And he was not alone. There were a few love letters after that which Julia came across.

There was heroism and beauty in people such as these who pitted themselves against the world and wrestled from it a meek existence. They were all fated to die in anonymity and obscurity, but so what? In their own worlds, they eked out moving lives and fulfilling existences.

The fact that she could find herself so absorbed in the lives of strangers, whom she would never meet, clearly revealed the extent of her own loneliness and offered a way to fill the unknown spate of time in front of her.

As for Ronnie, he was playing with a toy he had discovered in a package mailed almost three-quarters of a century before.

He discussed with her a few more of his discoveries, and, in this fashion, the next half-hour passed.

Eventually, however, Ronnie's blathering flickered out, and he felt—and looked—anxious. Mindful of the restrictions by which they were tethered, he told her that they should probably be getting back.

"Okay," agreed Julia, who grabbed a stack of envelopes for later.

Chapter Thirteen

I

Friday, November 20ᵗʰ, 5:08 pm

Bob drove to the police department downtown. He had no idea if Spence worked at that precinct house or at some other location. Chances were, he wouldn't be "working" at all that day, given the nature of his extracurricular exploits. But Bob thought it might be a good place to start.

Bob had passed the police department on a nearly daily basis for years, but had never been inside. He pushed through the front doors, crossing the path of several random police officers moving in one direction or another. Ignoring them, he walked over to a duty officer who was at the front desk.

"Um...hello?" began Bob, nervously.

"Yes?" said the duty officer. He was like every tired, overworked, underpaid local law enforcement officer Bob had ever met—only more so. This particular man had graduated from lifelong huskiness to middle-aged obesity; his whole weight trembled on legs that were like those of a piano—thin and short and altogether inappropriate for the weight they were supposed to bear. Added to this was a mysterious roll of fat on the back of his head—as if his body stored fat like camels do...like it was a double-chin that he had somehow misplaced.

"I just wanted some help finding someone," continued Bob.

"You mean, like paperwork to file a Missing Persons report?" the duty officer said gravely, his face settling into grim lines as he added, "You can fill out a form here if you'd like."

Bob blinked his surprise. "No, no, that's not what I meant," he said. "I just wanted to know if Detective Spence was here."

The name drew a faint note of amusement from the man and set Bob at a disadvantage. Clearly, their experiences of the same man couldn't have been more at variance. Nevertheless, Bob forged on. He spoke eagerly, persuasively, sounding a note of confidence that led the duty officer to treat him quite deferentially.

His sense of optimism was increased by a decisive incident. For no sooner did Bob learn that Spence had in fact come into work that day than his informant told him that he had just left.

"You probably passed him on your way in," he added.

Bob's eyes seemed to search the man more closely as he said, "Are you sure he just left?"

"Yes."

He turned to the duty officer with sudden decision. "Maybe I can catch him in the parking lot. What kind of car does he drive?"

The man, struck by the suddenness and vehemence of his appeal, gave Bob the information.

Bob visibly controlled himself. His voice dropping back to its calmer note, he said, "Thank you. Goodbye."

Panicking, his chest tightened. It ached as he ran outside, features set, his whole face drawn into an intense fixity of vigilance. But to Bob's strained attention every car looked at first like the one described to him—then abruptly none did. His eyes wavered between all the sedans and trucks and minivans and SUVs. He wheeled around and ran to the other side of the building to look at the other branch of the L-shaped parking lot. At length his attention fixed on a car pulling out into the street. It was Spence's.

Seeing the car like that had the disorienting quality of a chase in a dream, a nightmare. No matter how fast he ran, he felt as if he were wading through molasses. He tried to get back to the car he was driving. Though consuming only thirty seconds, it felt as if it had cost him thirty hours. With his pulse racing and a fire in his mind, he stuck the key in the ignition, slammed closed his door and gunned the engine.

Such was his haste that he failed to look both ways before swinging the car out into traffic. He just missed being hit by a passing truck by the narrowest of margins. Its irate driver blared the horn.

For a minute or so, he feared that he had lost the trail. The only thing he could do was drive in the direction he saw the car take and guess where it might or might not turn off. With his heart clutching up, he sped through the streets, his eyes scanning every road and vehicle in his path. A flood of adrenaline and alarm washed through him as, time after time, he came up empty-handed. He was losing faith. Just on the point of giving up, though, his gamble paid off. Several car-lengths ahead, he saw the vehicle again.

Thanks to the traffic lights, it had been waylaid at several key junctures, giving Bob just enough time to catch up to it.

Trying not to make himself conspicuous, he maintained a two- or three-car distance. By doing this, he thought he had escaped detection. He must have, since the car in front of him didn't appear to change its speed or direction in response to his own looming presence. Because of that, he was unwittingly taken on a tour of Spence's chores as he stopped off at a bank drive-through.

In any case, he pumped the brakes, bringing the car he was driving to a complete stop behind a white van. Both vehicles idled behind Spence's car as they all waited in line.

Spence was soon finished, though, and the line advanced. After Spence pulled back out into traffic Bob turned the wheel, slammed his foot hard down on the gas pedal and the car shot forward. He only narrowly missed the bumper of the van in front of him.

He didn't care. He couldn't lose Spence. He might lead him to his son. Within seconds he closed the distance between the two cars. Bob worried that he might have gotten too close, and dropped back to a safer distance. Meanwhile he moderated his speed, sinking back into the blend of highway traffic. Spence seemed utterly unaware that he was being tailed—especially as his pursuer bobbed and wove between intervening cars.

Because of his anxious, erratic driving, Bob nearly lost his quarry when he turned onto an off-ramp that opened out onto a quiet suburban area. Was this where his son was being kept?

Bob followed Spence at a distance, hoping that he wouldn't lose him in one of the many maze-like lanes and avenues that enmeshed the neighborhood. Spence didn't drive much farther before he pulled into a white pseudo-colonial two-story house. As he turned into the driveway, Bob coasted past him. He drifted to the curb four houses away and braked softly. He cut the engine.

He lowered his passenger-side window and listened, as he tried to fix on Spence through the rear-view mirror. He expected Spence to climb out of his car, but no. His garage door yawned open and his car disappeared inside. As the garage door eased down behind him, it made clanky, metallic sounds—as if the house that had just absorbed him was now metabolizing him.

Bob's heart started to race as he wondered if Billy was in there, could he really be so close?

He didn't know what to do next. He didn't know if it was a form of paralysis or not, but he resolved to bide his time and watch. Perhaps someone would come out of the house, perhaps someone would go in. Maybe something would give him a clue regarding what to do next.

The waiting began, each silent minute compounding the strain. The fast-approaching deadline to save his son was uppermost in his mind. How much longer would he hesitate? The mounting stress, the nagging sense of diminishing time abraded his nerves.

7:02 p.m. was the deadline. Had he come home sooner yesterday, then the twenty-four period would have reflected that. But, due to random circumstances, he had made his way home by 6:45 and first spoken to the kidnappers by 7:02. So now 7:02 was the deadline—a time that had unwittingly become the hinge upon which his whole future would pivot. Whether it would swing toward life or death he had no way of knowing.

It was just past 5:18 p.m. now, and he was getting increasingly nervous. Night was already getting underway. As the day was drawing down, it was like the net was closing. He could feel it tightening around him.

The sunset, he reflected, was painfully beautiful— like the chemical combination of an old master's pigments, which he'd arrived at by crushing up rubies to get a particular shade of crimson.

It was beautiful, but beautiful as only death is beautiful—just as the autumn leaves broke into blinding colors just before falling from the branches and dying.

Gripped by this thought, he grew anxious. His hands shook; the trembling spread to his stomach. He was getting antsy, just sitting there, staring at the house. Something had to be done; time was being lost.

"It's now or never," he thought to himself, climbing out of the car.

Whether circumstances would break in his favor, he could only guess. But he had to do *something*.

Chapter Fourteen

I

Friday, November 20ᵗʰ, 5:19 pm

He crept up to the house as stealthily as possible. He listened at the door, trying to gauge whether anyone was directly behind it or in the room beyond. To his ears, it sounded like no one was inside. So he decided to try the doorknob. It would obviously be locked, but maybe he could b—

"Huh?" he marveled to himself as the door opened.

Perhaps it was a trap.

With sweat beading up at his hairline, he toed open the door. He winced as it protested under the pressure of his foot with a raspy squeak. Stealing a look beyond the narrow crack he had made between the door and doorjamb, he saw that the room was indeed empty. His blood spiked with adrenaline, he opened the door further and entered the house.

It was just at this moment that he thought it might be prudent to take out the pistol in his jacket pocket.

His arms locked in front of him, sweeping left with the gun, then right, he advanced from the foyer to the living room, his gaze roaming anxiously around himself.

His glance, making a swift circuit of the room, rested finally on a door that hovered on a far wall. From that part of the house, he caught sound and the suggestion of movement beyond. What was the room on the other side? A study? A family room, perhaps? He didn't know. Since there was clearly someone on the other side of the hinged door, he wouldn't have the luxury of easing into the room—as he had just done with the living room.

He proceeded slowly, the sound of his feet over the carpet affecting the silence like a mayfly suspended on the surface of a lake, not breaking the surface tension but creating a tiny ripple as it moves. In this painstaking fashion he finally came up to the door. His sinews were taut, his muscles ready, each nerve a tripwire stretched out to full tension.

Psychologically, he seemed prepared for anything at that moment—even the unthinkable. If he miscalculated and some thug found him, he felt capable of murder. All of his nerves twisted together became a sort of waxed fuse that, when it went off, would trigger an explosion of motion and force.

His nerves hardened for the coming struggle. He had no notion of what awaited him, but he steeled himself, silently counted off three, two, one, and then burst past the threshold into what was unmistakably a dining room.

Over the gun sight he saw something that brought him up short: a family. They composed themselves idyllically around a dinner table.

He felt the sweep of some secret inner tide, his blood sloshing through his body, setting at a faster rhythm the ceaseless trip-hammer of his heart.

Everyone at the table raised their heads as if swayed by one impulse, and met his eyes.

"Where's Detective Spence?" he began, with a sharp sense of his awkwardness.

What appeared to be the father of the family cleared his throat. With thin lips set in a tight scowl, he said, "I'm Detective Spence."

Fear contested with shock for possession of Bob's face.

"No, you're not," insisted Bob.

And in reply to Bob's glance of interrogation, he sounded a faint note of irony by saying, "I'm the only 'Detective Spence' who lives here."

Bob pushed on haltingly: "The man I'm looking for is Gregory Spence— He— He's a detective at the Sweet River Police Department— He's an older man— A much larger man—"

Then, fighting to regain his equanimity, he demanded: "Show me your wallet." When no one moved, he repeated the command more loudly, whereupon everyone gave a start.

To his own ears his voice sounded harsh, malevolent. He was glad he had risen to the challenge of "acting" that the situation called forth from him. Even though he knew it was important to project a certain commanding malevolence he shivered at this note of brutality when he saw the look of fear in the children's eyes.

All the adrenaline of the chase and the confrontation crashed down around him and his bravado suddenly deserted him. Bob tried to merge his look of perplexity into his previous expression of menace.

As he concentrated his attention on the husband, the man's wife shivered away from him in a tremor of self-effacement as she tried to edge toward her children.

"Do not move!" he said, drawing out each word, the gravity in his tone lending an earnest emphasis to his statement.

He had to stall for time. Bob studied the room, the geometry of the situation. What was he supposed to do now? He turned the matter over critically.

His makeshift hostage ventured to say, "You clearly made a mistake."

Bob weighed it.

He took a deep breath. He knew he had to remain calm. He had blundered and blundered badly. Nevertheless, he had to command the situation, or risk chaos—and an accident the dimensions of which he feared to even contemplate. He took another deep breath, blew it out and said, "Take your wallet back."

The father of the house did not move as Bob handed back his wallet, but lifted to him a deep gaze of hatred.

Superficially the man seemed compliant, but Bob thought he detected beneath the surface of the man's apparent tractability a hidden stir.

Mindful that the father might have a service revolver close at hand, he lowered his attention to the area around the man quickly. He didn't know if detectives wore shoulder rigs under their coats or not. Everything he knew about police officers came from novels or movies. In any case, he didn't appear to be wearing one—as his coat had been removed and his shirt remained free of any such hindrance as he sat down to dinner.

The man seemed to Bob's watchful perceptions to be quivering on the verge of mutiny.

Bob was sufficiently self-possessed to recall the handcuffs he still had in his jacket-pocket. He presently fingered them through his coat with his free hand; and this gave a new turn to his thoughts. He hastened to put in motion the plan that was quickly evolving.

He surveyed the children. No, this was no "fake family" used in some elaborate ruse to trick him. After all, the only male child in the family was a "lower-case" version of his father. The large ears and prominent Adam's-apple of the parent were echoed in the son, as was the strange crease in the forehead, the bluntness of the nose and the dimple on the chin. Bob could imagine him fittingly referred to as "Junior".

No, for what he had in mind, he considered Junior ineligible. Next his eyes passed on to one of the two daughters. Both were pale with caramel-colored hair and fair eyes. Bob focused in on the younger of the two.

In an effort to be invisible she had remained silent, lowering her head, lifting her eyelids just far enough for a veiled glance at him. But now he brought her out of her invisibility by addressing her directly—an act which restored color to her previously inconspicuous figure, as measured by the blush which looked like a sudden sunburn.

"I want you to do something for me," he began.

"W-what?" she stammered out.

"It's real important you do it right—for your family's sake. Okay?"

"Okay," she said, in a near-whisper.

He closed the two steps between them and gave her the handcuffs. "Here. Put one cuff on your father's wrist—"

"What are you trying to pull?" objected the father.

"I'm trying to get out of here without anyone being shot," returned Bob. Addressing the little girl, he continued, "Put that handcuff on your father's wrist. Yeah. Just like that.... Okay. Now you," he said, directing his remarks to the father again, "lean over and put your hands by the base of the table."

The table didn't have legs, but a large thick base atop of which rested the wooden plane upon which all their dishes sat. Bob exploited this. He made the man lean over and hold hands with his son under the table. He then instructed the girl to place one handcuff on her father and one handcuff on her brother, binding them together, with the base of the table between them.

Afterward, he produced his key ring. With only one available hand, he couldn't detach the handcuff key, so he had the girl carry out this task as well. Once she pried it off with her fingernail, Bob grabbed the key ring back and announced, "That's the key to the handcuffs. Go, Sweetie. Run upstairs. I want you to hide in your bedroom and count to a hundred. Then come back downstairs and undo the handcuffs on your father and brother, okay?"

"Okay."

He thought he detected a faint glimmer of amusement in her eyes as she fell in with his orders.

His face paled with anger and humiliation, the father bent over passively as he glowered at the intruder.

"Don't worry," said Bob. "You'll be free soon. And I'll be gone."

He stood there as the tense silence pooled in the room. Finally, the little girl had made it to the top of the staircase and disappeared into her room to count. So Bob left.

He rushed out of the house and jumped into the car he had driven there. He tramped the accelerator to the floorboards, and the vehicle responded with a shudder, then a surge of power.

As he looked back at the house he had just left, however, he felt a twinge of uneasiness. For an obstinate impulse of resistance moved his former-hostage's wife to action; for no sooner did Bob glance back than he saw her face peering through the window, doubtless memorizing the description of the car he drove and its license plate.

To get rid of the car seemed now his most pressing necessity. First, though, he'd have to get out of the neighborhood.

As he drove, his head ached with misgivings. If the man he left back there was the real Spence, it opened up a new field of conjecture.

In the light of this discovery he studied the facts with a new intensity, seeing details impossible to see before; yet seeing them through a kind of murkiness, as if fear were a darkening medium into which he had been plunged bodily.

He brooded, his thoughts troubled with this new development.

His head was spinning. Or was it the situation around him that was turning at breakneck speed? He knew he'd have to stop and think about the situation deliberatively, systematically; but for the moment it was whirling him about so fast that he could only clutch at its sharp edges or be tossed off again. He carried away only one definite, immediate fact: though he placed great reliance on his father's judgment and experience, William had known no more about the kidnapper than Bob himself had. Of course the man would have guarded his identity! With a twinge of self-reproach, Bob realized he should have thought of that before.

It still made sense, though, that the man was in law-enforcement. Everything pointed toward it: knowing whether or not his victims contacted the police, his access to records of the criminals he recruited, his act of identity theft against the real Detective Spence.

As he was puzzling over these pieces of information, he stopped at a red light. The car that pulled up next to him snatched him from these musings. In it were two policemen, their faces in profile.

He looked aslant at them. One of the officers, in return, cast a more pointed glance at him. Bob summoned up a look of blank introspection.

He wanted the policeman to assume he was oblivious of them. It appeared to work, for when the light turned green both cars resumed their respective journeys, one veering left after a block.

Bob thought that it was a miracle that the call hadn't gone out yet from the real Detective Spence, who was doubtless even now phoning his colleagues at the police department.

It would probably only be a matter of minutes.

Bob realized he'd have to ditch the car immediately.

First, he'd have to find a means of escape; so he located a bus stop and parked the car three blocks away from it and around a corner. Cutting the engine, he sat there for a minute. He shook his head to clear it.

It was all happening so fast.

Throwing a quick glance around the car to make sure that it contained no clues to his identity, he prepared to climb out of the vehicle. In passing, he reflected upon how fortunate it was that it wasn't his car. He had previously fretted over the fact that he had abandoned his own sedan hundreds of miles away and taken the automobile of the men who had tried to kill him. Now he was glad that the circumstances had fallen out as they had, for, in finding the car, the police would not be able to trace it back to him.

Remembering the suitcase with his son's ransom money, he grabbed it before closing the door. It would look odd, carrying it in the street. But he had no choice now; his son's life depended on it. So he hefted his burden as he hurried from the vehicle, propelled away from the abandoned car like a human bullet from its spent shell casing.

At the bus stop, he plopped the cumbersome case next to him on a bench as he sat down and waited for the next bus. He had no idea where it would take him. It didn't really matter, so long as it spirited him away from the car— and the real Detective Spence's house. After five minutes he started to feel vulnerable, sitting out there by the street, his face and figure open to any passerby's scrutiny.

He kept darting glances up the street, hoping that the vanishing point of the road in the distance would soon produce a bus. Instead, it held out only the deceptive images of large trucks and vans, which, as they approached, offered the occasion for grim disappointment.

It also produced smaller vehicles—a steady stream of them. Among their number was a police car. Surprise abruptly pinched off his breath as he reflected that it was the same car he had seen earlier at the light.

As it passed him he tried to feign a personal preoccupation, a look that hinted that he was too deep in his own perplexities to spare a glance at a police car.

Had they already located his abandoned car?

Were they now making sweeps of the area for suspicious pedestrians?

As he turned these questions over in his mind, his eyes fixed on the police car. It had closed to within twenty yards when evidently one of the two the officers in the car had recognized him. Bob composed himself the best he could to deflect their glances. But the car zeroed in on him like a shark. Suddenly it drove into a nearby parking lot and swerved in a semi-circle, screeching as it spun and exited back out into the street.

They were doubling back toward him.

Bob had to leave.

After a moment's indecision, he rose from the bench. Running would generate suspicion. Resisting the urge to sprint, he walked briskly away with measured haste.

The suitcase hobbled him physically as he tried to walk down the street. He moved as rapidly as he thought acceptable onto a side street. Once he turned a corner into it, his stride quickened. He sped with all the agility the suitcase allowed him.

The police rushed in full pursuit toward the fugitive.

In a residential area now, he struck obliquely through a yard. He made for the relative protection of an alleyway behind the houses.

He turned into a street, his pursuers close behind.

He almost staggered as he ran under the impulse of a great inner force.

He gasped for breath as he sprinted, choking on too much air. It was a terrifying feeling. Carried away by the sense of confusion, by the emotion of fear, he couldn't think. In a strange way, though, he was in full possession of his physical senses. They were unusually keen and alert—as in a person suffering fever. Something in the awful disturbance of his organic system had so exalted and refined them that they perceived things never before noticed. He felt the wind upon his face and was conscious of the separate sensations of his muscles as they worked in harmony to propel his body forward. He looked at the unfamiliar neighborhood around him, saw the individual houses, the trees and the cars that sat in the driveways. He saw the very license plates upon them: the numbers, the letters. He noted the colors of everything, the textures—and the slanting rays of the setting sun as twilight deepened into evening.

Looking back to gauge how far away the police were, he realized that he was running toward the setting sun. The sun, he reflected, sets in the west. He was running toward it, so he must be heading west.

West! he thought.

Beyond that, he had no ideas. Where was he running to?

He required a fixed point in the blinding chaos.

A landmark! his mind suggested. *Run toward a landmark, somewhere where you can get your bearings.*

But, no, moving in a maze of conflicting moods, his judgment clouded by the riot in his brain, he instead stole the opportunity of his pursuer's brief disappearance by jumping into a bush in somebody's yard.

I can hide here, he thought. *When they drive past, I'll double back and go in the opposite direction.*

To his complete surprise, the primitive ruse worked. Because as he dove into someone's large bush (in a yard with overgrown landscaping), the police car, rounding a corner, sped past.

Bob waited in his hiding-place for only a few minutes after the car vanished. Knowing there was no time to waste, he extricated himself from the bush's sharp, stabbing branches and stole away.

But to where?

Chapter Fifteen

I

Friday, November 20th, 11:11 am

Though Julia was fascinated by the letters, escape from her prison remained paramount. So, as they walked back to her cell, she resumed her survey of the building's architectural details. She still saw no overt escape-route, but she somehow sensed that it would all fall into place later.

She tried to disguise her surveillance by striking up a conversation with Ronnie about the letter room. Owing to the effect of the letters, perhaps—or the shared danger they engaged in by exploring the building somewhat—Ronnie lapsed into a confidential mood.

He busied himself with various odds and ends after they got back to the cell, and then said impulsively: "The look you had on your face when you saw me playing with that toy reminded me of someone."

"Really?"

"Yeah. You seemed just like— Well, the look, I mean— It was just like my sister, when she saw me doing something stupid."

"Is that who I remind you of?" asked Julia.

His expression changed to one of great perplexity. Then at last he said, "Yes. You look an awful lot like her."

"I thought it must be something like that."

"Like what? What do you mean?"

"The way you look at me. I started to get the feeling that I reminded you of something or someone."

An inviting silence, and then recklessly: "Ellen was her name." His voice was low and there was a new note in it. His features, too, were suddenly transfigured. He seemed years younger as he harked back to that lost time.

In thinking back on that period of his life, he was molded by memory into a new form, his spirit rising to fill the larger outlines it had known then. This man, who normally prattled and fidgeted, now sat motionless and spoke simply, sincerely, evoking by some power the miracle of that serenity which a lost age kindled in him.

For those few minutes that vanished world claimed him so completely and he yielded to it so absolutely that he seemed lifted out of the gray drab nightmare-of-a-setting around him.

He talked to Julia as if he were thinking aloud. He spoke in a voice shot with quiet intensity, his face irradiated by the light of some distant memory.

"Well, what happened to her?"

"Ellen was murdered," he said, the blood ebbing from his face. "She was only nineteen. We lived in a bad neighborhood. It wasn't safe sometimes, especially at night. She went out to the store and was killed in a robbery."

"I'm sorry," whispered Julia.

It might have been the utter humanity of his disclosure, or the childlike way in which he spread his past before her, Julia stared at him as if she were seeing him for the first time. He seemed remote from the ugliness of his surroundings, and she realized in an intuitive flash that this effusion revealed the extent and degree of his emotional isolation.

If a date could be affixed to the beginning of that isolation, it might be that first day he went to prison for killing the man who, according to rumor, shot his sister. He was just seventeen, but he was tried as an adult. By the time his case made its way through the glacial slowness of the criminal justice system, he had attained legal majority, anyway—so off he went to serve a ten-year sentence for first-degree manslaughter. (Luckily, the jury had enough sympathy for his plight—and saw enough evidence of the dead man's guilt—that they took mercy on Ronnie by not returning a verdict of murder.)

In any case, it was this prison sentence which brought him into close contact with all sorts of underworld characters.

Ronnie hinted darkly at nightmarish degradations, at horrific infamies. Eventually, though, he learned to ingratiate himself with others, to form alliances. Survival demanded it.

That's how he met Larry. The effect of this situation was that Ronnie was wholly under the older man's influence.

As for Julia, she had wondered about how two such different people happened to be working together.

The circumstances underlying any human bond are always a profound mystery which nothing can wholly explain. Even though the two men were bound together in allegiance, their relations wore that irksome character of mutual forbearance whenever they were in the same room at the same time.

To Ronnie, Larry was blustering, a nuisance and a bully. To Larry, Ronnie was a fool, Ronnie was stupid. This was his theme, and he repeated it endlessly with innumerable variations.

Yet, for all that antagonism, they worked with each other. Because they were bound together by a common misfortune—like anyone who happened to have been in the army or in prison with a comrade: a common suffering which constituted the foundation of their relationship. Apart from it, however, the two men couldn't have had less in common.

Or, at least, that was her reading of the situation.

This fact was illustrated no better than by the quality of their various looks at her. It may have been that she reminded Ronnie in some way of his sister, but, whatever the explanation, the effect was to stir in him feelings of warmth and deference altogether inappropriate to their presumptive roles of captor and captive.

A sort of sympathy flowed from him to her. Moreover, he did not assume an air of superiority or restrained hostility, or behave as a being gloatingly aloof from her degraded sphere.

That role was left to his partner.

As for Julia, though, she didn't want to think of Larry. So she steered the conversation back around to Ronnie's sister, Ellen. He seemed glad to resume talking about her.

She thought it was touching that his sister occupied his thoughts all these years later.

She went over the conversation with Ronnie, seeking to identify herself imaginatively with his existence. She looked on, moved by the change she saw in Ronnie's demeanor. It touched her on the tenderest spot of that nurturing, maternal side within herself to see this large, apparently dangerous man efface himself before the memory of his sister.

He was a strange bundle of contradictions, she thought. That is to say, he did not quite come into line with the ways of the world. Like a tumbler in a lock that refuses to align itself with the other tumblers when the key is inserted, he stood in the way. And because of that, the door to the mystery would not swing readily open.

Not fully a criminal, not fully a saint, he was utterly removed from every imaginative scheme into which she might try to fit him.

There were two men in him: one, an antisocial being, a criminal; the other, a warm, demonstrative little boy. Each aspect of his dual identity was like a facet in a gem, both ever-present—if she squinted her eye and turned the jewel to hit the right angle in the light she could, at any moment, see either characteristic. The effect was similar to those holographic pictures one sometimes sees in a child's card, which change depending on the slant one gives them.

Maybe Ronnie was conscious of this fact himself. Fearing that he was perhaps exposing too much of himself, he demurred somewhat, because during the whole outpouring he did not look up at Julia.

It scarcely mattered to her.

Ronnie's reminiscence about his sister had the effect of centering her thoughts on her own family again. Because of that she wanted to ask him how her son was doing, how he was holding up.

She began in a collected manner, which nevertheless suggested one or two rehearsals, as she said, "I have something I wanted to ask you."

"What is it?"

"Is my son here?" she asked, with measured deliberation.

"Yeah."

"Is he okay?" she said, her voice a plea.

"He's fine. He'll be alright. Everything'll be alright," Ronnie said with conviction. "You'll see."

She was grateful that Ronnie tried to assuage her worries. It was the first time since she had been abducted that she experienced the faintest glimmer of optimism. Fear pressed in around her on all sides, but strangely, it did not touch her centrally. There was some inner defiance, some quality of resistance that shone deep down inside her like an ember. And like any hot object smothered by twigs and brush, it soon sent up wisps of smoke. In just such a way her hope was kindled when Ronnie said that, her optimism fanned into a flame.

II

The memory of all the years she had spent as a wife and mother flashed in a second of time before Julia. Ronnie, too, seemed to be caught in an excess of nostalgia. He had at last openly admitted to the fact that his prisoner bore a striking resemblance to his sister.

The same almond-shaped eyes, the same sun-touched brown hair, the same pert little nose.

He was beside himself when he first saw her. For an instant there was the illusion that he had stepped back in time, or rather, that Fate had rendered an appellate decision that Ellen be allowed to grow up and grow older. Sooner than he would have liked, however, reason was restored to him and he realized that Julia was merely a random lookalike—and not even a perfect one. Chief among the flaws was the disparity in age. Then there was also her voice. To stare at the face of Ellen and to hear the voice of Julia was as disconcerting as listening to the voice of someone you've only heard on the radio or on the telephone, and the shock at the incongruity when you finally see them and their face looks nothing like what you had imagined.

So many lookalikes of famous people, no matter how much they resemble a particular celebrity physically, can't overcome this challenging vocal disparity.

Thirdly, Julia was slightly taller than Ellen. Fourthly, she had a tiny mole under her left ear which looked like a small smudge, as if an accident had taken place during the duplication process and a tiny portion of the ink had come off onto the copy.

All that notwithstanding, he was thunderstruck.

Perhaps he shouldn't have allowed himself to stare for so long. But he couldn't help it.

In any case, he was glad that an opportunity presented itself for him to get this off his chest. It was a relief to venture on to new topics and to leave the story of his past behind.

Eventually, both people—captor and captive—fell back upon the letters that they had brought with them from the back room.

Time stole away unheeded, till Larry came into the cell and Ronnie announced:

"I have to go now."

"Okay. Bye, Ronnie."

Having intercepted a disapproving glance from Larry, Ronnie shrank back into himself.

Rigid with tightly controlled anger, Larry sued for Ronnie's attention.

"Yeah?" said Ronnie.

Replying stiffly, Larry said, "Can you come over here for a minute?"

They walked to the other side of the room, whereupon Larry began to remonstrate angrily.

"Shut up," he admonished sharply. "How many times do I have to tell you not to use names?"

"I'm sorry. It won't happen again."

"You're damned right it won't happen again—"

The next series of comments were lost to Julia as they descended into more muffled tones.

Finally, they resumed a more audible level and Julia heard:

"You better get back to the boy now," Larry said in his measured, deliberate tone. "He might need to go to the bathroom or something."

The tone was so final that Ronnie obeyed, although he paused for a moment before turning and going meditatively out of the room.

An intense thrill shook Larry at the mere contemplation of being alone with his prisoner again.

He seemed to tremble with anticipation and excitement.

As Larry moved back over toward Julia, he stared at her with his dead, hooded eyes—a look beyond description.

She studied his stony expression, but it was implacable. She thought it best to ignore him and retreat to a far corner of the room. He followed her. The atmosphere became tense, dramatic. Julia felt the constriction in her stomach.

As for Larry, his clenched features attested to some inner compulsion, some rallying of the will.

His shadow passed over the room like a weather front. The room seemed to drop ten degrees in warmth as a shudder passed through Julia.

She blanched, making a convulsive movement with her whole body.

Somehow, even though her attention was partly on her circumstances, partly on her son's whereabouts and well-being, she was aware of Larry's reaction to her. Beneath his brusque, cold-hearted exterior, his secret response was that of a rapist suddenly made aware of a hitherto-dormant appetite.

Responding to the unspoken urge on his features, her flesh crawled.

He stood staring at her with his soulless eyes. There was no hint of feeling in them—they were just cold and calculating.

In those tense moments when she was confronted by her captor's crude carnality, she reflected upon what a perversion it was in light of what real warm human intimacy is.

Long-forgotten incidents flashed upward from her memory: episodes that happened to her from the first moments when she met the young man who would later be her husband.

They were still teenagers, still in school. They knew—even then—that there was a change coming over both of them—not just in relation to each other, but with respect to each one's relationship with the world.

For a while both were committed to pretending that they were still children. As a result, the surface of their thoughts had been fully occupied by their studies. Yet at a certain depth a secret drama was always at play in their minds. Occasionally a chance encounter of their eyes in the classroom or in a hallway would bring a part of that hidden life to the surface. Both tried to suppress it, bury it back under the banal details of a gray world. They held fast to the theory that merely by containing themselves to banalities, they could neutralize all the indecent assaults on the mind committed by the soul and the heart. Both tried to isolate themselves in their own parallel lives, comforted in the assurance of insulation from contacts with the rough and dangerous world of living emotion.

As with electricity, however, a contact was eventually, accidentally, established when the two lost their grounding. It happened one day in class. Toward the end of the lesson, he had dropped a paper and a crosscurrent from the heating system carried it to the foot of her desk. In the act of retrieving it, he arrived at where she was sitting. He faced her vacantly. Trying as hard as he could to look past her, he nervously rushed over to get the paper that had slipped to the floor below, plunging almost as quickly as his heart. In an effort to recover from his telltale awkwardness, he bent down to retrieve it. She followed suit, and their hands, groping for the same thing, accidentally touched. Suddenly a torrent of feelings rushed through them as their fingers met.

His hand didn't spring back from her touch in shock. Like electricity, that happens with a relatively small charge. With a larger one, the exact opposite effect is observed, as when your hand becomes seemingly welded to the point of contact as the body becomes part of the circuit. It was just so with Bob. His fingers closed over her hand and, over the opposition of his will, remained there.

Then came a fuller, more lingering flash of those eyes, which arrested him, a light passing over them, full of secret thoughts and anxious expectations. Julia herself registered an impression from him, for one shadow of collusion in his eyes, one slight pressure of his fingers told her that he was at last, in spite its inadvisability, prepared to abandon himself to her. Struggling against the lower impulses of her nature, she ended the touch, pretending that she hadn't noticed it at all. She feared it was futile, though, to hide the fact that all the unspoken mysteries of attraction trembled in the air between them. Nevertheless, she broke the spell and grabbed the paper. Sitting back up, she righted her blouse and realized, with a shock, that the whole episode had transpired in a scant few seconds, by conventional time.

No one else in the room seemed to have noticed anything unusual.

It was as if for a moment she had been transported out of herself. The inner person had been allowed to come to the fore. It's then that one lives in a different tempo, another world.

After recovering her self-possession, she scarcely heard anything else as class resumed. Eventually, it came to an end. Everybody hastened to the door, even the teacher. Bob pretended to busy himself with his book bag as he stole sidelong glances at a tarrying Julia. She hazarded a quick glance at him, too; and, for a moment, both of their eyes met, each sharing a furtive look of delicious conspiracy.

When they were at last in the room by themselves a strange thing happened. Not the least hesitation in being alone with each other, not the slightest shyness or doubt of any elapsed interval, clung to them. Having experienced a sample of the chemistry they shared with that touch under her desk, they both seemed ready to be carried bodily along in the swift current of spontaneous emotion.

Julia's thoughts were abruptly torn from these observations by the approach of her captor. She resented him for forcing her to leave the upper air of her memories for the firm ground of reality. Because as she was reminded of Larry, she was drawn back into the vulgar world of this kidnapping, forced from her natural element into something unsavory and abrasive to her nature.

She wished she could withdraw back into her own interior world; but, even if she tried, she understood that the escape would not be complete, for one region of her consciousness would be occupied exclusively with the menacing figure of her captor. She noticed that she was once again the subject of profound consideration by him.

Fear throbbed in her like a new mysterious pulse.

As for Larry, he watched her and admired the beauty of her hair, the provocation of her breasts. For all that, he could only think about her rebuff of him earlier, her refusal to talk to or acknowledge him. It awoke a cold anger in him, an icy determination to humiliate her.

In a state of nervous irritability, his breathing became heavy.

Things were rapidly approaching a crisis when something fantastic happened—salvation. The door flew open. It was Ronnie.

"What do *you* want?" asked Larry, in evident frustration.

"There's been a change. We have to go to the house."

"What are you talking about?"

Flashing a glance at their captive, Ronnie nodded for Larry to follow him over to the door. After Larry gave reluctant assent, the two mumbled for a few moments before returning to Julia.

"We're going to have to tie you up again," said Ronnie, with a sympathetic expression on his face.

"Why?" she asked.

Not directly answering her, Ronnie went on, saying, "It won't be for too long. We'll be back soon."

Despite this development, she allowed herself to be guided back to the chair, where she was directly tied up again. Larry did the tying, and it was too tight in places.

Julia complained, but there was little Ronnie could do under the circumstances. Still sympathetic, though, he uttered, "It won't be for long."

The two men passed gravely out of the room.

III

Julia wondered what was behind the sudden departure of her captors. It seemed so rushed. Had something gone wrong? Was Billy tied up? Did they take him somewhere?

In spite of Ronnie's avowals to the contrary, she would have several hours ahead of her to think about it. She struggled once again in the attempt to escape. But no matter which way she twisted and turned, it was useless. Larry had done too efficient a job.

Time passed. It was afternoon, then dusk. She could feel the darkness of late autumn tinge the room a more somber hue. The silence and stillness enfolded her.

It was early evening by Julia's estimation before they returned—or, rather, before Larry returned. Up till then, she was hoping that Ronnie would come back for his shift. But he didn't.

She had mixed feelings about this. Though she dreaded Larry, she preferred that Ronnie look after her son.

Larry started untying her.

"I thought for sure that it would be Ronnie's shift," she muttered.

"Our time was interrupted by—Well, never mind. It doesn't matter. There was an interruption. So we're going back as if nothing happened. So you have me for some hours more."

Julia noticed something in Larry's left hand: her key chain. She recognized the small novelty soccer ball and tiny picture of her son affixed to it.

"How did you get those?" she asked, abruptly.

"Get what?"

"Those keys. They're mine."

"Never mind. Here. You're free."

"Did you go back to my house?" she pressed.

"No more questions," he warned, giving her a severe look.

"Ronnie said that you'd have to go back to the house. Was that *my* house he was talking about?"

"Do you want me to re-tie you—and gag you?" he asked.

"Um...no," she demurred.

"Then do what I tell you and *shut up*."

With that, he walked away to a chair on the other side of the room. Julia was puzzled. But she was grateful to be free. Her extremities felt numb. It was an odd sensation to feel the blood rushing back to her toes and fingertips. As she thawed, Larry made a great show of ignoring her. He sat down and pretended to read.

She was grateful that whatever incident had intervened seemed to have thrown a chill over Larry's previous behavior.

Yet maybe she made too hasty of a judgment on that score. Because, within the hour, she could sense that a change had occurred in him. It was in his eyes, in his silences. His demeanor was made more ominous by its simplicity, its frigidity. The expression in his eyes became more and more fixed.

Gradually fear crept over her as an atmosphere of constraint hung like a threatening storm over the room.

She remained on guard, on edge. Nevertheless, she felt a wave of fear ease through her.

She wished she could just ignore him as she did before, but she couldn't. Her attention, directed by a series of sidelong glances and furtive looks, followed his slightest movement, his subtlest shift.

Why?

It was more than just caution in the face of possible danger. She looked because she *had* to look. For horror has its attractive power, like beauty. Her heart beating violently, her pulse racing, she couldn't tear her attention away from her captor.

As for Larry, the reaction was somewhat different. Larry had little understanding of female mannerisms: they were a strange haiku too subtle for him to comprehend, a pattern in a key too high to fall within the narrow compass of his consciousness. Yet he was stirred, deeply and thoroughly stirred. His senses ached for touch, connection. He had no more understanding of the hunger than an animal. He moved to its dictates less like a man hearing a melody than like a hound snapping its neck at the sound of a dog whistle.

Julia, unmistakably human, was deaf to the sound of the supersonic note that moved Larry as he at last walked up to her.

The room felt smaller now. Larry seemed to fill the room and grow larger. It was as if the air was being drained from the room to feed Larry and Julia had trouble pulling oxygen from it to breathe.

"You want your keys back?" he asked, his eyes probing her face.

"Yes," she gasped.

Pulling them from his pocket, he handed them over to her.

"Thanks," muttered Julia.

"No need to thank me," he said. "I just felt like there was no reason not to be nice."

Julia accepted the remark in silence.

"You want to be nice back to me, don't you?" It felt as if all the air were sucked out of the room.

When she spoke it was barely above a whisper, her voice the merest echo reaching up from some remote inner depth. "Don't you dare touch me."

"Shhh. Be quiet," he said, his voice flat and cold.

"Don't," she continued quietly, her voice tense but controlled as she stared at her captor. Suddenly her mouth went dry, her heart raced. She winced to feel his shadow creeping over her like frostbite over her extremities, inching its way toward the center of her body like gangrene. A great vein stood out on his forehead, his features tense and his left eye twitching with rapidity. He was standing over her and she could feel his quick, eager breaths on her face.

"Where's Ronnie?" she asked immediately in order to gain time.

But he was deaf to her perfunctory question, his face set, the light of a cold implacable will shining in his eyes.

Moving backward, she hit a chair and stumbled. Larry took the advantage and fell to the ground on top of her.

"Get off!" she exclaimed.

"Shut up," he breathed, struggling with her.

To her shock and relief, Ronnie abruptly appeared— as if in answer to a prayer.

Larry's gaze swung to him. Ronnie met his look, knew what it meant, and retired a few steps.

"Larry, I need you for a second," uttered Ronnie, barely above a whisper.

"Later."

"No. Now." Ronnie, shocked, embarrassed, looked to the right.

"I said later. Get out."

He stopped, took a deep breath, tried again. "Larry—"

Larry snapped his eyes over at him. "I *told* you to get out!"

His rage choked him. "No," insisted Ronnie.

Larry was perplexed and then enraged by Ronnie's steadfast refusal to leave. Ruled by impulse, he decided that the best way to rid himself of the pest was to ignore him and abandon himself to his lust. Ronnie seemed beside himself with the fact that his appearance in no way abated his partner's desires.

Julia strained away from Larry, her face averted, hands fisted at her sides. Lust accentuated the coarseness of Larry's features, the crude sensuality of his lips. As he pressed himself against her, a feeling of revulsion rose in her. Her throat tightened, a sour taste erupting in her mouth.

She was terrified, her eyes pleading. Her horrified gaze fixing on Ronnie, he trembled and quaked. In that stare that seemed to penetrate his own body, the fear was communicated to him. He had to stop it, had to make it end!

Her voice, sharp with urgency, swelled with panic as she called out to Ronnie.

He thought of all the times Larry had yelled at him, humiliated him, taunted him, and rage welled in him. But more than that, he thought of her: Her figure was so pathetic, her plight so harrowing that he was on the edge of blind rage.

Ronnie yanked Larry up and off Julia by main force. After Larry struggled to find his footing, Ronnie seized his neck with a sudden nervous strength that amazed Julia.

Ronnie's swift transition from inertia to violence was so mysterious to Julia that it reduced her to paralysis. She just lay there, trembling from head to toe, feeling totally inadequate to the situation.

Larry doubtless felt something of the same inadequacy. This reversal of roles was so totally unexpected that it needed all of Larry's control not to reveal his panic, his fear. But Julia saw it in his eyes. Men of Larry's stamp, men who bully others, are often the biggest cowards when confronted with physical danger.

Yet it was too late for him. The struggle was surprisingly brief. The pressure applied to the windpipe, the restriction of blood to the brain via the carotid arteries quickly incapacitated Larry. Although he thrashed about and tried to strike Ronnie, his blows—administered at too close quarters—produced no effect. Meanwhile the pressure from Ronnie's hands around his throat was inexorable. Larry could feel the energy ebbing from him, the life seeping out of his body. His face, at first mottled with red patches, soon grew pale. Like an ice cube, white at its center with a galaxy of captured air-bubbles, each one of his eyes swarmed with flecks of light that swelled into a blinding effulgence. At that point, for a fleeting moment, his eyes looked strangely spiritual—as if he were trembling on the brink of an insight, a revelation. Whether he ultimately received it or not remained an open question as his eyes became unfocused and finally glazed over.

The only sound from him was the involuntary sigh that escaped his lifeless body as it collapsed on the floor below.

Julia held her breath, suppressing the cry in her throat.

Breathing in quick, shallow gasps, she rose from the floor and waited with her back against the wall.

She stood there, marking time.

Meanwhile, the room lapsed into silence as Ronnie stood, contemplating his act. He had turned on Larry, he reflected. Guilt attended that betrayal. More than that, fear. He shuddered violently with a sense of what he had done.

He seemed to have lost his bearings. Julia tried to meet his gaze, but the focus had gone from his eyes.

IV

When Julia worked up the courage to speak she tried to thank him, but her tone seemed too sharp, too unnatural. As if her voice were not her own, but someone else's to which she could only listen. She paused to try and gather herself, but her ribs were still shaking, her nerves were still jittering. For the first time she entertained the prospect of escape. Not fanciful, vague plans for escape. But *real escape.*

She nurtured the secret resolve to try to get Ronnie to help her. By doing so, however, she risked making him blame her for what had happened. If he did that, all was lost.

From this gloomy survey of her situation, she came back to the thought of its crowning difficulty: to turn the death of Larry to her advantage without inadvertently making Ronnie resent her. She knew it would be difficult, but it didn't shake her resolve to try.

She hesitated. Doubts, misgivings, advantages surged like an unruly froth across her mind. It seemed so callous. Yet, why not? She had to do *something.*

Although she allowed these self-recriminations to drift through her brain, she gave them little weight.

One fact of deeper significance was operative in her: her maternal impulse to bend all circumstances toward the goal of saving her son.

In the meantime Ronnie settled into a crouching position over Larry, pulled thoughtfully at his lower lip for a time and then lapsed into profound meditation. He was weighing the options: If he stayed where he was after having betrayed his partner, he would have to pay the consequences. If he left, he'd be safe; but, by fleeing, he'd be leaving his captive and her child to an uncertain fate.

His heart quailed at the thought of abandoning such helpless people.

Meanwhile, he gazed out ahead of himself, glassy-eyed, staring vaguely in front of him not as one whose glance is fixed on any particular object, but as one who is trying to gaze into the middle-distance to determine if it is starting to rain.

A sort of awe, a sense of the close company of Fate upon him kept him silent and uncommunicative.

He felt empty to the depths of his being.

His mind searched among the possibilities of the situation. Meanwhile, with the undertow of his mind he sensed the expectation that was being entertained with regard to him by the woman in front of him.

Finally, changing a tone which jarred even on his own sensibilities, his brow contracted as he found his voice and said, "I don't know what's going to happen. I'll probably get us all killed, anyway. But let's go."

"You're going to set me and my son free?"

"Come on," the hoarse answer came back.

A sense of relief rushed over her. As for Ronnie, he rose unsteadily, hesitated for a moment, then looked at Julia before pressing forward.

She could see that the rescuer in him had flamed into life. Scheme after scheme raced through his head and was reflected in his eyes. Stern resolve brooded over the troubled mayhem of his thoughts and subdued them. With a shaking hand, he fished in his pocket for a key ring. For what seemed like an excessive length of time, he trifled with the door's lock.

"Hurry." Her voice rose a notch. "Please."

There was sense of some danger that was quickly approaching and that stirred in her a greater feeling of the need for urgency.

Finally, Ronnie got the door open. Shivering at the prospect of what lay ahead, both of them pressed out into the hallway.

They moved with quiet celerity through the building.

"Where are we g—?"

He made a movement enjoining silence and went up to the stairwell.

Was Billy on the floor above?

Julia was about to speak, but he silenced her again with a quick movement. When she at last spoke—as they ascended to the floor above her old cell—her voice was a whisper.

"Is there someone else in the building?"

He waved her into silence again. "Please don't speak or we might get caught," Ronnie finally cut in.

She didn't like the pitch of pessimism in his voice but she forgot all negativity when they arrived before a door.

Ronnie took out his key ring and unlocked the door. Then the fingers of his hand came together with the palm to form the fleshy socket in which the doorknob rested like an eyeball.

Apparently, Billy's cell had a window. Although, since evening had drawn on, it scarcely shed any light in the room. As for the makeshift cell itself, her son was in a long, rather low-pitched room. When she finally saw him he made her heart turn over.

Whereas his pallor seemed to be cast upon him from above as if by a ray of light from God, it was in reality merely the sickly beam from a single light bulb, hanging from a stanchion over his head. He sat there in a pool of soft light.

It was strange for her to see her son's face drained of youthfulness, of whimsy, of life almost. He looked almost green in the light, with none of his robust boyish radiance.

Tears welled in her eyes as she rushed toward him. Billy.

Seeing Billy like that was unbearable, its poignancy touching her heart like a cold hand. Her eyes went from head to toe to hand to finger. He didn't look like he had been hurt.

He opened his eyes sleepily. Then they flashed with recognition.

"Mom?" he asked, unsure what was transpiring. She could tell he was trying to be strong, her brave little man.

They looked at each other. She read at once a whole volume of fear as she scanned that little face. She clasped her hands and stood wringing them in silent agony as Ronnie set about untying him.

After only a few minutes, he was done.

A warmth spread into all corners of her being as she grasped her rising son to herself. As she held him like that the love she had for him consumed her. She inhaled the sweet, dusty smell of her son's hair and felt all of the muscles in her body expand with relief.

She had to fight off the urge to hold him to her forever, to never let him go—so, reluctantly, she let him withdraw from her embrace.

"Are you okay, Billy?" she asked.

"Yes."

"They didn't hurt you?"

"I guess not," he returned.

"It's going to be alright, Billy. I promise."

Ronnie looked about anxiously. While Julia took a moment to rub her son's arms to foster circulation in them, Ronnie stared off, pulling at his earlobe nervously.

"We have to go," he coaxed her.

"Alright," she acquiesced. Then to her son: "You have to be very quiet now. We don't want anyone to hear us."

As Billy nodded, there was a sound at the door. Ronnie swallowed. She saw something cross his face.

Now that she had her son, and had switched from a vocabulary of logic to emotion, she was lost to all reason, and realized nothing now but the necessity for flight.

Before she had covered ten yards, though, she was brought up short. Because as the door in front of her opened, she realized that they were saved.

"Thank God, it's you," she cried out.

Instantly an exclamation broke from Ronnie. As for Julia, she was relieved by the sight before her. "Thank God!" she cried. "Detective Spence!"

Chapter Sixteen

I

Friday, November 20th, 5:39 pm

In flight from the police, Bob didn't know where to go. *A landmark*, his mind repeated. *A public building, a store, a museum, anything.* From there, he'd be able to phone a cab to come and pick him up with as little suspicion as possible.

Consequently he was moved away from the residential area he found himself in toward a more commercial section of town. He didn't know how long he ran, or how much time it required but he finally made it to a branch of the public library.

He stood outside the entrance until he had recovered his breath. After he did, he reflected upon the fact that, as people milled about, he was safe, obscured, hidden among their number.

He needed a car now. He quickly formulated the plan of going to his home and using his wife's car. It would just be sitting there in the garage. But to get there first, he'd require a taxi.

In the lobby of the library, there was an ancient bank of payphones. Unthinkingly, he picked the receiver and started dialing. Only when it had started ringing had he remembered that he had a cell phone. How had he forgotten that? He was tired. (In the muddle of his brain, it had slipped his mind that he had his father's cell phone; but, for the most fleeting of instants, he had forgotten and assumed he was still carrying a tapped phone.) These reflections were dispelled when an operator came on the line. He asked her to give him the number of a cab company. "Which cab company?" she asked.

"I don't know," he replied. "You pick."

But then she told of her inability to pronounce an opinion. It was against telephone company regulations.

"So you can't help me?" he huffed.

"I'm afraid I can't."

"Okay, then, uh...Yellow Cab," said Bob, considering every city he'd lived in had a company with that name.

The operator said that—for the price of a few coins—he could be connected to their dispatcher.

On the point of telling her he'd use his cell phone, he realized that, in his mental state, he might not remember the number she'd foreseeably give him. So he didn't want to disconnect the call. After acquiescing and feeding some money to the machine, he heard ringing and then a new female voice said, "Yellow Cab."

"Yeah, hi, I need to be picked up at . . ."

Just then he realized that he didn't know the name or address of the library.

Waylaying a passerby, he asked what this library was called.

"The John W. Parks Library," returned the Good Samaritan.

"Thanks." And then to the dispatcher: "I'd like you to send a taxi over to the John W. Parks branch of the library."

"What's your name?"

"Eber— Eberhard," lied Bob.

"And where are you going?"

Bob gave her his address.

"Okay. I have a driver only five minutes from you. He'll be there in just a bit."

Bob waited in agony, torturing himself by watching traffic and imagining a whole series of police cars which, as they drew nearer, were revealed to be ordinary civilian vehicles. The last one he mistook for a police cruiser was the taxicab itself.

Drawing a sigh of relief as it swung around to let him in, he signaled to the driver and started opening the door. The driver gave Bob a start when he put on the brakes and started climbing out.

"You need help with that suitcase?" he asked.

"Uh...no. No, thank you," said Bob. "You don't have to put it in the trunk. I'll carry it with me. It's no problem."

"Okay," responded the driver, who climbed back into the car.

Bob was silent for most of the drive. He merely studied the streets as the taxi drove on. Eventually, he got his bearings and figured out what suburb outside of the city he had been in. Using that as a reference point, he could discern how much time he had left before he would reach his home.

His chest rose and fell like the sea. And, like the sea whose tides are ruled by the moon, Bob's chest seemed to rise and fall the more violently when he drew nearer to the source of his unrest, to the cause of his hope: his home. He had the taxi drop him off two blocks away and walked the remainder.

He moved, a haunted, hunted figure with all his life in his eyes as he drew closer to his house. He was stirred by all the old associations with his home and family as he crossed that threshold into his old life.

These images, at first so alluringly held out to him, so seductively offered up, were quickly yanked away as he made it closer and noticed an unfamiliar car parked in front of his house.

The perception that his house might not be empty came to him with a sharp pang of surprise.

II

Taking in all the details of the neighborhood he knew so well, his eyes rested on the car he didn't recognize.

His glance traveled from the car to some of his neighbors' homes. Could the presence of the vehicle be explained in terms of a person paying someone in the neighborhood a visit? But there was a problem. There was plenty of space in front of all the houses of his neighbors. After all, even allowing the fact that the car might have belonged to someone else's visitor, no one's driveway looked so full that it would necessitate taking up space in front of *his* house.

There was another fact that militated against this harmless, non-paranoid interpretation. He could tell who was home and who was not from the lights on in their houses. After all, in the gathering darkness of dusk, lights were coming on in the windows. In those houses where no lights shone, he could infer that no one was home. Several houses were obviously empty.

So there were no parties, no surge of guests visiting a particular house. So why the extra car parked there, and—most significantly—parked in front of *his* house?

He warily surveyed his surroundings. He shifted his attention from the car to the house. Yes, judging by the fact that there appeared to be a light on, it was reasonable to assume that someone was in there.

Chastened by the fact that his last efforts failed lamentably, he decided to be more careful, more circumspect. He wouldn't just rush into a house as he did before—even if it *was* his own house.

Meanwhile his mind had been feeling its way toward a conception of the problem and struggling toward a solution. There could be no frontal assault (even if he thought he were capable of it), no warning to his pursuers. Whatever he did, he would have to rely on subterfuge. But, in what form? He had to make a clear appraisal of his circumstances and the possibilities before him.

His thoughts came rapidly. It would be suicide to rush in there without knowing how many people were inside. Yet where else—in the position he was in—could he go? He had to hide, but he couldn't go inside his home until he was sure it was empty, safe. Because of that, he realized that he'd have to draw whoever was in the home out. He could do so, he reflected, by precipitating a crisis. That was the objective; it remained how to achieve it.

He was in no position to phone the police and tell them about the men who had broken into his home. He didn't want the police. Yet, then again, neither would the men inside the house. Drawing on his own feelings, he could infer theirs. After all, hadn't he been told not to involve the police? The fact that they set a proscription against it didn't support the notion that the whole police department was corrupted and bought—not entirely, at least.

He was suddenly consumed by an extraordinary possibility.

He paused, the thought coming into focus.

He decided to mount a trap. He had no time to second-guess, to refine his strategy. For an idea crossed his mind, which he immediately put into execution.

He started by reaching beneath his jacket and hitched up his shirt, feeling for his undershirt. He tore at it and wrenched loose a strip of cloth. Later on, he would take the time to peel off the rest of his clothes and remove the article of clothing completely. As for now, he was content to yank what he could from his body and tear it into a sort of makeshift fuse.

His heart was beating unsteadily as he crept over to the strange car and located its gas tank. Finding a stick on the ground not far away, he popped open the compartment, unscrewed the lid, opened it and, having tied the cloth around the end of the stick, he poked it past the steel trap of the fuel port and shoved it down until he was sure that he had at least gotten *some* gasoline on the cloth. Pulling the stick back up, he unfastened the cloth and now had a flammable wick. Tying the dry side of the cloth onto the end of the stick, he poked it back into the tank that led to the fuel line. All he needed now was a match. He didn't smoke, so he didn't carry matches or lighters. Momentarily panicked, he decided to leave the wick in place as he turned his steps toward his shed.

With as few movements as possible, he hugged the wall of his house and stole past it into his back yard. Dropping to a crouch, he crept over to the small outbuilding where he kept his lawn mower and gardening supplies.

There he looked madly around for something to use. Perhaps he had a book of matches somewhere. Frantically searching, he found nothing. Almost on the point of giving up, he happened across a lighter that his father-in-law—a smoker—must have left there.

He hoped desperately that he wouldn't be observed as he ran back to the car. But he couldn't allow himself to think about that possibility. The most important thing now was the fire. He shut his eyes, set his teeth and went to work.

"Damn it!" he muttered to himself, marveling at the relative chemical stability of gasoline. It didn't explode into flame as he had hoped. Nevertheless, he was patient and kept applying the lighter to the tip of the cloth. Just on the point of yielding to defeat, something happened: a single thread started to smoke. At last, it ignited. Bob leapt back as the flame crawled up the length of the cloth and down into the gas tank.

He just had time to take cover behind a distant hedge in a neighbor's yard as the sound of the explosion swelled behind him. As he turned to look, his face was locked in astonishment. From his vantage-point, he commanded a clear view of his house and the car in front of it. Though the chassis was largely undamaged, the glass shattered under the impact of the explosion.

The scene was set. Within minutes he could hear sirens in the distance as a helpful neighbor obviously reported the vandalism. The sirens he initially heard probably weren't police. They were most likely fire engines. But the police would follow in their train.

The diversion had its effect. Through the smog of burning materials that billowed up into the sky, he could make out motion from an upstairs window. A curtain moved. Then the front door tentatively came open as a male face peered out at the vandalized car. Then another.

There were at least two men inside.

Bob had a sinking feeling that his plan had gone off the wire. This sentiment was confirmed when not only the people inside his house reacted to the explosion, but so, too, did neighbors. Furthermore—due to his destruction of their car—the men went inside, located Julia's keys and set about stealing her car.

A feeling of exasperation possessed Bob as he watched while the garage door rolled up and they pulled the car out.

"My God, no!" thought Bob, anxiously, hoping for a fleeting moment that their own car would block their exit.

But no. They merely backed the car down the driveway and swerved onto the grass to avoid the smoking wreck in their path.

Shifting the car into gear, they sped away moments before the first fire truck arrived.

God, what am I gonna do now? wondered Bob, reflecting upon the fact that the car was his only purpose in coming back home.

Handed a setback, he determined to overcome the crisis and find another car. But from where? He had blundered again badly—and not just by losing the car. Wincing at the buzzing excitement of the growing crowd, he reflected upon how stupid he had been. Maybe, in all the commotion, he could slip into his house unnoticed.

He kept his eyes averted to the grass in an effort at being inconspicuous as he walked toward his house.

The house-front raised before him its expanse of yellow aluminum siding and burnt-umber brick accents, and he was struck by the incongruity of its thoroughgoing domesticity, of its soft lines and suburban surfaces.

Inside, his house held out the intimate welcome of its fireplace and familiar furniture. Everything in it emanated the atmosphere of peace and stability that had prevailed before the events of the last twenty-three hours. His favorite chair invited him to sit down, his television set made what blandishments it could in the effort of getting him to stop, relax.

Of course, he couldn't stop and relax, and pretend that everything was as it used to be. And that's why it felt so strange: everything was exactly as it had been when he had left. There was nothing extraordinary in that, of course, but it seemed extraordinary to him. He expected some change, however trivial, to correspond with the worlds of experience which had separated him from his last appearance there. But everything was the same. The same brown carpet, the same burgundy drapes, even the same odor of fresh lumber and old coffee.

He stood in the foyer for much longer than he normally would have, trying to absorb the ambiance of the home.

He encountered no one and no sign of overt change.

At last he headed up to his study, and reflected with a pang of queasiness that this was the very room that issued the intruder he had confronted.

Getting a hold of himself, he decided to turn this opportunity to account, to exploit this brief respite by accessing the information he could obtain by using his computer. As he settled into the chair at his desk, he reflected upon a number of things. According to Bissel, the kidnapper representing himself as Gregory Spence might very well work in the police department. But, the fact remained that Murex's name kept cropping up in a more-than-suggestive way. Considering this, he wondered if it was reasonable to assume otherwise than that Murex was involved. So Bob resolved to give them a call to see if he could establish the man's true identity.

He needed to log onto the Internet to find their telephone number. As he turned on his computer monitor, his apprehension started to rise. None of the customizations on his computer were in place. Most of his screen icons were missing, and those that were there were in different places. An illuminating impulse urged him on. He looked at the exterior of the computer, the metal housing of the machine. It was the same model as his computer, but it was missing a stain where his son had touched it briefly with a pen whose indelible ink refused to come off. His gaze widened; his muscles tensed. He realized at that moment the computer before him was not his. It had been switched out.

Why?

Was that what that man was doing when he startled him by coming home too soon?

He'd have to pursue these questions at greater length later, for, just then, he managed to log onto the Internet. Going to a search-engine, he located several telephone numbers to Murex. Since it was now past regular office hours, he hoped he'd be able to talk to someone and get some information.

Chapter Seventeen

I

Friday, November 20th, 5:52 pm

Bob's picked up the telephone on his desk and dialed the first number on the list.

A recording intoned: "Murex is now closed. Our business hours are from 9:00 a.m. to 5:00 p.m., Eastern-Standard time, Monday through Friday. If you would like to leave a message with a particular person and you know their extension, please dial it in at this time. If you would like to listen to a directory, please press '9' now."

Bob pressed the number 9, but the random list of names meant nothing to him.

Disconnecting the phone call, he turned back to the computer and, after a brief search, located Murex's home security division. It was more likely that they'd offer twenty-four hour access to operators. So he dialed their number.

"Finch home security. How can I help you?" a male voice asked.

"Finch?" wondered Bob, at a loss. "Is that a subsidiary of the Murex Corporation?"

"That's correct, sir. How can I help you?"

Bob thought for a moment, then abruptly decided to abandon the line of questioning he'd initially decided to pursue. Instead, he wanted to see what information he could garner by gambling as he said, "My wife's the one who got this account. I got the Murex name from the receipt. I just wanted to know if you already have our address listed in your system."

"I can help you with that," said the young man. "Can you give me the name and address?"

"Yes, Ebersol is the last name. The address is 1002 Weeping Willow Court."

"Um...hold on a second, if you will," rejoined the operator as Bob overheard the clicking of a computer keyboard. The young man returned with the declaration, "Yes, here we are!"

"So then the address I gave you is listed in your system?" asked Bob.

"Yes, it's right here, Mr. Ebersol. Is there anything else?"

"As a matter of fact, there is. As I told you, my wife set this whole thing up so I have no idea how it works. I didn't even know that men had come out to set up the system. I mean, I didn't notice a keypad by the door or anything like that so that I could arm or disarm the system."

"Are you serious?" asked the operator, befuddled. "You should have a standard keypad display. It's listed on here."

"Well, it's not by the door," continued Bob.

"It's supposed to be. That's strange. I could place a maintenance call and have someone out to your residence first thing in the morning. Then we could g—"

"I'd appreciate that. But I'm more interested—now that I have you on the line—in how the system works. My wife never tells me anything. Is it a standard setup? Or are there cameras involved? She mentioned something about cameras."

"Well, we do offer that service. Unfortunately, some people have had bad experiences with baby sitters, abusive nannies, and so forth. So they ask for hidden mini-cameras. Not many people, of course, request it, but—"

"Is it listed in our package?" persisted Bob.

"Hm. Let me check." After a few more keystrokes, the young man said, "Yes. I see it right here. That's strange."

"What is?"

"Well, you have two cameras listed. But neither of them appears to be associated with children's playrooms or bedrooms or anything like that. Odd."

"Why? Where are they?"

"One appears to be...um...hold on a second. Yeah. Here. One appears to be in the living room and the other appears to be placed outside the backdoor."

"And listening devices?"

"We have a listing here for those, too. You have four."

"Are any in the upstairs study?"

"Uh...hold on. Um...no. No, sir. Just in two bedrooms, the living room and the kitchen."

"That sounds like quite a security apparatus," remarked Bob, sarcastically.

"It's not the usual package, no. In fact, I've never quite seen this setup before."

"Can you tell me who put in the work order?"

"Of course. Yeah. Here it is: it was keyed in at the request of a certain 'F. Bledsoe.'"

"Is he someone who works there?"

"Not in this department...not that I'm aware."

"Can I have your name?" uttered Bob. "You've been so very helpful, I think I'd like to compliment you to your manager. Can you patch me through to him?"

"Oh, thank you, sir," responded the young man, the tenor of his voice changing to a sunnier register. "You don't need to do that. My name's Dennis, by the way. Dennis Landry. But if you insist—"

"I do. Patch me through."

"Thank you. Here goes. I'm placing you on hold for a moment while I transfer the call."

"Thanks again, Dennis."

The young man's voice was directly replaced by muzak as Bob waited on the line. After a two-minute interval, a deeper voice, with a more gravelly timbre asserted itself.

"Hello, Charles Houghton here."

"Hi, Mr. Houghton. I asked to be sent through to you to compliment one of your operators. Said his name was Dennis."

"Dennis provided excellent customer service?" asked the man.

"He did. So I wanted to pass the word along."

"We appreciate positive feedback. It'll be placed in his file."

"That's good. But I do have one other reason for asking to speak to you," ventured Bob.

"How can I help you?"

"Dennis mentioned an 'F. Bledsoe' on my account. I was wondering if I gave you my information, if you could tell me how to get a hold of him."

"I could sure check. Hold on a moment for me."

After the preliminary information was exchanged and computer screens were accessed, the manager said that he had no idea who "F. Bledsoe" was. But he could confirm that it was inter-departmental.

"What does that mean?" asked Bob.

"Well, he doesn't work for Finch, but he does work for our parent corporation. That's strange," Houghton abruptly interrupted himself.

"What is?" asked Bob.

"The work order came through a different channel than it's supposed to. I have the code here."

"Do you have any contact information for Mr. Bledsoe?" pressed Bob.

"No, but I do know where he works. It's—"

"It's at Murex, right?"

"Right. But he's in an entirely different division. He shouldn't even have access to our system."

"What division is he in?"

"That's the thing. The code associated with his name links him to the Criminal Profiling division. They shouldn't have anything whatsoever to do with us."

"Do you have a phone number?"

"Uh...no," mumbled the manager, still clearly perplexed by the irregularity and scarcely paying attention to Bob by this point as he toggled back and forth between screens on his computer in search of an answer.

Bob, however, was satisfied with the lead, and said, "Thank you, anyway, Mr. Houghton, did you say?"

"Yes, Houghton."

"Thanks. You've been extremely helpful. Bye."

II

At last Bob had a name: F. Bledsoe. This was such an exciting discovery that he received it with a racing heart. He decided to turn back to the Internet. Keying in the names "Murex" and "Bledsoe", he wanted to see what would come up.

In startlingly short order, he found articles where both key words appeared. He discovered "F. Bledsoe" was a certain Frank Bledsoe. He, in fact, ran the Criminal Profiling division for Murex and was a consultant for several different law enforcement agencies.

Apparently, he was a thirty-year veteran of the police force and was once up for the spot of commissioner. Why he never acceded to that position, Bob couldn't determine. But, for whatever reason, he had retired from law enforcement and joined Murex six years ago.

The banal articles describing the man were in such contrast to Bob's feelings that he could only read them in bafflement.

After a certain point, he started to wonder if this man had anything whatsoever to do with his case, but then he saw it: on the fourth article where the man was mentioned, he saw an accompanying photograph. It was the kidnapper! The man he had previously known as Spence.

Frank Bledsoe!

Bob asked himself if this unremarkable man could be the monster who haunted his life. And looking at him, as he stood there in the photograph, Bob was bound to admit that it seemed extraordinarily improbable.

With the gray hair, the froggish face and oversized belly, Bledsoe looked more like a grandfather than a malicious criminal.

Bob sat there for some minutes just staring at the monitor, trying to assimilate the information until a police siren warbling in the distance to jarred him from his trance.

Standing up, he moved over to a window in the room. He stared out at the front yard between the slats in the venetian blinds. From that vantage-point he surveyed the wreckage of the vehicle he had vandalized, the car now a smoking ruin.

With the strobe effect of the fire engine's lights still dancing in his eyes he noticed how dark it had gotten, even since the brief time he had been up in the study. Because after the inferno of colors from the burning sunset, night settled like falling soot over the landscape. Yet no soot could have been darker than the shadow of hopelessness which suddenly fell over Bob. His mind turned anxiously back to his son. As he stared at the lowering sky, it brought him back to a sharper sense of his central peril: dwindling time.

But more than dwindling time. Because a second source of danger came to his attention as he peeked out the window. There, across the street and a few houses down, he was shocked to see the same tan sedan from the supermarket.

A dark silhouette visible behind the windshield told him that someone was inside it, watching. It took him nearly a minute to absorb what he saw, to shake off his disbelief. He had no idea that they could scramble more people to follow him so fast—especially after the precipitate departure of the other men. Yet there it was: a car staking out his house.

His thoughts flew to the kidnapper, his enemy, Frank Bledsoe. The men Bledsoe commanded were like so many channels through which his influence streamed to his target. Like fingers reaching out to grasp him.

Bob nearly staggered away from the window, hoping no one had seen him. If they hadn't, he still might have time to escape.

With that thought, he quickly set about snuffing out what little light the room had. He scrambled back to the computer to shut it off. As he clicked out of the page with the Murex article, the computer's "wallpaper" came back into view. Once again he was reminded that this was not his computer. He dimmed the brightness of the monitor so it was barely visible.

Too anxious to ask why it had been switched out and too scared to leave his home to confront the dual menace of questioning policemen and watchful henchmen, he used the computer as an excuse to vacillate for a moment, to mark time as he examined it. Sitting back down at his desk, he squinted at the monitor as he scrolled through files on the system.

One particular file caught his attention. He opened it and was shocked to see countless images of child pornography.

"What the hell?" he uttered, caught in a fresh wave of chaos.

Bob was nauseated.

He closed the file, but only found more like it. He clicked again and again. There were countless records. He searched through the related documents with rising perplexity.

And then he found something to tie it all together: a suicide note. As the meaning of the words coalesced in his mind, a shadow crossed his heart and clouded his otherwise set features. Bob read on, and the whole contemptible nature of the situation rushed over him. Shaken, pale, he realized that the note wasn't supposed to have been written by him, but by his wife.

Julia!

According to the bizarre scenario they had created, *he* was the pervert, the reprobate, the monster driven by dark lusts, who attacked and killed his own son. She, the tortured wife and mother, had gone after him with the intent of exacting vengeance. At the end of it all, however—moved by a manic desire to join her slain son in the Afterworld—she decided to take her own life.

The discovery of this document shot its light along dark vistas of fear. Because it established that Julia was central to their cover-up. She wasn't just some unfortunate bystander as Bledsoe had allowed him to believe. To the contrary, she was necessary for their plans. Had Bob known, he would have never allowed her to withdraw from the situation and wait out the dénouement on the sidelines.

It all made sense now! When he initially drove his wife to her sister-in-law's house, the cell phone he had been given was used to track him. Until that moment, the possibility had never brushed his mind that his wife could be in danger.

He felt cold all the way to his bones.

Alarmed, he picked his desk phone up with the intention of dialing his sister-in-law's house. He realized, however, that he didn't have her phone number memorized. It would be in the address book Julia kept downstairs in the kitchen drawer under the coffee maker.

He started downstairs to get it and was waylaid by a ringing of his doorbell.

III

The appearance of a police officer elicited a panicked response. Thinking about the situation objectively, it made sense that the police would canvass the neighborhood to see if anybody had seen or heard anything suspicious prior to the act of vandalism.

Bob was so deep in his thoughts that their appearance seemed sudden. He was at a disadvantage. He couldn't speak to them. If he did, he risked alerting the kidnapper's contact on the inside—which would be fatal to his son.

Whatever he did, he'd have to avoid the police. The doorbell kept ringing, now interspersed with insistent knocking.

I have to get out of here! he thought in hysteria.

Bob was so eager to escape that he almost forgot the ransom money. Tiptoeing back upstairs, he grabbed the suitcase. In a moment of lucidity, over the protests of the still-ringing doorbell, Bob quickly decided to do two things: get a heavier winter coat, and transfer the money from the suitcase to a book bag. After all, he was still wanted in connection with terrorizing a member of the police force. It would be sensible to alter the description they put out about him.

Rushing to his bedroom closet, he grabbed his coat; and, making a detour into his Billy's bedroom, he searched around desperately for a book bag. His son, to his frustration, had had his backpack when he was abducted. It required some searching, but he finally found an old one at the back of the closet.

Unclicking the hasps of the suitcase, he disgorged its contents into the backpack. Throwing the overstuffed bag over his shoulder, he stole down the staircase.

To his shock and dismay, the police were still standing on his front porch.

He thought about several ways to outwit both the police and the surging curiosity of his neighbors so he could exit his house. In the end, he opted for the simplest one—stealing out of the side door. The police cars and fire trucks were focused on the front of the house and the hidden camera of the kidnappers was trained on the back.

He still had to be careful that his movements wouldn't attract undue attention. The darkness of the deepening night helped provide some cover as he crept from his yard into his neighbor's. He only felt reasonably safe after he had placed a block between himself and his neighborhood.

Where to go now?

He needed a car.

Bob felt the blood well into his head in a surge of desperation. He had no idea where to get a car. Suddenly, he remembered the car from the night before, the car of the intruder who met his death at the foot of Bob's staircase. He would use *that* car. He had left the keys in the ignition, after all. He would just return to it.

He had originally left the keys in the car in the hope that some helpful aspiring criminal might drive the car off and further place a further distance between Bob and the corpse. Now, less than a day later, he desperately hoped that his wish had not been fulfilled.

As he walked to the park where he had left the vehicle, he vacillated between hope and despair. Meanwhile, with bittersweet anguish, he marked the swing where he had swung his own son, the corkscrew slide down which he had pushed him, the merry-go-round where his wife had spun him, as in some abstract game of roulette. His insides twisted in anguish.

Yet his thoughts focused again as his eyes fell on the car.

It was still there!

His heart gave a leap in his chest as he ran over to it. It was just as he had left it. But, what about the dead man in its trunk? The fact that there was a cadaver made the outline of reality that much harsher.

Was that just yesterday? He couldn't believe that everything that had transpired had been compressed within the space of twenty-three hours.

Overcoming a twinge of mortification, he took the keys from the ignition and brought them around to the back of the car. Popping the key in, the trunk-lid hissed open like a vacuum-packed can, exhaling air. As it did so it seemed like an animal with bad breath. Clearly, the corpse's bowels had loosened between the time he had left it and the time he returned. Furthermore, sour gases would be escaping from the corpse's open mouth as the process of decomposition got underway. And his mouth was open, as Bob could see from his three-quarters' angle of the gray waxworks figure of the corpse's face.

Bob had to step away for a moment. He took a deep breath of fresh air. It was all he could do to control his nausea when his stare again centered in on the man in the trunk.

It had taken all the strength Bob had had to load the corpse into the car in the first place. Now that rigor mortis had set in and the body had stiffened in an inconvenient position, he realized that it would be much harder to get him out than it had been to put him in. He felt a wave of nausea and apprehension gripping him as he examined the body to see if there was some way to jimmy it out.

A grimace of effort contorted his features as he pulled on the dead man's body. He strained at his task and muttered invectives under his breath, but he didn't make much progress with the intractable corpse.

Just at that juncture, Bob slammed the trunk-lid shut as he spied a woman who was walking her dog scarcely twenty paces ahead of him.

"Good evening," she said, as she caught his eye.

"Evening," he responded, hoping against hope that her rat-sized canine wouldn't start sniffing around the car.

It did. But the matronly woman tugged at its leash until it came to heel and the two went on their way.

For a moment Bob considered resuming his attempts to dislodge the corpse from the trunk. Yet he abandoned all hope of doing it when he reflected upon the fact that this woman had seen him. He mulled that over. Even if he *could* manage to pull the body out of the car now, when it was discovered the police would ask the neighbors questions. He would be identified eventually— especially given the fact that his home was a mere few blocks away.

No, he couldn't dump the body here now. He reluctantly went back around to the driver's side door, opened it and slipped behind the wheel.

With a shudder, he stuck the key back into the ignition and started the engine. Stamping on the accelerator, the car bucked. Nervous, he forgot to release the handbreak. Doing so, the car jolted forward.

"Jesus Christ!" he muttered to himself, as he turned on the lights and pulled out into the street.

IV

He was intensely angry with himself for not having been able to remember his sister-in-law's phone-number, or for not having had the clarity of mind to steal the address book in his escape from the house. It made little difference now as he drove. The silence was conducive to thought. As he pressed further into the city's streets, he went back in memory not only to his many mistakes and missteps back at the house but also back to the documents he had stumbled across on the computer in his home office. There grew upon him the urgency, while he turned these thoughts over, of seeing his sister-in-law.

Within a few minutes, he was in front of her house, which she shared with a husband and three cats. Her name was Katie. With her curly blonde hair, blue eyes and a weak chin, she bore only the slightest of resemblances to her sister. Bob had opportunity to remark upon this fact again as she opened her door.

"Is Julia here?" Bob looked at her with a mixture of barely-masked fear and rising panic.

Her answering look of confusion confirmed his deepest fears and he woke to the crushing assurance that his wife had been captured. He tried to mask the feelings he experienced at this news, but he paused and she saw him struggling with new thoughts.

She was struck by his look of pale excitement, and an impulse of concern made her say: "Bob, is anything wrong? Come inside."

"Is Phil home?" he asked.

"He's in the bathroom. Why? Come inside. Tell me what's wrong."

He returned her look of curiosity with one of veiled

frustration. He *wanted* to take her into his confidence, but he couldn't.

"No, everything's fine," he spoke evasively, wondering a little at his own duplicity. "It's just that I was in the neighborhood and I thought Julie might've stopped by here."

He wasn't completely sure that he brought it off, however. For her eyes were on his face, and under her gaze he felt an acute sense of disquiet.

"Are you sure everything's okay?" she pressed, struck by his frowning agitation.

Bob sighed out his frustration.

Katie seemed about to speak, but he evaded her appeal by a sudden turn. "I have to run," he said, cutting her short as he made a slight gesture of impatience.

She stood there, in his way, however—irresolute. He wanted her to accept his reticence at its face value, but she wouldn't. She felt in Bob the lurking sense of something unexpressed.

Sounding the expected note of sympathy, she continued: "You don't know where Julia is?"

He had a moment's embarrassed hesitation. "Um...no."

His face was serious, with a slight shade of annoyance as she pursued, "You haven't been fighting, have you?"

"Yes, we had a fight," he returned. He needed to hasten their conversation without raising alarm.

"About what?"

Developing at once upon this theme, he told her that they had had a spat over finances.

"She *has* been wondering lately," said Katie, "if she should get a job."

"She told you that?" wondered Bob, embarrassed.

"I don't know if that has anything to do with wanting more money. But she's bored at home, now that

Billy's at school. She keeps complaining that she should have finished up architecture school. She's probably just feeling a little stifled, shiftless."

"I always thought she liked staying at home," said Bob.

"Well, she loves her family, of course," insisted Katie in a conciliatory tone. "It's only natural, though, that as Billy gets older—"

"Well, anyway...that's what we were fighting about," rejoined Bob, who then went on to add a few more phony details.

He put it all lightly, with a lightness that seemed to his high-strung nerves slightly, indefinably overdone.

He had to go. He was losing time and he needed to find his family. "I have to go. I'm sorry."

He longed to believe that Julia's disappearance could not be explained in terms of her capture, but no other possibilities came to him. All his vaguest fears had suddenly taken definite shape.

Nothing was left now but to phone the kidnapper. Up until then, Bob had shrunk away from phoning him until he had cleared a way through his own perplexities.

Now he had no other choice—and no time.

At least he had the money and that gave him courage. Yet once Bob gave the ransom money to the kidnapper would he just kill them all? Isn't that what the set-up on his computer implied?

Who knew what else they had planted in his house?

In any case, he'd have to phone the kidnapper now. Bledsoe.

Yes, Bledsoe was his name. Bob had that going for him, too. He knew the identity of the kidnapper.

But what from these scant materials could he devise to protect his family between now and the dropping off of the money?

With his thoughts still inconclusive, he sat in the parked car a block from his sister-in-law's house and pulled out the cell phone.

To his horror, he noticed that it was turned off. *How had that happened?*

He felt a cold sweat break out on his forehead as he considered the possibility that the kidnapper had tried to contact him and not been able to reach him.

It had never occurred to him that, by some accident of the first magnitude, by some monumental act of carelessness, he had disabled the cell phone.

He hoped that this mishap hadn't cost his loved ones their lives.

Panicked, he turned the phone on and dialed. His fingers greased with fear slipped over the number pad as he cursed their clumsiness.

A hatefully familiar voice pronounced his name.

Bob held his breath for a moment. "Yes. It's me."

"I was starting to get worried. You were getting dangerously close to the cut-off time."

"Well...I'm here now."

"You have the money?"

Bob wavered, as if for the first time conscious that he might be able to gain an advantage by lying. Crafting an alternate version of the events, he said, "Those men you sent to 'give me further instructions'...They disappeared, chasing my father," he risked. "I'm not sure they were entirely glad they found him."

"Well, what happened?"

"I don't know. I waited. I didn't know what to do. Before they showed up, I approached my father myself and told him about the situation. He gave me the money."

"He had it with him?"

"He put it in a suitcase and it stayed in the living room right in front of us—until the men came."

"What happened to it?"

"There was so much confusion, so much chaos. I didn't know what was happening. My father ran off and they gave chase. I waited, as I told you. But they never came back. I still don't know what happened."

"So you left?"

"Yes. I took the money with me."

"You have it now?"

"I couldn't disobey orders," he said, resignation in his voice. "You asked for the money, so I took it." His feint of obsequiousness broke down, though, as he added, "No thanks to the men you sent—who seemed to be not only after him, but after me!"

Bledsoe did not appear to resent the implicit accusation. He went on in the same tone of imperious persuasion: "Well, I can't account for any mistakes that may have been made in the frenzy and confusion of the situation. But you did the right thing to take the money and run. Good. I haven't heard back from my men yet. Truthfully, I can't wholeheartedly vouch for their character. I half-suspected that they'd take the money for themselves and run. Maybe that's why I haven't heard from them yet." He paused, and then went on in a lower voice: "In any case...it's necessary now to establish the point of exchange: You'll deliver the money to 529 Lamplighter Lane," he said with no quarter in his voice.

"Lamplighter Lane?" muttered Bob. "That doesn't sound familiar."

"That's because it's not in your town. It's two towns over in Holden."

"Holden?"

"Yes," said Bledsoe, who went on to give Bob some simple driving instructions. Afterward, he made Bob's grip on the cell phone tighten as he added in as casual tone as he could muster, "Would you like to speak to your wife before we disconnect the call?"

Bledsoe framed the sentence coldly, the shock calculated, the effect devastating. He knew he had struck the right note, for Bob's voice was suddenly weak. He had his son; now he had his wife. Bob wondered at the heartlessness of the man to so callously be able to inflict this last refinement of his misery.

Bob's face was ashen. He hyperventilated, fear and air swelling in his chest.

The tension was accentuated by Bob's silence. When he replied, he made a noise in the back of his throat and in a voice that was little more than a hoarse whisper. "So you *do* have her?"

"Yes. She's been a guest here since last night. It was a simple matter of picking her up from her sister's house . . ."

The muscles of Bob's jaw worked furiously as he listened. His face gradually paled and hardened. From pink it turned to a chalky white, and lines of concern deepened the furrowed eyebrows and sharpened the faint creases on his forehead.

He wanted to yell, he wanted to hit out at the man. He recalled negotiating with him and how he had extracted promises from him—all just to be made a fool of. But he realized he was in no position to press his complaint.

"So then you'd like to talk to her?"

"Of course," said Bob in a barely-restrained voice, swept by feelings of anger and futility.

"Hold on. I'll put her on the line."

A sickening hollowness spread through Bob.

"Julia?" he said, trying to control the fear in his voice, anxious now beyond any anxiety he had known before.

His mouth went dry and there was a swelling in his throat. Then, with a flush of joy, he heard her. Listening to her voice, her face hung for a moment before him.

"Bob...?" she began.

"I'm here," he said, with a tremor of emotion, swallowing over the swelling in his throat, "I'm here."

"I just want you to know that whatever happens tonight, I love you. I'll always love you."

"I have the ransom money, Julia. Don't ask me how I got it, but I got it. I don't want you to worry."

"I trust you, Bob. I know everything will be alright. I feel it." Her words carried a heavy weight of obstinate love and determined optimism.

He marveled at the quality and depth of her strength.

"I'll be there soon. You'll just have to ride out the next half-hour or so. But I got the money. I just want you to know that. I'll be there soon," he said firmly. "I'll be there soon."

Julia's voice was abruptly replaced by that of Bledsoe, "Would you like to speak to your son, too?" he asked.

"Yes," said Bob tightly, as he moved the phone to his other ear.

"Good. It's important to be reminded of all the people who depend on you. Here's your son."

"Billy?" There was a hitch in Bob's voice. He checked it, then soldiered on. "Billy, is that you?"

"Hi, Dad."

"Are you looking out for your Mom?"

"Yeah."

"Is she okay? Are you okay?"

"We're both alright, I guess," said the boy timorously. Then, with more emotion: "Are you coming to get us, Dad?"

"I'll be there soon, Billy. I promise," replied Bob. In a moment of tenderness, he added, "And I found your baseball card. I'll bring it with me."

"You did?"

His son broke into a moment of happiness in which the odd boyish note was once again perceptible.

Bob smiled unsteadily. Tears stood in his eyes.

"I'll be there soon," he repeated in a voice he tried to keep steady but that nevertheless trembled on the surface of a deep emotion. The kidnapper resumed the line. On a certain level, Bob couldn't hear him. He was too steeped in the sense of his family's nearness, absorbed in the contemplation of their voices, their inflexions. His heart trembled. He felt his happiness so near, so sure, that it caused him untold pain to have them snatched away from him. Now, at last, could he focus on the voice of the kidnapper. Bob wanted to yell at him, but some instinct of self-preservation choked off his voice. What emerged from his constricted throat in its place was a whisper: "Yes, I'll be there soon."

After terminating the phone call, he sat still, staring into space. In his eyes lingered the vision of the harried wife and mother who suffered under great duress waiting helplessly for her husband to rescue her; in his mind's eye, he still saw the brightened features of his son as he told him that he had recovered his baseball card.

Bob blinked, trying to force his mind to come together. He swallowed the lump in his throat.

He started the car back up and tried to keep his thoughts focused on the positive aspects of the situation: the fact that he had the money; the fact that he knew who the kidnapper was and could possibly, afterwards, take the evidence to the authorities; the fact that he had made the acquaintance of someone with press connections who might be able to institute an inquiry into the whole affair should things go wrong.

For all that, though, something gnawed at him.

He could feel the trap closing.

"I'll be there soon, I'll be there soon!" he could only go on saying; and with the repetition of the words the picture of his wife and child suffering agonizingly took shape again.

I'll be there soon!

Chapter Eighteen

I

Friday, November 20th, 6:27 pm

Bob had wondered what events had unfolded to see Julia kidnapped, as well. Julia, too, wondered at the events. At least, she had got to hear her husband's voice. To gain that one moment of heaven, though, she had had to wade through hell. The worst of it was when she had thought that "Detective Spence" was still her savior.

She had winced at the memory of her near-escape.

Her mind went back to that moment, the moment when the door opened and there he was. An authoritative quality pervaded his appearance, compelling admiration, but at the same time intimidating people—especially Julia. Yet it didn't matter, she reasoned. The man she knew as Spence corresponded admirably with the popular conception of a father-figure. He was solidly-built, had gray hair that was almost wholly white, and an air of confidence hung about him like a grandfatherly cologne. Julia had been relieved to see him.

She had looked over at her friend. Ronnie's eyes had met hers and she could see the light of fear in them.

With vehemence she tried to persuade "Spence" that Ronnie was her ally, her accomplice, that he had tried to save her and her son.

Even as she spoke, she had speculated on the mysterious change which had come over the detective and the certainty deepened in her that something was wrong. Once she recognized this, she awaited his next move with trepidation.

Threaded through the fabric of her impressions was the strange observation that he had seemed to take no notice of Ronnie.

"So there's no need for any violence," she said, noticing the gun in his hand.

"Oh, you mean because of him?" he said lightly.

Julia managed a nod. And then, with no further ado, he proceeded to shoot Ronnie in the head.

Her heart lurched in her chest as a spasm ripped through her. Ronnie fell like a marionette whose strings had been cut.

As the final darkness deepened around him, she turned her eyes to the man who had shot him. Julia stared at Spence's round, self-satisfied face in complete bewilderment and horror. His whole attitude suggested that snuffing out Ronnie's life meant no more to him than turning off a light-switch or shutting off a machine.

They had stared at each other and he saw the question in her eyes which she hesitated to put in words.

Something cold started in her stomach and spread to the rest of her limbs.

Suspicion darkened into terror.

There was something in his appearance that indicated a being of a wholly different order than just an ordinary police detective.

She drew back with an involuntary feeling of revulsion.

Suddenly, Spence's voice vibrated on the air—just one small sound picking through the cold tones of the night. "Now—" he said followed, after a measure, by "let's go."

She didn't trust her voice, but tried to respond anyway. The faintest possible "alright" came as if from a great distance, brushing by her captor's ear.

Whereas, before, she could never surrender herself wholly to the idea of immanent death, now, now that her last hope had finally deserted her, her whole interior being—her spirit, her soul, her life-force—collapsed. Her body reflected her new deflated state as her features drooped, her shoulders sagged, her whole body slumped.

She was shocked at the change in herself. Fear robbed her of all initiative. The ensuing paralysis demoralized her.

The last remnant of her will rebelled against this paralysis, because a frenzy of rage surged forth in her as her captor laid his hand on her son's shoulder to guide him to the door.

"Don't touch him!" she brought out with a low-toned intensity, her eyes filled with deep, uncompromising hatred.

Such was the force of her emotion that—counter to all expectation—he stood down and let *her* interpose herself between him and her son. Indifferent, he shrugged. Thus they moved toward another room up the hall.

As they walked, she reflected upon the fact that her son felt so small, so insubstantial. A pass of her hand over his shoulder alerted her to the fact that his little muscles were knotted. She tried to massage them with her left hand as she walked with him.

Turning from his hostage's stormy features, the kidnapper said, "Have your son sit down in that chair over there."

"What are you going to do?" she asked.

"You're not in a position to ask questions," he said, his voice taut with irritability. Then he added, "You're going to tie your son up."

"But I don't have anything to tie him with," she said in a feeble voice.

"Go back to where we just came from, gather up the rope that was used to secure him before. Then take Ronnie's keys off of him and go back downstairs to where *you* were being kept and bring back the rope from there. Meanwhile, your son is going to stay here with me."

Seeing the gun in his hand which was aimed at her son, she saw no option but to do what he said.

With a desolate expression, she backed away from her abductor and out of the room, resentful of the confidence he flaunted by "trusting" her to do whatever he said. Of course he could: he was threatening her son. The thought of physically leaving Billy again tore at her, but she had no choice.

As she entered the hall, the possibility briefly flashed before her of running and getting help. Such thoughts were dashed, though, before they even had a chance to lucidly coalesce, owing to the fact that he'd kill her son prior to her being able to contact anyone.

With a sense of futility oppressing her, she walked blindly down the hall.

The door where Ronnie lay dead suddenly confronted her. On the background of her present mood, this fact seemed fantastic. Was he really dead and just lying there?

Terror swept her. Could she go back into that room where that poor, foolish young man—the young man who had risked his own life to save her—lay dead?

She must.

Bracing herself, she pushed past the door. The room was just as they had left it minutes before—it was cramped, stale and seemed mutely to invoke annihilation.

She looked around the space critically—her mind set on passing over Ronnie's cadaver in search of the rope. But no matter what she intended to do, her eyes were irresistibly drawn to him.

She stood surveying Ronnie's body for nearly a minute.

He had been alive (she reflected), and now all that he was, all that he thought, all that he remembered (the images of his past, his life, his sister)—all were gone.

What did it mean?

She could feel the foundation of her sanity trembling. Is this what awaited her and her son?

A chill sizzling up her spine, she gave the corpse a wide berth and grabbed the rope which still sat on the chair.

Afterward, she wanted to run from the room. But her son's kidnapper had given her the task of getting the keys from Ronnie in order to unlock the door on the first floor.

What a cruel and purposely heartless duty to impose upon a person!

It cost her another five minutes to work up the courage to kneel down and fish around his pocket for the keys. Holding her breath, she set about her work—luckily getting them on the first try.

With her heart lodged in her throat, she hurried toward the door.

In the hallway, the breath exploded from her lips, Julia having almost forgotten that she had been suspending her respiration. Her lungs and heart throbbed painfully inside her chest as she stopped to catch her breath before pressing on to the stairwell and the first floor—where a second body awaited her.

For some reason Larry's corpse, when she came to it, didn't trouble her as much. Perhaps the difference in reaction could be that she considered him little more than an animal, anyway. His death therefore roused no more feelings in her than the slaughter of a cow in an abattoir. Both were unpleasant—and frankly unfortunate—but neither occasioned deep and probing existential questions.

It was unsettling to find herself thrust among so much death and carnage. Shaking and pale, she made her way back up to Bledsoe and her son with the rope.

"You're back!" he uttered upon seeing her. "You have the rope. Good. Before I forget, may I have Ronnie's keys, please."

Her nostrils distended a little due to the fact it cost her an effort to briefly touch her captor as she put the keys in his palm.

Accepting them, he directed his glance over to her son and said, "Now tie him up."

Julia was tormented by the look in Billy's eyes as she bound him back into the chair.

"And no games, mind you," broke in Bledsoe. "I'm going to check when you're done. If I see any hint of trickery, any loose rope or untied knots, I'll shoot him right there and then."

Julia carried out her orders to his satisfaction, judging by the cluck of approval he made a few minutes later as he tested the ropes himself.

"Good. Now that he's tied, it's your turn. Sit in that chair over there. Better yet: bring it here."

She did so, and he proceeded to range the chair next to Billy's. As he began tying her up, he commented, "There. Now mother and son can be together."

II

Bledsoe dragged a third chair to a location behind the sole piece of large furniture in the room—an old metal desk which occupied considerable space in a corner. It must have been left over from the time when the building was a functioning postal hub. Bledsoe inhabited it now.

Julia watched him almost as narrowly as an art student studying a model for a sketch. She did so surreptitiously, only watching him from the corner of her eye. As she did, she noticed that he seemed utterly remote from his two victims, less concerned with them than with the thoughts that filed through his brain. His intensity imposed silence.

Julia regretted that, because she desperately wanted to talk to her son, to find out how he was doing, to reassure him and make certain that he knew that she loved him. She feared, however, that, with the least chattering, their kidnapper might do something as abrupt and pitiless as what he did earlier to Ronnie. So, even though Billy glanced over at her a few times, she subtly discouraged his desire to talk to her.

This threw both of them into their own separate hells of solipsism. As time progressed, Julia retreated more and more into the gloomy recesses of introspection. She withdrew into herself making a final demand on her inner resources.

The only outward sign of the storm of emotion that was taking place within her was the tears that silently wet her face.

She had failed her son. At that thought her heart withered like a salted slug.

She had tried to escape, but gained nothing by it.

Julia's whole body shivered with fear like a terrible form of laughter convulsing her frame—laughter from the cruel leering devils of Fate which mocked her belief in the possibility of escape.

The cumulative effect of these realizations upon her was not an agreeable one. For all the time, behind her defiant front, this gnawing away of her confidence went on.

In this state of emotional tension, the tautness of her nerves had become unendurable. The only thing left for her to do was to retreat, retreat away from the situation, away from her anxiety, away from her terror—and jump through the trapdoor into the past.

As her thoughts strayed backward, they found their center in her happiest memories, her most fulfilling times—such as her marriage to her husband or the birth of her child.

It was strange being a parent, she mused. Before the actual birth, she could only conceive of the baby as an extension of herself. His birth, so she assumed, would be a doubling of the range of her personality, a broadening of the field of her influence. One can imagine, then, her surprise when he came into the world and bore no relation to her. He wasn't olive-skinned as she was, but fair like his father; his personality didn't hark back to her own, but was completely and inexplicably original. His nature was already so well-knit, so self-determined that, at times, she regarded him as something of a tiny enigma.

She looked over at him now, and still marveled at him.

He was being so brave, so strong.

God, what a strange effect having a child produced on a person! It expands you, make you see life objectively again—especially since you have to explain things to a child that you previously never had to think about.

For instance, she remembered teaching him the alphabet. Only then did she ask why the letters of the alphabet don't have a corresponding sound that makes sense. Like the letter H, for instance. It's pronounced "AyCH". It doesn't even make the sound it purports to convey. A child naturally hears "ayCH" and logically thinks it should represent the "CH" sound in English. But no. That would make too much sense. Likewise, with other banal, everyday things. For example, why are the ads that businessmen hand out printed on square pieces of paper, yet are called "circulars"? Her son seemed perplexed by this when he first learned the term. Or—in learning about American history—why are the people aboriginal to this continent called "Indians" when they have no relation whatsoever to India?

How sloppy life is, how inexact. An adult doesn't really understand this until he or she has to explain it to a child.

But what they cause in confusion, they more than make up for in joy. This is never more apparent in the madness that inclines a parent to indulge a child in toys. In a way, a mother or a father get to relive (if only vicariously) their own childhood through their offspring and redress previous grievances. After all, Billy had no idea that he was bought a particular yo-yo because his mother was denied one by her mother decades before. Or the tinker-toy cars. Though he showed no interest in them, they were purchased because, at some point in his own youth, his father had coveted ones very similar. This trying to "correct" the past by way of a child is clearly insane. But then isn't that why the euphemism exists for onlookers who whisper about "older people" in their dotage experiencing a "second childhood"?

Yes, if they were crazy, then so be it.

The experience of having a child was worth it. It expanded you, it created new dimensions in yourself that you never had before. Because if she had given birth to her son, then he—in a sense—had also given birth to her, as well. Or rather: Birth to that more well-rounded, more faceted person that she was now.

III

As time passed and Julia emerged more and more from her transport of introspection, she darted glances back up toward her captor. She studied him, but his expression revealed nothing.

All he would do was alternately sit there and gaze into space abstractedly or dial on the keypad to a cell phone and listen.

Meanwhile, as for her and her son, silence and darkness encompassed them like a scene on which a curtain had fallen. In fact, the setting, the dustiness, the refuse which resembled abandoned props—all suggested that she and Billy were merely in the wings of some horrific play. Fear, apprehension, terror and misgivings held center stage in their turn.

As time dragged on, she could feel her stomach tighten. The sense of being on the threshold of some impending event oppressed her.

The same sense of anxiety must have affected her captor as well, for with his most recently attempted phone call she watched as irritability blazed through him.

She grew more anxious when he started to pace the room.

His apparent anxiety jarred on Julia, who shrank deeper into herself physically as he passed by, irrationally hopeful that he'd be less conscious of her presence.

Masking the extent of her attentiveness, she marked the fact that a nervous quality pervaded him, informing his attitude and gestures, and it was this that worried her.

He glanced at his watch. He moved uneasily across the floor.

"I have to check something," he said suddenly.

He turned—a study in impotent rage—and crossed to the door.

Julia was excited by the prospect of his leaving, but thought she gave no indication of this fact. Perhaps, despite herself, her eyes shone with anticipation. For, before leaving, he turned and looked at her so searchingly that her glance wavered.

His voice was vibrant with menace as he said, "I'll be right back. Don't do anything stupid while I'm gone."

After he closed the door behind himself she sat there, reviewing the possibilities, looking around mechanically, till a memory of the keys in her pocket focused her attention. No, she didn't have Ronnie's keys anymore, but she had her own. Larry had given them to her. She wished that she had had a miniature Swiss Army knife on the key-chain. She'd seen novelty items like that before. No, the only implements that could answer to the purpose of a knife were the keys themselves. Maybe, she reasoned, she could wriggle in her ropes until she had enough play to slip her hand into her pocket to obtain the key-chain.

Still, she worried. What if he came back and caught her?

She hesitated for some seconds.

Her fear, however, goaded her into overcoming her paralysis and finding a way out of the nightmare. Her son's life depended on it. She took herself in hand, and tried to concentrate her attention.

Once she could no longer hear her captor in the hall, she advanced resolutely toward her objective.

After a minute's struggle, she managed to get just the tips of her fingers into her hip pocket. At first she feared that she wouldn't have the leverage to get the keys out; but, by lifting her leg somewhat—as far as it would go—she just barely succeeded.

Billy, noticing her effort, said, "Mom, what are you doing?"

"Shhh," she hissed, hoping that his remark wouldn't be overheard.

Chastened, Billy sank back into silence as he watched his mother yank the key-chain from her pocket and start rubbing one of the keys against a length of rope on her thigh.

It wasn't the most efficient cutting device. The edge of the key she was using was dull, after all. But, by slipping it between the filaments of the rope and pulling, she was able to make a little headway. Unfortunately not enough, because even though the length of rope she was working on had started to fray somewhat, she didn't have enough time to bring the project to a successful conclusion before the man she knew as Detective Spence returned.

She immediately set about slipping the key chain under her leg and out of view. She winced as it jingled a bit, but the sound was obscured by the closing of the door.

Julia swallowed with a dry throat as he gave her a hard look. After satisfying himself that nothing was amiss, though, he walked back to the desk.

She watched him in evident perplexity. The man's attitude expressed irresolution and stress.

She wished she knew what he was thinking about.

The intensity of his features frightened her. It was evident that he was arriving at an unpleasant decision regarding something, for his movements denoted great deliberation.

What she couldn't have known was that she and her son were the subject of his fevered thoughts. Because, as time passed and he couldn't get in touch with her husband, he was coming more and more to the conclusion that Bob had failed. Perhaps he was even dead. In light of that development, he would have to kill the lady and her son.

Who should he kill first? The boy? If he did so, the woman would scream and thrash about and probably capsize her chair.

But if he killed *her* first, what would the boy do?

Which scenario would present the least amount of problems?

With icy impartiality, he turned these considerations over in his head in a troubled silence.

It was similar in quality and texture to the silence inhabited by Julia and her son. They were bowed down by the sheer weight of it.

When the silence had become almost unendurable, a telephone-ring pealed through the room.

Everybody started at the sound—perhaps even more so than at the gun-shot that had ended Ronnie's life.

She remarked the fact that a change seemed to come almost instantly over her captor as his features relaxed from beetle-browed anxiety to tentative self-confidence while he spoke in low, even tones.

She felt that she was safer if she didn't eavesdrop, so her consciousness once again withdrew into itself. Absurd, chaotic thoughts trooped through her mind. Irrelevant musings rose before her—such as the fact that her legs felt numb, or the circumstance that she could still faintly taste peanut butter in her mouth from the crackers she ate earlier, or—and this was strange—the regret that she had never finished school since money had been so tight and events in life had intervened to force her to drop out.

Why did these reflections choose now to bubble up from her brain like a strange sort of mental foam? But the froth was abruptly swept away when she suddenly heard Billy exclaim: "Dad?!"

The utterance exploded like a bomb in the middle of Julia's private ruminations.

She looked over at her captor and saw that he was pressing the cell phone up against her son's ear.

Bob?

Immediately, Julia began to tremble. Excitement, wracking in its intensity, pulsed through her.

What was Billy saying to him? What was he saying to Billy?

Her mind was too frenzied, her nerves too raw to be able to make it all out.

Then the kidnapper resumed the phone for some moments. After only a brief spell, he pressed the phone to *her* ear.

As she listened to her husband, her captor stared at her with an intensity which goaded her almost beyond endurance.

Slowly, and with difficulty, her mouth formed phrases in reaction to the comments her husband was meanwhile making.

She could only absorb the information he was giving her imperfectly, retaining only one word in three, but from that she gathered that—somehow, by some miracle!— he had obtained the ransom money and was on his way to rescue them.

Whereas before the room's squalor had reduced her to its own level, now she appeared to glow in the darkness of this background; a new quality pervaded the room. The air was suddenly crisper, the colors abruptly more pronounced, the debris littering the floor somehow less disturbing.

"I'll be there soon!" her husband said.

"Yes!" she returned, beside herself.

"I'll be there soon!" he repeated emphatically, the phrase echoing in her ears long after the actual phone call had ended.

Meanwhile, her captor—almost as excited as she was—assumed his seat behind the desk and settled himself for a final review of his plans.

Chapter Nineteen

I

Friday, November 20th, 6:31 pm

For Bob Ebersol, Time attained a new significance: it became an implacable enemy who fought to undermine him at every step. This fact was underscored as he drove, his hands at the ten o'clock and two o'clock position on the steering wheel. Vaguely aware of this, he winced that even the car lent itself to metaphors about his ever-present consciousness of Time.

He had to save his wife and son.

He was cognizant of the foolishness of delivering himself into his enemy's hands. He knew it was inadvisable to put himself in a situation in which he was even more at the man's mercy. But he saw no choice.

As he drove there, his thoughts revolved in a turmoil of indecision. He wished he had had time to contact someone at Murex, to figure out some way for *them* to put some pressure on Bledsoe from the inside. He might have been able to persuade someone at Murex that he and the corporation had areas where their interests converged. They could *both* take on Bledsoe. After all, if this one rogue operation compromised the rest of their legitimate business, it would be in their interest to take him down, to turn on him. He hadn't had time to assemble his facts, though, no opportunity to organize a plan that would gain him leverage.

If only there was some way to ensure that he and his family just wouldn't be killed the moment he handed over the money, some stopgap measure to offer some particle of assurance.

There was nothing for it now but to go on.

Because of the highway, Bob was forced to drive in ever-wider concentric circles until he at last came to the outskirts of the city. As he drove, he fixed on the yellow lines in the middle of the road. They reminded him of the threading on the inside lip of a Mason jar. Initially he felt that by following the grooves he was getting closer to lifting the lid on the situation. But, the more he drove, the more he realized that he wasn't driving in the direction of loosening the lid, but tightening it, as all the forces arrayed against him were finally closing down on him.

He felt suffocated as the air itself seemed to thicken and swell.

Only one thing gave him strength: the anticipation of seeing his family again. There was a haze before his mind in which floated his son's image, all the memories associated with his wife, flashes of their time together as a family.

He went through his memories one by one like a miser counting gold coins.

He was so absorbed in this process that he failed at first to notice the tan sedan following him at a discreet distance. Looking in the rearview mirror, his face dropped.

Since he hadn't reached his destination yet, he had time for some thought about this singularity. Firstly, the car wasn't driving erratically, wasn't speeding. It was moving at a clip equal to his own. That was the problem. If Bob slowed down, the sedan slowed down; if he sped up, the sedan sped up at an equal pace.

Secondly, it was the same make and model as the car he'd seen earlier in front of his house and earlier still at the supermarket.

But there must be millions of them on the road, his more logical side weighed in. *You're just being paranoid.*

For all that, though, he couldn't shake the feeling that he was being tailed.

It could have been Bledsoe's thugs, he considered, although that seemed unlikely on several counts, not the least of which was the fact that whoever drove the tan sedan showed up too soon after the other men had driven off in his wife's car. Moreover, there was, so far as he could tell, only one man tailing him now, not the two he had seen fleeing.

A darker shadow passed across his imagination: it might be the police.

Christ! And I have a corpse in the trunk! he thought in panic.

He couldn't risk being apprehended—not now, not at this point, when precious seconds mattered.

What am I doing? he said inwardly. *I don't even know if it's the same car from before. I can test it, though.*

He did so by turning off the highway and seeing if the car would follow him into the quiet residential area he happened to veer into.

Bob had never been in that particular neighborhood before, and had no business there now. The car continued to pursue him.

He drove on aimlessly until he came to a fast-food restaurant. The glint of a sudden decision shone in his eyes. It occurred to him to make a feint of ordering something as he drove into its drive-thru lane on the side of the building. When the tan sedan followed him, he stepped on the gas. His car raced forward, swinging wide to avoid hitting a nearby truck as he veered back out into the street.

He doubled back and tried to find his way to the highway again.

Yes, he was without question being followed.

The thought registered that, whoever was following him, wasn't very good. They didn't seem to care one iota about being inconspicuous at this point.

So maybe it *wasn't* the police.

Wouldn't they have tried to pull him over by now?

If not them, then more of Bledsoe's henchmen?

None of the possibilities were pleasant.

As he tried to make sense of the situation, he wheeled around a corner, then another, desperately trying to lose the sedan.

He thought he had gained a little headway, but it accelerated, trying not to lose any more ground.

"Where the hell is the highway?" Bob muttered to himself.

Bob entertained all sorts of time stealing scenarios in which he'd slam into another motorist, or accidentally strike a pedestrian crossing the street. His preoccupation with these possibilities diminished somewhat as he finally found an onramp and regained the highway.

How much time had he wasted, trying to get away from his pursuer? His blood turned to ice as he contemplated the passage of precious minutes and the threat under which his family languished.

"Damn him!" he nearly hollered, as his hatred grew of the driver who had made him waste so much time.

He was almost prepared to ignore him for the duration of the trip—but, knowing the risk involved if Bledsoe saw that he was followed and it turned out to be the police, he realized that that option was untenable.

What could he do?

Suddenly a vague hope surfaced when he noticed that the car had slid into the right-hand lane. He was in the left-hand lane. Two circumstances arose simultaneously: there were no cars directly behind him for quite some distance and there was an exit coming up.

Seizing his chance, he slammed on the brakes and watched the tan sedan fly past him (locked in by cars in front of it and in back of it). He then put the car in reverse and backed up to the off-ramp he had just passed.

Putting it in drive, he barely missed getting hit by a station wagon that was bearing down on him.

"Thank God!"

II

Having successfully evaded his pursuer by getting off the highway he drove ten more miles, then came to an access road on the right.

The lonely road opened up in front of him with all the gloom of Fate unfolding a path down which he was meant to go. He had no choice but to travel it. As he did so, he felt ever-greater pressure such as a diver might feel on descending to lower and lower depths in the sea. Gravity seemed to compress the nearer he got to his goal.

Perhaps owing to these forces, he started to torture himself with questions—chiefly: Would his wife and son even be in such a plight now had he just passively gone along with everything, had he not gone and given into the flash of a primitive instinct and killed that first man, setting into motion a whole host of unforeseen events? Driving up to his final destination now, memories of that mutiny returned to him charged with the new weight of guilt.

It was in this state that he finally stopped before the address where a steel gate barred the way. Flanking the gate in either direction was a twelve-foot fence, angled outward at the top with barbed wire. As forbidding as it looked, the gate was unlocked. It swung inward.

Tall lampposts were arrayed across the featureless property. Their mercury-vapor lights shed a sour yellowish glow over everything.

He followed them for a while, to a squat three-story building finally offered its huge labyrinthine menace to his gaze. There were several outbuildings on the same property, as well. They could be in any one of them—or none of them at all. He didn't know.

The car drew up with a jerk of finality.

Worried about his ability to cope when so much was riding on him, he hesitated a moment before getting out of the car. He gripped the steering wheel tightly, so tightly his knuckles turned white. Perhaps to hold onto something as his world turned upside down. Or maybe he held onto it to hold onto *something*—after he had failed to hold onto everything else he had ever loved.

III

A light in the window caught Bob's attention as he surveyed the property. *Was that where they were?*

His heart pounded at the thought of what was before him, one part of him scared and uncertain, the other part rigid with determination. A furious core of certainty was growing within him. Bob took a deep breath and exhaled slowly. He had come this far, he told himself. He had found resources within himself to do things he could have never before imagined. If there was any deficit for what he had to meet in the upcoming minutes, he would have to bridge it, overcome it. He could do it, he told himself. He *had* to do it.

That resolution, however much it appealed to his intellect, didn't quite assuage the visceral misgiving he felt.

With each step he took toward the entrance of the building, the shorter his breath became, the more his heart pounded.

He didn't like the icy feeling that was beginning to settle over his stomach.

The wind picked up. His teeth chattered. He was glad in retrospect that he had outfitted himself with his heavier winter coat.

Even so, the wind leached the heat from his body. Or, perhaps, it wasn't the wind. Perhaps what he felt was his very substance, his very life-force slipping away.

No. Rigid determination to save his family drove all self-defeating thoughts away. He couldn't afford to be weak while his family's situation was so precarious.

The windows looked down on him with an air of vigilance and menace that dead windows always seem to have.

Arriving at the entrance, he found that it was unlocked. His senses roused to their primal limits, he paused a moment to listen for anybody who might be hiding. Satisfied that no one was waiting for him on the other side of the door; he stepped inside and closed it against the cold.

IV

Quietly, he pressed forward. The prevailing smell, which confused the nostrils with the simultaneous suggestion of dust and antiseptic, reminded him of a hospital.

As he entered the lobby, his face sharpened to distrust. The situation of his being caught in an ambush presented itself to him as a very real possibility.

His senses painfully alert to every nuance of his environment, he scanned every shadow, weighed every sound. Keeping close to the wall, he advanced. A door in

245

the middle of a hallway, to the left, offered a view of an office. It was empty. He continued on, treading silently.

Guardedly, he moved toward a door at the end of a long corridor. He cleared his furred throat and slowly eased it open. As he looked beyond, he shuddered to the depths of his being. He was abruptly gripped by a terror which seemed to throw him off his balance.

A man was in there, on the floor—dead. The man's eyes stared vacantly at the ceiling and his arm was twisted in a strange way.

Who the hell is that? wondered Bob.

Where were his wife and son?

Inside the room, the tension hung about the air like a vicious strain of influenza striking Bob with a fever characterized by pallor, nervous stomach and sweating. There he stood, every nerve pitched to the highest tension. The blood rushed to his head and sounded like a million people marching around him.

The fog penetrated Bob's head. He prayed, but he didn't know what he prayed. His voice was an inaudible undertone as he muttered like someone mumbling from rote over a rosary.

"Please God, please God, please God . . ."

There was a tumult in his spirit. He felt horribly unprepared for an outcome he could not guess.

He was taken out of himself by a voice from a nearby stairwell.

Bledsoe's commanding voice boomed across the hollow space. "I'm up here, Mr. Ebersol. On the second floor."

Chapter Twenty

I

Friday, November 20th, 7:01 pm

Gripping the bag with the money in one hand, Bob reached over and felt the gun in his coat pocket with the other hand. The upward flight of the staircase echoed the mounting anxiety inside him as his fear was raised another octave.

To his astonishment, he made it to the second story without incident.

Looking down the hallway to his right he saw movement. Bledsoe.

He beckoned to Bob and indicated which room he was to enter. Bob did so, with a heavy gait and a pounding heart. Entering the room, Bledsoe received his victim with an affability which implied he was in fully in charge, running the show and clearly expected the outcome to be in his favor.

"I congratulate you on making it!" he said. "For a little while there, I was starting to doubt. But you did it. I'm sure they're glad, too."

Bledsoe tipped his head in acknowledgement of the bound hostages.

"Julia? Billy?" A quaver found its way into Bob's voice. He took a steadying breath.

He saw his wife tied to a chair, she looked pale and her clothes were dirty, but he didn't see any bruises or blood and she appeared to be physically unharmed. Billy was pale, too, but less dirty than Julia. He sat there so quietly that it broke Bob's heart.

Even through the stir of his mounting confusion, he was aware of the change his presence had on Julia. Seeing him for the first time, color rose into her face, and her eyes clung to him poignantly in an access of desperate appeal.

All Bob wanted to do was run to them, and hold them. He wanted the tangible reassurance that they were alright and he never wanted to let them go.

It was hard to deny them his full attention, but, for the time being, he had to. Determined not to let Bledsoe see that he was emotional, aware that any sign of sentiment would be interpreted as proof of weakness, he decided to play the part of a brave man. If he was going to survive the next few minutes and save his family, he knew instinctively that he could only do it by abandoning himself to a role.

The concentrated stress of the last twenty-four hours told on his features, the pressure taking its toll on him physically, emotionally, mentally; and while Bob Ebersol, the father, didn't have to acknowledge it, Bob Ebersol, the meek supermarket manager seemed to proclaim it with increasing boldness.

Shut up! Don't lose it now!

The meek supermarket manager had to be kept at bay, suppressed, his voice stilled.

All through the horrible journey of the last twenty-four hours Bob had felt the dead weight of this second person inside him, weighing him down, adding to his exhaustion.

And while he accepted his own assessment of himself, he knew instinctively that if he was going to survive—or, more importantly, if his *son and wife* were going to survive—he'd have to jettison this weaker, indecisive, whining voice like so much ballast.

Survival depended on it.

Even if he were wrong, even if Bledsoe were not in fact fooled, at least the feint of bravery and self-assurance seemed to produce a stabilizing effect on his family. Because his look, his self-confidence, the simple fact of his presence, restored Julia's shaken balance. Just under her composed features he saw the tumult of her fear and doubt, because her eyes, which she kept resolutely fixed on him, confessed her misery. Aside from this one lapse—her face was otherwise impassive. She was being strong for her son.

As for that son—

He seemed fine; and, save for a slight redness of the eyelids and pinkness of the nose, his appearance revealed no mark of abuse.

He was, however, more pale than he had ever seen him. The change in his appearance gave his father the measure of his fear.

He raised his eyes entreatingly to his father's and Bob read in them forbearance and an unquestioning belief in his father's abilities.

Collectively, then, their eyes—those of both mother and son—were bright with anticipation of deliverance, of hope.

Bob was so outside himself, so divorced from his center, that all his actions seemed unreal. The only thing that gave them the faintest appearance of reality was his family's belief in his strength. Their eyes transmitted a secret power to him, a secret faith.

Despite that, though, he still couldn't ignore the utter pathos of their position.

Seeing his family like this he felt a sudden rush of indignation. The kidnapper's presence was an outrage to his pain, an affront to the finer feelings which bound him to his family.

For all his disgust, he struggled to contain his excitement. He needed all his willpower to keep from running over to them.

Instead, Bob moved his hand back toward the comforting weight of the gun in his pocket. Bledsoe caught the motion, allowed a disappointed expression to lower over his features and said, "You'll be good enough to put your weapon on the ground in front of you."

Surveying Bledsoe's appearance now, he realized, as his eyes traveled down, that the kidnapper was training a gun at his chest.

Bob's eyes widened. Then they glazed with resignation as he reluctantly surrendered his gun.

Still conscious of the two other sidearms concealed about his person, he wondered when he'd be able to make use of them as the kidnapper continued talking. Because Bledsoe was in the process of asking for the money and directing attention toward the backpack in Bob's sweaty hand.

Bob, trying to mask his anxiety, handed it over. Throwing the bag onto an adjacent desk, Bledsoe fingered the tabs, unzipped the zipper and lifted the cover to disclose the neatly-wrapped stacks of bank notes.

"This is it, then?" asked Bledsoe.

"Yes," said Bob, without expression.

"You did good," Bledsoe said quietly, with even a measure of respect, as he looked at Bob.

All phony hospitality ebbed from his features as his eyes locked on Bob's again.

"I almost wish I could hire you myself," he remarked as he moved over toward Billy. The barrel of his gun stroking the boy's temple, Bledsoe's finger curled around the trigger.

Bob tensed. With rage and excitement struggling in his breast, he forced himself to say, "You can just let us go now. You have everything you wanted."

"No, not everything," said Bledsoe, hotly. "The money was only half of what I wanted done. The other half...the other half— Well, let's just say that there's a reason you're not dead right now."

"What the hell more could you want?" begged Bob.

"I still don't know where your father is. That was part of what this was all about. It was the majority of what I wanted, actually. But he decided to...complicate things."

"So you really were just using me this whole time to get to him?" wondered Bob.

"Of course I was using you!" shot back Bledsoe.

After all, Bob was just an automaton to him, a robot. If Bledsoe thought of him at all, it was only as the chance instrument of his dark aims.

It was then that he laid his plans before him with a cold lucidity, describing to a stunned Bob the broad outlines of his machinations. He uttered the words in a level voice, as if he were summing up the results of a business conference.

"So you see? You were supposed to kill Sutton when you 'chanced upon' him in your house," said Bledsoe. "And how about the phone number I left on the cell phone I gave you?" he added, pausing after each word.

Then in a rising tone he enumerated certain of his more clever activities. Bob learned that the map found in the car he'd used was planted there purposely, he learned that he was supposed to track the ownership of the house to Murex, and—most intriguingly—that the men who threw him in the trunk of the car were given strict instructions *not* to frisk him. It seemed that Bledsoe actually *wanted* his unwitting courier to shoot them (so he couldn't risk their depriving him of his gun).

The idea was incredible, yet it took such hold of him that he could scarcely steady his lips to say: "How would you possibly know that I'd do what you wanted? You couldn't possibly know what I would have done!"

Bledsoe met the question with an easy smile. "To the contrary," he said. Bob's rebellion was what he expected, what he relied on.

"You just made better sense as a courier. Who can trust criminals with money? They might have done what your father did. You, however— I didn't know anything about you. I didn't have to, though. You're a family man, a 'regular guy'. I could trust to the probability that you'd make a far more reliable bagman. I wouldn't have to go hunting for you, you'd go hunting for me. You wouldn't let any obstacle stand between you and the delivery—not with your family's lives hanging in the balance."

As Bob took all this in, he realized that, all along, he had merely followed the line this monster had traced in behaving the way he had. He was a marionette manipulated by a puppeteer. Every move, every action had been calculated; every moment staged to create a general effect; and he had played out the scenario just as it had been engineered.

He stood there, disgusted, thinking about the kidnapper in the shadows, controlling and shaping every move; watching from the wings as his plans came into focus.

His reason stunned, his emotions drained, he asked Bledsoe what he would have done had the killers murdered him somewhere along the way.

"Oh, that?" he said lightly. "You had me worried there, within the last few hours, that something like that might have happened. I couldn't seem to get into touch with you."

He then went on to assure Bob that he took the most elaborate precautions to ensure that, no matter what the circumstances, he'd have a story available to satisfy the inquisitive. Like a puzzle-piece falling into place—though

Bledsoe didn't explicitly address it—Bob now understood the significance of the back-up narrative that he had stumbled upon by discovering the forged documents on the computer. For, as Bledsoe said vaguely, countermeasures always have to be put in place. He *had* to have a back-up scenario for what had happened to Bob and his family if things went off the wire.

Of course—for his own purposes—he didn't want Bob to die. He wanted him to succeed. It was admittedly a risky strategy based on probabilities, but it was all he had.

"I mean, I tried to stack things in your favor where I could," he added, "by telling Mostellar and Rhys, for instance, not to frisk you—as I said. Or by jamming their guns."

When Bledsoe mentioned jamming their guns, Bob realized that the guns secreted on his person were worthless. The confirmation of his fear sent a tremor of alarm through him.

His expression of astonishment slowly settled into a pale grimace. At last, he understood: there was a game being played and he had lost. Up until that very minute, that very *second* perhaps, he had looked upon the discovery of his wife and son as the end-result of his search for truth. He felt like the legendary character of Theseus. Like the Greek hero who stood in a maze littered with skeletons, his only way out was the thread he used to record his movements in the labyrinth. In archaic English a "clew" was a "spool of thread," and writers adopted the metaphor from Greek literature as a way to describe evidence that led to the solving of a crime. Over the decades, "clew" became corrupted into "clue". Just so, Bob metaphorically poked the spool, yanking on what he assumed was an emerging thread. Now it assumed a different character altogether, because there he stood, yanking—only too late recognizing it for what it was: a loose thread pulled, a seam undone—a whole life unraveled.

Grasping, he made a desperate appeal to Bledsoe's humanity.

"Just let Julia and Billy go," he said, "I'll stay."

The captor's face was unstirred, however, by any moral consideration or ethical qualm.

"No, the simple fact of the matter is: I need them—in order to get you to do what I ask," said Bledsoe.

"But I'll do what you want. You don't need them. That's my point!" Bob's voice had become thin and hollow.

"Please don't argue. It's already been settled, long before this moment. They still have a part to play, just as you do—as corpses," answered Bledsoe, tonelessly.

"What?!" wondered Bob as terror quaked through him.

"The service you provided by killing everyone linked to me on that previous job was only part of what you were supposed to do. But how could I let you and your family stay alive as yet another link? No, that's not part of the narrative."

"What is the narrative?" asked Bob, beside himself.

"You're a serial killer. I have the identities of the men you've already killed. The forensics can be used to tie you to the crimes. I could have killed them myself, but— you did it for me. So, you see, by shooting you, I'll be a big hero, a hero saving the world from a dangerous serial killer."

"But you still need me to find my father. You have to keep me aliv—"

"And your family?"

"What if I refuse to g—"

"Oh, that was never the deal. It was never 'Do-what-I-say-and-they-live'. It was: Do-what-I-say-and-I'll-kill-them-quickly-and-mercifully. If you don't, they'll die long, lingering deaths. It'll all be attributed to you, anyway—you being a 'dangerous serial killer' and all."

Panicked, Bob tried to make a play for time, saying, "But there's only one problem: Murex has already been briefed on the situation. Your own people have turned on you."

For the first time, Bledsoe seemed at a disadvantage. Bob's remarks were so unexpected that he hesitated before replying:

"You're bluffing."

"Am I?" countered Bob, observing the fact that the gun trained on him had wavered. Unfortunately it hadn't moved off target far enough to miss him if Bledsoe pulled the trigger. Nevertheless, he went on: "How do you think I knew your name when I came here, Mr. Bledsoe? Where do you think I was directly before coming here? To the people at Murex you're an embarrassment now, a liability."

"You're lying," he said, with an indrawn breath.

Bob held his ground. "Where do you think I got the money? Those are all marked bills. The money's worthless. I was just sent here to get you on tape."

The furrows in Bledsoe's brow grew deeper. He had obviously been caught off guard.

Stalling for time, Bob continued: "I was just so surprised that you went on and on like that. They said you liked to talk, you liked to impress people with your brilliant plans"

"Ebersol," began Bledsoe.

"I'm grateful to you for speaking so clearly," he raced on, "and speaking into the microphone, no less. By the way, there's a car out in the parking lot receiving a direct transmission from me, so even if you take the microphone and destroy it, the tape's already got what you said up to this point."

Bledsoe, to Bob's horror, moved over to the one window in the room and peered out into the darkness.

In those brief instants, Bob allowed his eyes to wander over to his wife. Her heart fluttered when their eyes locked. Though she was in no position to communicate directly, her glance touched him like a sunbeam. It was as if her whole being dilated and gathered in her eyes.

Their souls met in that instant's silence.

"Do you see it?" Bob asked, feigning courage, buying time.

He didn't know what he was buying time for, short of just gaining enough time to catch his breath and settle upon a course of action. If for nothing else, he enjoyed throwing the pompous man on the defensive. He felt that if he could keep him off balance long enough maybe he'd make a mistake.

Something made a noise behind Bob. It was probably just the wind as it clattered up a drafty hall. Moved by rising paranoia, Bledsoe risked a quick look and snapped his neck to try and fix on the origin of that sound, shifting his attention from his captive to the distant door at the far end of the room.

Seeing the previously indomitable man's anxiety rise and come to the fore, Bob's composure was somewhat restored. It was gratifying to see Bledsoe's confidence shaken, to hear his flat, smug tone replaced by a more thoughtful, hesitant note.

"Well?" continued Bob. "Did you see the car down there? Or have they hidden it? No, never mind. You probably only see the car I drove down there anyway. They probably wouldn't be so amateurish as to park in plain sight."

"Look, Ebersol—"An edge of fear sharpened Bledsoe's voice, fear that hadn't been in evidence throughout the entire nightmarish ordeal.

Suddenly the aspect of the whole scene changed. Bledsoe's whole manner suggested that he had been joking all along, that the situation was part of a larger misunderstanding. A sense of strangeness overtook Bob. It captured him so completely that, for a brief spell, he thought that perhaps he was telling the truth and men of executive position at Murex were plotting Bledsoe's downfall.

He developed this theme at length. So engrossed was he that, for those moments when he was in the charade, he had nearly forgotten his wife and son who were listening to the whole exchange in bemusement.

He was surprised that several of these shots in the dark seemed to hit their mark. It was in this manner that some of the information given by Bissel received such unexpected confirmation.

If he had intended to use these facts to stun Bledsoe, he had succeeded beyond his expectation.

As for Bledsoe, though, a change came over him as he tried to rally. Bob couldn't tell what was simmering in his mind, but he could tell that something was, because, with a swift transition of mood, he said, severely: "You're telling me that Murex is taping me, or the police are?"

"Is there a difference anymore?" hedged Bob.

Bledsoe, looking in another direction, fretted until, moved by a sly curiosity, he turned his eyes critically upon Bob.

"So then you spoke to Glendenning?"

"Yes," lied Bob.

"And Holt?"

"Of course," he said, covering the prevarication with a cold dignity.

Meanwhile Bledsoe regarded Bob doubtfully. Yet Bob kept all expression off his face. Bob could feel Bledsoe's eyes on him, gauging his reaction.

"And you even spoke to Pat Bolingbroke?"

"Yes."

"What did he say?"

"What does it matter what he said?"

With that, Bledsoe brightened with a little glow of triumph as his arrogance resurfaced.

"What?" said Bob.

"You made your first mistake."

A pause opened up as Bledsoe let that sink in.

Finally, Bob risked it by saying, "What are you talking about?" Whereupon Bledsoe said with telling emphasis: "Pat Bolingbroke is a woman, not a man."

"So?"

"I asked you what 'he' said, and you didn't correct me. You have no idea who Pat Bolingbroke is, do you?"

Suddenly, his fraud was uncovered and all powers of his deception withdrawn. Bob's ears heard no outside sound and his vision decreased to a pinprick with this fresh and catastrophic setback. Previously equating his behavior before with "playing a part," he abruptly staggered into the darkest element of that scenario and he went blank like an actor with stage-fright, struggling to remember his lines.

If he had expected Bledsoe to play the role of supportive stage manager, whispering lines from the prompt-box, he was sorely mistaken. All the man did was smile archly, almost sportingly—acknowledging to Bob that he had almost succeeded in his attempt to rattle him.

A black wave of despair washed over Bob.

He had been determined to succeed. He'd staked everything and was hard set on seeing it through. Now, that all was lost. Something inside him collapsed. He looked pale, beaten, his face heavily lined. He had been living on his nerves ever since this nightmare started; and now his stores of energy were at last depleted. Losing that last shred of hope was like waking up from a hypnotic trance. He realized that what he had been grasping at had been a delusion, and that the real horror and tragedy had been waiting patiently for him all along, just waiting there — till he woke up.

A very definite effort of will was required not to surrender to it wholly. Nevertheless, his legs felt rubbery, his knees weak underneath him.

Bledsoe straightened his posture and regained his self-possession, preparing to bring the affair to a triumphant conclusion.

"You've succeeded in at least one thing: You made me realize that, maybe, it's best to forget your father altogether—chalk it up as a loss—and move on. It'd be stupid to protract this thing and keep you and your family any longer. I only have one last thing to do," Bledsoe said, with an air of finality.

As he pronounced this death sentence, Bob felt as if Bledsoe must be talking about someone else, speaking as if he were discussing the affairs of someone in whom Bob was totally disinterested.

This couldn't possibly have anything to do with him! He was just a supermarket manager. Bledsoe couldn't be standing there, telling him that he was about to murder him in cold blood. If what he were saying was true, Bledsoe wouldn't be standing there like that, with such little dignity, with his belly hanging over his belt.

The whole thing belonged to a dream.

But if a dream, then a dream from which he was soon to wake up. Because the loud report of the gun sounded in Bob's ear like the clear note of Fate.

The distinct sense of the end of all things came to him.

II

Something was wrong; consciousness had not departed from him. If anything, his senses sharpened, his awareness of his surroundings heightened.

Was this what death was like?

No, it can't be!

For, he was still unmistakably in his body.

He turned around and a figure moved into view: his father. He was shocked to see him there. It seemed almost impossible—but there the fact remained.

In that crowded moment, Bob was aware of many things at once. His father's face, his lips set in a hard line; the kidnapper, shot, convulsed as an eruption of blood spread across his chest; his son and wife sitting there, startled, throated moans escaping their mouths. Their wide, stunned eyes fixed in shock on the fallen body of their captor.

When Bob looked down at Bledsoe, he saw the man's brutal face set in an expression of helplessness. At length, he stopped struggling, and a dark and final silence settled over him.

There was a ringing in Bob's left ear. Before he could process the information rationally and attribute it to the report of a gun in an enclosed space, he momentarily wondered if the high-pitched buzz he heard was the sound of his own body's shivering—as if it had produced an accompanying hum like a tuning fork.

"Come on," his father said as he pressed close to him, "let's get your family untied."

"Where did you come from?" asked Bob shakily.

"I tracked you."

"How?" he said, and in his voice the older man caught a note of wondering admiration.

"The same way they tried to track you. The cell phone. I gave you mine, remember? I used that as a transponder. I stole their idea. I followed you . . ."

"You...followed me?" returned Bob, for his fear had obscured the significance of certain events at the time of their occurrence, but now, owing to his father's presence, it emerged with increasing clarity. "You followed me...in a tan sedan?" continued Bob.

"So you did see me?!" wondered his father.

Bob managed a pale, watery smile.

"How could I miss you?"

"You almost got me into an accident back there."

"And you were parked just now in the parking lot outside?"

"Yeah. Why?"

Bob emitted a pale laugh, thinking back to the coincidence that probably saved his life, picturing Bledsoe's expression when he looked out the window and indeed saw one car too many. Reflecting on the coincidence that lent his lie the force of conviction, he asked his father why he hadn't called him.

"I tried," answered his father. "But the call wouldn't go through for some reason."

With a grimace, Bob recalled his turned-off phone.

On the point of explaining it to him, he instead found himself—to his own surprise—asking him another question: "Why did you come back?"

"Let's start untying them," said his father, nudging him. Because Bob felt himself drifting strangely, but he couldn't help it. The older man, meanwhile, commanded the situation as Bob fought to recover from his daze. Eventually, however, he recovered his faculties and lent a hand in untying his wife and son.

As he did so, his father explained in halting tones that it was only with the realization of the danger in which he had placed his son, but his grandson as well, that had roused him to the sense of his responsibility. Given his part in the affair, he couldn't tolerate the prospect of any danger befalling them. So he had come back to intercede on their behalf. He had had to bring into play everything he had learned over a lifetime of criminality; from somewhere deep within himself he had had to call upon faintly remembered instincts; but he had successfully done it—tracked his son.

Meanwhile Julia emerged from her bonds. She stood up and faced her husband. For a moment they looked at each other in silence, as if the thoughts between them were packed too thick for words. Because there came a moment when no word seemed to fly high enough or dive deep enough to utter the sense of safety and comfort each gave to the other.

He wanted to find an expression, then, a gesture—but settled on an embrace. As he pressed her to him, grasping her as if she were his only handrail as he dangled over an abyss, his breath came quickly. For the first time everything in Bob, from head to toe, seemed to be feeding the same full current of sensation.

Julia held her mouth up like a cup to his lips. And he drank deep of the passionate tenderness within her.

Until he pressed her against himself, he didn't realize how numb he had become physically. The currents of sensation that passed over his body as he touched them bore comparison to a limb whose circulation has been cut off and which springs back to life rapidly after the bonds are removed.

He dimly perceived that she must be experiencing the same sensation—albeit from a more physiological perspective.

As he stood there he took in with a new intensity of vision little details that he had never noticed before: such as the flower-petal texture of her skin which was the color of moonlight, or the tiny "frown" on the tip of her nose which appeared when a smile creased it, or the faint freckles spattered on certain unexposed portions of her skin like seeds inside a watermelon whose flesh has been exposed by a knife. All combined to convey the glorious sense of her presence.

All the while, Bob's father struggled with thick clumsy fingers on his grandson's ropes. As he finally got the last one untied, Billy got waveringly to his feet, whereupon

Bob took him into his arms. After the boy held him for some moments, Bob sought his attention and said, "This is your grandfather, Billy."

"Nice to meet you," said William, smiling radiantly upon the boy as he threw his arms around the child. When he came away, however, there was blood on Billy's shirt.

For a moment, Bob wondered if his boy had been wounded. It took a second for him to realize that, no, it hadn't been Billy who was shot, but the little boy's grandfather. He had been quietly bleeding the whole time, suppressing his own pain to free his son's family.

Bob's heart twisted with struggling impulses. He was ecstatic to have his wife and son back, but mortified to see that his father was wounded. Regrettably, the sound he had heard previously wasn't one gunshot but two, as both weapons discharged almost-simultaneously; for Bledsoe had apparently squeezed off a shot before he fell.

"Dad!" Bob called. Just then the old man— lightheaded with the loss of blood—collapsed.

Bob hastened to his side. Upon examination, William's pulse was irregular and very faint. For a few minutes Bob could detect only a feeble sluggish throb at long intervals, followed by a rapid fluttering so indistinct that he was unable to count the pulses. His father's hands were cold and clammy, and his arms inert as lead.

No wonder it had taken him so much longer to untie Billy. It must have cost him a tremendous effort to keep his hands steady, his fingers nimble.

Bob's emotions exquisitely balanced between love and confusion, he knelt by his father and said, "Dad, can you hear me?"

"I can hear you," he brought out with an effort.

"I'm gonna call an ambulance. Hold on. We'll get you patched up. You'll be okay; I promise!"

"Put that phone away!" demanded William, almost angrily.

"I have to call—"

"No. I'll be gone by the time they get here, anyway. I want to go. Let me go, Bobby."

"No, Dad. You don't know what you're saying!"

"*I know what I'm saying*," he uttered with vehemence.

"Dad—"

"I love you, Bobby."

"No—"

"I love you."

He continued to consider his son between half-drawn eyelids.

The older man was filled with an overmastering emotion. As for Bob, he was shocked. For him, it seemed like a travesty of miscasting. This man before him looked so unlike his real father. William seemed to shrink before him. The pain of dying told on his features—they were drawn, wasted by exhaustion, tautened by pain. In stress his face settled into older lines and his features reflected his true age.

As Bob sifted these impressions, his father continued weakly to say that he had done what he could to deflect the course of events.

"It's okay, Bob. I know I wasn't always there, but," William paused to cough, "I'm glad I could do this, for you and for them," he nodded his head in Julia and Billy's direction.

Bob's disturbed face and shaken voice underscored the pang of compunction he felt as he said, in a breaking voice, "Dad, hold on."

The older man resumed speaking, but then broke off as the strain of talking was evident. His face convulsed in pain.

He seemed increasingly remote, as if his mind were less occupied with his immediate surroundings than with the thronging memories that must have then been assailing him.

"You know what I suddenly remember?" William fought to bring forth. "That day...so strange to think of it now." Then he continued, pouring all of his soul into the broken phrases: "You were just a little kid—a five year-old—and we were at a park, looking up at the clouds. I remember that day. I've kept it with me all these years. Do you remember that day?"

"Yes, Dad," said Bob, as he felt a fullness in his throat. His breath came unevenly as he added, with a crimp in his voice, "I remember."

The older man watched it pass before him, the long ghostly pageant of memory.

"That, I think, was the happiest day of my life," continued his father.

His voice shook with rising emotion as he uttered, "Mine, too, Dad."

"No! You have more happy days in front of you—with your own son. Take the money and start that new life you always wanted to start. Do it! And then get out of here." He was struggling to breathe now, his breath coming in short, fluid-filled gasps.

William stopped speaking and his brow cleared.

Having withdrawn beyond the reach of pain and struggle, he inhabited a mood of tranquil detachment now, as if he suddenly floated above his circumstances in a haze of wisdom and opiatic apathy.

The expression of his face was pained yet tender.

For the first time Bob understood what the man himself had suffered. In that moment of self-searching Bob realized how myopic and one-sided had been his conception of his whole childhood and, by extension, his relationship with his father.

Now his father was gone.

He crouched there in tranced rigidity, holding his dead father in his arms.

As Bob looked up, he saw his own son, with a sudden hole in his life that he hadn't even known was there. As if the bullet that killed his grandfather had made not one hole but two. The second "hole," as it were, would be less bloody for the boy, though—as if the bullet was so hot and fast that it instantly cauterized the wound it had inflicted so that it didn't bleed. As for Bob, however, he would experience bleeding. Because that's what Bob suddenly felt in his chest: a wound that throbbed, the rush of blood to it being the only clue to him that the pain centered around his heart.

"Bye, Dad."

A haunting silence had established itself in the room around him. Bob didn't know how long he remained like that, holding his father. All he knew was that, as he crouched there, a new and terrible knowledge slowly transfixed him.

This was Death. And as he stared down at his father's face Death had ceased to wear its mask.

But if Death itself was present, so was Life—two monumental figures crossing his horizon, as if for the first time.

Life!

He and his family were alive. They had survived.

There was relief in that knowledge. It swept Bob with the ecstasy of music. He was confused, he didn't know what would happen next, there would be so many radiating consequences to what had occurred—but it all seemed so irrelevant when balanced against the realization that they had survived. Joy echoed and swelled and surged in him till he seemed no more than the skin atop of an overmastering euphoria: the soul in him not just his own soul, but part of the larger impersonal soul that constitutes the life-force in all living things.

He was humbled before it, reduced to a child by it; a child in mysterious communication with forces beyond himself—with eternity, God, chance, fate, all of it. Especially Love, more than anything else, because, as he felt the hands of his wife and son on his shoulders, a slow, deep, luxurious sense of well-being invaded him.

He disentangled himself from his father with due solemnity and drew himself up to a standing position. He made a slow, ample gesture indicative of his need for his family's embrace. As he swept them in his arms, he lifted his face up to the ceiling and listened to himself breathing explosively, surprised at the sound of his own respiration.

His wife, now safely in his arms, no longer felt as if she had to be strong. Brave for so long, she finally shattered into wrenching sobs as her husband enfolded her in his arms. As he did so, he wondered what the future held for them. Should he do what his father advised? There seemed no reason why he couldn't keep the money.

Bob, on this point, did not pretend to any fixed opinion; one feeling alone was clear and insistent in him: his old life was receding, and a new and strange life was breaking on the horizon.

After his wife had spent the majority of her tears and recovered somewhat from her strain, they all moved as a family to the door, though none of them could believe it. The moment they had hoped and prayed for was finally at hand.

As for Bob, he said: "I don't know how we're even going to get home. The car I drove here has a corpse in the trunk."

Producing her car keys, Julia said, "They drove my car here, I think."

"Are those your keys?" he marveled.

"Yes."

"How did you get them?"

"I'll tell you on the way out. Let's go."

Then, having glanced around the room with an air of mild curiosity, as if he had never seen it before, Bob grabbed the money and followed his wife and son as they walked out the door.